HAARVILLE

For Andrew and our greyhound Sally (aka Sally Bally Beebo, aka Noddles) – my very own perpetual sources of silliness, love and zoomies – J.D.

Kelpies is an imprint of Floris Books
First published in 2023 by Floris Books
© 2023 Justin Davies
Author photo courtesy of Bob McDevitt
Map and illustrations created by Francesca Ficorilli © 2023 Floris Books
Justin Davies has asserted his right under the Copyright, Designs and Patent Act 1988 to be identified as the Author of this Work

Also available as an eBook

British Library CIP data available
ISBN 978-178250-844-1
Printed in Poland through Hussar

Floris Books supports sustainable forest management by printing this book on Forest Stewardship Council® certified paper

MIX
Paper from
responsible sources
FSC
www.fsc.org
FSC® C167221

HAARVILLE

JUSTIN DAVIES

Kelpies

Contents

1. Fearty's Perpetuals   9

2. Olu Pays a Visit   15

3. The Customer Isn't Always Right   25

4. Tittle-tattle   34

5. Up, Periscope!   46

6. Marching Orders   53

7. Room to Let   60

8. Black Cats and Broomsticks   69

9. Gushet House   77

10. Three's a Crowd   87

11. Ice Warning!   94

12. Pollock Row   103

13. A Light Tower Alight   111

14. The Accused   120

15. Whoever Heard of the Haarville Hoard?   129

16. The Storyteller of Crab Gulley   135

17. Repelled and Expelled   144

18. The Edge of the Ledge   154

19. Smash and Grab   163

20. Sail Away   173

21. When Snoozing Means Losing   183

22. Jailhouse Rot   192

23. Baggit & Son's   197

24. Rhymes of the Ancient Mariners   207

25. Round and Round the Merry-go-round!   215

26. All Aboard!   228

27. Anchors Away!   239

28. Hatched   244

29. Raft Race   252

30. The Ninth Wave   260

31. Clam Rock   269

32. An Eye for an Eye   281

Glossary   290

About the Author   293

Acknowledgements   294

1.

Fearty's Perpetuals

The eye stared up at Manx Fearty from his palm. He half expected it to wink at him, but of course it didn't. How could it? It had no lids to blink with.

Manx tossed it into the air, catching it expertly between his thumb and index finger, before rolling it around in his hand. If it had been a real eyeball, there'd have been stringy tendons and gloopy muscly bits hanging from it. And instead of being hard, it would have been soft and slippery, like one of the freshly laid turtle eggs Professor Oliphant had taken him and Fantoosh to examine on one of his "aquatic zoology" classes at the beach.

He dropped the glass eye back into a tall jar, where it made a satisfying *clink* against the shards of wave-washed glass collected over years of beachcombing. The eye rolled to the side, ending up with its seagrass-green iris staring out at Manx. He'd always been fascinated at how his great-granduncle Fabian

Fearty's glass eye was the same bright green as Manx's own real ones. Apparently, all the Feartys had had the same green eyes, pale pink skin and identical mussel-black hair. And even though Manx had never met any of them, he liked knowing he looked just the same.

"Keeping an *eye* on me as usual are you, Fabian?" said Manx, laughing to himself as he reached for the scent diffuser he'd been busy repairing all afternoon during his shift at his family's shop, Fearty's Perpetuals. It was a finicky job, and a couple of minutes playing with his great-granduncle's false eye often helped to loosen his fingers.

Nimble fingers were definitely required for the next part of this repair job, because fishing out the tiny fragment of golden-hued amberose with a set of miniature tongs, then carefully cleaning it, wasn't easy. One thing was for sure: Mr Pothery, the owner of Haarville's parchment shop, wouldn't be pleased if his mother's diffuser wasn't working when she went to spray her favourite dog rose scent on her one hundred and fourteenth birthday next week.

As he adjusted his grip on the tongs, Manx wondered what his great-granduncle and the rest of his long-deceased relatives would have made of his current repair efforts. Generations of Feartys had earned their living by keeping the town's vast array of perpetual devices in working order. According to his guardian, Father G, none had been as skilled in working with their unusual source of power, amberose, as Manx's mother Matilda, who'd known exactly how much of the sweet-smelling substance every device needed to work perfectly.

Manx's father, Fintan, had also been something of a genius when it came to perpetuals. Or rather, he had been until a perpetual egg poacher exploded in his face only days after Manx was born. That unfortunate accident robbed Manx of one parent, whilst a violent case of fish fever a few days later robbed him of the other. Everyone had begged Matilda not to scoff an entire bowl of pickled herring roe at the wake following her husband's barrel burial, but the inconsolable young mother wasn't for listening, and down the fish eggs went, scoop by vinegary scoop. Until down she went too, sunk for ever by grief and her grumbling guts.

Matilda's death was unique in that it hadn't been amberose-related. The rest of the Fearty clan had perished in a multitude of fiery explosions or other gruesome accidents — untimely deaths were an occupational hazard when working with a dangerous substance such as amberose. Not a single Fearty had lived to celebrate their one hundredth birthday, and in Haarville that was considered very unusual indeed.

"It'll be my turn sometime," whispered Manx, as he put the tongs down to wipe his sweaty hands on his apron. "But not today." He straightened up and admired the tiny piece of yellow-gold amberose (one-sixteenth pebble-weight to be exact) he'd successfully fished out from the diffuser, and liked to think his parents and ancestors would have been proud too.

Manx breathed deeply, savouring the heady, sweet scent of the shop. Decade upon decade of amberose devices gently humming away had left an indelible smell. It had sunk deep into the dark wooden panels lining the walls and the green woollen curtains hanging at the bay window. Even the oak floorboards, salvaged centuries before from a wrecked ship, now gleamed like honey on hot toast, imbued with years of amberose.

Everything Manx wore smelled richly of the substance too, even his favourite yellow oilskin smock, which he'd found washed up in Limpet Bay last year. With a bit of mending it could now fend off the very coldest wind, the absolute wettest rain, and the thickest, most bone-chilling winter fog – but it was no match for fragrant amberose.

And it wasn't just clothes. The substance seeped into hair and skin too, meaning that he and Father G permanently emitted a semi-sweet aroma. It was a handy benefit that they fully embraced, as it saved Father G the bother of procuring perfume and meant Manx could skip bath day occasionally. Well, if he smelled so pleasant already, what was the point?

The perpetual carriage clock hanging near the entrance chimed four times. Manx draped white sheets over the shop's two display cabinets, then flicked the sign in the window to

and locked the door. Where was Father G? Four o'clock on Saturdays meant fresh pastries from Bonbeurre's Bakery, and Manx had already decided he deserved at least two of Madame Bonbeurre's famous rowanberry jam puffs.

If Father G was running late, it meant he'd almost certainly got carried away at Nine Stitches buying up bundles of gull-feather boas and yet more mother-of-pearl fripperies, egged on, no doubt, by Betsy Lugstitch. The shop owner's idea of a perfect Saturday afternoon was to charm Father G into purchasing more accessories than he could possibly need for a year of performances as his glamorous drag queen stage character, Gloria in Excelsis. But as long as he'd remembered to stop at the bakery, Manx didn't mind how many feather boas and necklaces his guardian had bought for his show that night.

The winkle-shell curtain separating the shop from the house jangled in a sudden current of air. Manx darted back behind the counter, through the curtain and into the kitchen in anticipation, but had to swallow down the saliva pooling inside his mouth because Father G was bursting to say something. He'd obviously run all the way back to the shop and was breathing heavily, sweat glistening on his dark brown face and bald head.

"What's going on?" Manx was genuinely concerned that his guardian might pass out, and if he did there was a chance he'd topple forward into the delicious jam-oozing puffs, which would make them really quite difficult to eat. "Here," he said, pulling out a chair, "sit down."

"It it-it's amazing," stuttered Father G, loosening his

13

purple silk cravat and unbuttoning his shirt collar as he collapsed into the chair. "It's incredible." He looked up at Manx. "You're never going to believe it!"

"Correct," said Manx. "I'll never believe it if you don't tell me what I'm supposed to never believe."

"I'm sorry, Manx," said Father G, fanning his face with his hand, "it's just that this hasn't happened in Haarville since, well, since *I* happened in Haarville."

Manx's tummy grumbled. Both boy and stomach were in need of a jam puff. And fast.

"Is this one of your guessing games?"

"No," said Father G. "But if you think I'm excited, you should see the rest of town!"

Manx sighed, resigning himself to stale pastries. "Come on! What's going on?"

Father G took a deep breath. "There are strangers in Haarville."

Manx almost toppled over onto the puffs himself.

"Outsiders," said Father G. "Two of them! They came over the causeway."

"The causeway?" repeated Manx.

"Yes, the causeway."

"The causeway that's so dangerous only a deranged squid searching for a lost tentacle would attempt to cross?"

"There's only one causeway, Manx."

Manx felt himself go giddy. He held himself steady against the table.

"But... there's been no outsiders in Haarville since..."

"Since I arrived," said Father G. "Forty years ago."

14

2.

Olu Pays a Visit

Manx could hardly wait to find out more information about Haarville's mysterious newcomers. Even Father G was restless, with the result that his alter ego, Gloria in Excelsis, was dressed and ready with a full face of make-up faster than ever that evening.

On any other Saturday, the transformation would take hours, with Father G fussing over which gown to wear for his regular weekend suppertime drag show at Lumpsuckers, Haarville's ever-popular fish bar and restaurant. Choosing the perfect wig was usually a major operation, with his entire collection called into service before the perfect match for "the mood" was found.

But there was no such dallying this week. Manx dashed around with armfuls of shell necklaces, boas and high heels, whilst Father G grabbed at random and threw them on. The result was, of course, nothing less than spectacular, which left Manx wondering if his guardian needed to make quite so much fuss every weekend.

Manx was relieved that he hadn't spent ages tweaking

and poking at Father G's wig, because en route to Lumpsuckers a brisk wind blew along Front Street, almost toppling it from his guardian's head, and whipping several long blonde strands loose.

As expected, the restaurant was far busier than usual, with people crammed together at the tables. The air was thick with gossip and the aroma of fried haddock. Condensation streamed down the windows and dripped from the ceiling.

Father G wasted no time in taking to the small stage, whilst Manx set up the perpetual gramophone with one of the few records his guardian had managed to bring with him to Haarville. The vinyl was a bit scratched from years of use, but the singer's beautiful voice still rang out loud and clear. Manx often wondered what the original singers would say if they could see Gloria – all six-feet-whatever of her, not including the towering wig – twirl around the stage, glittering and sparkling, miming the words to their songs.

Father G said his drag queen act had once been hugely popular in the Out-There. It usually went down well in Lumpsuckers too – especially when the music ended and Gloria began telling jokes and picking out customers to join her on stage. But tonight, despite turning out another fabulous performance, not even Gloria in Excelsis could compete with the news of the new arrivals. Hardly anyone was watching the show, and Manx found it almost impossible to force his way through the heaving mass of diners with his tip bucket.

Eventually, he gave up and stood on one of the upturned fish barrels that served as seats, searching the restaurant for Fantoosh. He caught a glimpse of his best friend's striped, knitted dungarees at the far end of one of the communal benches. Fantoosh's dungarees, much like Fantoosh herself, were unique. They'd been knitted by her dad from scraps of dyed wool, and as she grew, he added more colourful stripes to the bottom of each leg.

"I give up," Manx sighed, squeezing in next to Fantoosh and leaning over to pinch the last fish ball off her plate. His friend gasped and made a show of being outraged, but Manx didn't need to apologise: Fantoosh always ordered one extra of whatever she was eating, knowing full well that he'd appear to snaffle it. He munched the salty treat for exactly four seconds before swallowing – the optimum time to achieve maximum taste and crunch satisfaction from one of Lumpsuckers' famous fried snacks.

Having wiped his mouth on his sleeve, Manx emptied that night's meagre tips onto the table. "There's not even enough in here for a couple of stale limpet buns."

"You can't blame this lot," said Fantoosh, raising her voice over the excited chatter. "The outsiders are almost bigger news than when I broke the town record for limpet picking."

"Only almost?" laughed Manx.

"Maybe they're *slightly* bigger news." Fantoosh's eyes shone copper-bright in the flickering gleam cast by the perpetual lanterns, and her light brown face glowed warmly. "Oh, alright," added Fantoosh, smiling. "They're the biggest news since *for ever!*"

It was true. Nothing this momentous ever happened in Haarville. The only problem was, not one person claimed to have actually seen the new arrivals. There was no word on where they were staying. By closing time there was even a wild rumour that it was all a hoax.

Manx and Father G stumbled round the corner back home to the shop, exhausted from shouting to be heard in the boisterous atmosphere of the fish bar.

"I hope I haven't damaged my delicate vocal cords," whispered Father G, as he unpinned his beehive wig and laid it gently on the shop counter. "And they'd better be listening to me next week or Gloria will never again grace the stage."

"Don't worry," said Manx, "by then we should know more about these outsiders, Gloria will be as popular as ever, and we'll have enough tip money to buy limpet buns all week."

On Sundays, Manx liked to rise early and spend some time alone in the shop. With the sound of Father G's snores echoing down the stairs, he fixed himself a quick breakfast of cold and slightly stale rowanberry jam puffs. They were still tasty, if a bit claggy on the tongue. He then took his cup of gutweed tea through to the shop and began cleaning the mechanism of an ornate perpetual crumpet toaster.

This was an especially important device as it came from Gushet House, home of one of Haarville's oldest and most reclusive inhabitants, Ma Campbell. She'd been toasting her morning crumpet with it for decades, and since the elderly lady was one of their more important customers, it was vital that Manx took extra care.

Unfortunately, Manx couldn't concentrate long enough to hold the tongs still. He glanced at the dark stain engrained in the wooden countertop – it served as a grim reminder of the blood spilled when his grandfather had lost control of a perpetual knife sharpener. Not being in the mood for a deadly amberose-related accident this morning, Manx decided to leave the crumpet toaster and work on an easier perpetual, but before he'd even put down his tongs, there was a sharp rap on the door.

Rat-a-tat-tat.

Rat-a-tat-tat-tat.

"Olu!" Manx cried, leaping off the stool to unlock the door. He held it ajar and the orange tip of an oystercatcher's long beak poked inside, followed shortly after by the rest of the bird. Olu padded on his webbed feet into the middle of the shop, then stretched his wings and ruffled his black-and-white feathers. Slowly, he turned his small head first left, then right, and then finally looked up at Manx, cocking his head to the side so that one red eye stared out.

"Feeling peckish?"

Olu tapped the floor with his beak once.

"Shame," said Manx. "There are some tasty crumbs left over from breakfast."

The bird stared.

"Thirsty?" asked Manx. There were plenty of puddles outside, but he knew Olu was partial to a drop or two of Da Silva's finest cockle cordial.

Olu tapped again. Once. And stared.

Finally, Manx understood.

"You've heard about them, then? The visitors?"

Olu tapped twice, still staring. Then the bird let out a squeaky, whistling call. Manx often thought an oystercatcher's call was like the sound a baby otter made when caught in the beak of a sea eagle, and now, as the whistle echoed off the display cabinets, it made his skin prickle.

"Have you seen them?"

Two more taps.

"And do they seem friendly?"

Olu paused for a moment, then tapped.

Just once.

Then the bird wandered off, beginning a circuit of the shop, stopping occasionally to tap the wooden panelling as if checking for death-watch beetles. Olu visited at least once a week, but was normally content to perch in the window, either observing the passers-by outside on Kipper Lane, or watching Manx and Father G at work at the counter. Manx wasn't certain how long oystercatchers lived, but this one had been paying visits to Fearty's

Perpetuals for as long as Father G had been in Haarville, and possibly far longer than that.

Olu strutted into the middle of shop, head flitting this way and that. Manx had never seen the bird so skittish.

"It's alright, Olu. Everything's fine here."

Olu gave Manx a final stare, then made for the door, tapping it lightly. Manx unlatched it.

"See you soon," he said, as the bird vanished into the swirling mist.

Turning the key in the lock, Manx frowned. Olu was rarely wrong about anything, which meant if his feathers were ruffled by Haarville's new arrivals, then there had to be something decidedly fishy about them.

Unusually, there were no customers that morning, and after a few hours Manx poked his head out of the door. A thick haar had filled Kipper Lane and was rolling uphill towards Nethergate. The dank, heavy sea fog that gave Haarville its name was just the sort of weather that discouraged even the town's hardy folk from venturing out, and when Father G returned from a quick nip round the corner to Da Silva's grocers to fetch provisions, his raincoat dripped a damp trail from the door, through the shell curtain and into the kitchen.

"I have some news on the outsiders," he declared, spearing a fried ragworm segment with his fork as they sat down to lunch. "They're lodged with our esteemed Burgmaster."

"With Lugstitch!" Manx almost choked on a chunk of sea carrot. "Who told you that?"

"His wife," replied Father G. "Betsy was at Da Silva's collecting a mountain of groceries. Apparently the outsiders went directly to Burgh House when they arrived in Haarville, and Lugstitch took them home with him. Betsy's furious at having to cook for two extra mouths *and* do all the work at Nine Stitches."

Manx could well imagine Betsy complaining about having to look after the newcomers. Whenever he was at the outfitters being measured for new breeches, she would moan about how her husband left her to run their shop alone whilst he paraded around Haarville as Burgmaster, barking orders at people like a constipated walrus.

"There must be something special about them if they're staying with Lugstitch," said Manx.

Father G chewed another ragworm segment. "All I know is that I wasn't greeted so warmly when I arrived in Haarville: the only place I could find lodgings was Phlegm Town."

"I didn't know that," said Manx. He rarely ventured across Parten Brae to the dingier, more run-down part of Haarville, but if the wind was blowing in the wrong direction, everyone was treated to a blast of Phlegm Town's many foul stinks and putrid pongs.

Father G pursed his lips. "The Elders were clearly discombobulated to discover a twenty-something, six-foot, brown-skinned, female impersonator in their midst. They'd never seen anyone like me before. I'd probably still be festering there if your grandparents hadn't sponsored me as an apprentice here."

Manx felt a familiar tingle down his spine. It happened whenever his guardian spoke about the family he'd never had a chance to meet.

"It's true," Manx said. "You own more dresses than trousers, and you wear make-up most days. You're not like anyone else in Haarville. But then, who is? Look at Fantoosh. Who else wears plaits that long? No one has hair like hers!"

Father G smiled. "Nor as untidy as yours. But I'd bet my tin of finest samphire tea that when Fantoosh's ancestors arrived in Haarville after being shipwrecked, the Elders back then had no idea what to do with *them* either. They'd probably never met anyone who'd sailed from the Indian Ocean before!"

"How they treated you is so unfair," said Manx. "Every Haarville family came from somewhere else originally. Even mine. There wouldn't *be* a Haarville if my ancestors hadn't been shipwrecked here after they left Ireland."

Sometimes, Manx wondered whether the Burgmaster and the rest of Haarville's Elders had forgotten that it was *his* ancestors, Sarah and Finnick Fearty, who founded their town over two hundred years ago, after their ship, the *Amber Rose*, was wrecked just off shore. When other families who were stranded in Haarville over the years took on the tasks of building houses, furniture-making, fishing or blowing glass, Sarah and Finnick had used their skill with clockwork mechanicals to provide the town with useful devices. They also discovered that the unusual substance storm-tossed onto the beach with them the night of their shipwreck could be used to power these devices, and named it amberose, in honour of their lost ship. The Feartys had kept everyone's perpetuals in working order ever since, which was just as well because no more amberose had ever been found.

"There must be something unusual about these outsiders if they're being treated so well by the Burgmaster," Manx continued. "One thing's for sure, Olu didn't like the look of them."

Father G wiped down the table and pushed his chair in. "Ha! I'm sure they can't be all that bad." He ruffled Manx's mop of hair. "I'm going out to sweep the yard," he said. "Will you watch the shop?"

Manx headed back through the curtain. He really hoped Olu was wrong, but the bird's unusual behaviour had left a nervy flutter in his stomach. And now it was lodged there, it didn't want to leave.

3.

The Customer Isn't Always Right

By half past three on Sunday afternoon, Manx had completely given up on any customers appearing and decided to close early. He'd just started dusting everything down when the door opened.

Looking up, Manx instantly jumped back against the counter, sending his sea-glass collecting jar tottering over. Its contents spilled out, waterfalling to the floor. He watched as Fabian's eyeball rolled away towards the man towering in the open doorway. The late-afternoon haar had followed him in, giving the impression that he was smouldering.

The man was tall – easily as tall as Father G in his heels – and clad in a dark leather, ankle-length coat. A broad brimmed hat, also leather, was pulled low over his face, leaving only a pointy black beard visible. He held his hands close to his chest, clasped together. Manx thought immediately of a praying mantis he'd seen in one of the town library's encyclopaedias.

Raising a handkerchief to wipe the end of his red-tipped nose, the man lifted his head, revealing pock-marked cheeks and puffy, bloodshot eyes. Then, having cleared his throat, his mouth opened slowly in a yellow-toothed smile. Teeth which, Manx decided, went well with his sickly-looking face.

"Do I have the pleasure of finding myself in Fearty's Perpetuals?" he asked, exhaling heavily, sending an invisible cloud of bad breath wafting across the shop.

Before Manx could reply, Father G brushed through the curtain and strode towards the stranger, accidentally scuffing Fabian's runaway eyeball further across the floor. A polished brown boot shot out from under the stranger's coat and stopped it. The man bent, leather creaking, and retrieved the eye with pincer-like fingers.

"This is Fearty's," said Father G.

The man's nostrils flared as he looked Father G up and down, then he turned to Manx to examine him too.

"Remarkable," he said in a whisper, as if to himself. "I do not need to ask if you are Master Manxome Fearty."

Manx winced at hearing his full name spoken.

"It's Manx," he said.

The man smirked. "How cruel of your parents to leave their child such an unpronounceable name." He made a show of looking around the shop. "But how generous of them to leave you this remarkable establishment." His eyes narrowed suddenly. "It is you, Manxome Fearty, whom we have come to see."

"*We?*" asked Manx.

By way of an answer, the man moved aside, dispersing

the cloud of haar still drifting in through the door. As it cleared, a boy appeared. He was Manx's height, although thinner and not quite as pale-skinned. But that wasn't the remarkable thing about him. Nor was the fact that he was dressed in an identical, if smaller, version of the leather coat worn by the man. The wholly astonishing thing about this boy was that he had exactly the same head of thick, unruly black hair as Manx. And identical green eyes.

The boy stepped forward. His coat squeaked as he folded his arms, a scowl that could curdle seawater fixed firmly on his face. The man flashed his grim yellow teeth again.

"May I present my son, Nathaniel Baggit. And I am Ninian Baggit."

Manx eyed the visitors warily.

"You're here to see *me*?" he asked.

Ninian Baggit strode across the shop, coat-tails swinging. "That can wait," he barked. His spider-crab claw fingers reached out. "First, I should return this most curious object." He rolled the eye between his bony thumb and finger whilst the boy looked on, his scowl replaced with a look of pure surprise.

The elder Baggit dropped the eye into Manx's waiting hand. "Did it belong to anyone you know?"

Manx retrieved the jar and carefully placed the eye in the bottom. "My great-granduncle."

The younger Baggit let out a sort of squeaking gasp, and his father glared at him, which silenced the boy instantly.

"Nathaniel's great-grandfather left him something equally small and useless," said Ninian Baggit. "Nevertheless, it's wonderful when our loved ones leave us their most precious belongings." He looked around the shop. "Is it not?"

Manx wasn't sure how to respond, but he sensed saying nothing was best.

Baggit stroked his beard, tugging on the end until its tip formed a needle-sharp point, then coughed once. He patted his chest theatrically, and coughed again. "This dreadful fog you seem to endure here really gets to one's lungs."

"Manx," said Father G, "fetch Mr Baggit some water, will you?"

"How very kind," gasped Baggit. "Although a hot tea would be of considerably more comfort."

Father G's eyes narrowed for a moment, before he forced his mouth into a brief smile. "Of course, we're always considerate of our customers here at Fearty's Perpetuals. Please, come into the kitchen."

Baggit followed Father G through the shell curtain, leaving Nathaniel and Manx glaring at each other. Then the boy slinked after them, brushing past Manx with a grunt.

"Manx."

"Huh?"

"Would you pour the tea, please?"

Manx, who'd been sitting in silence whilst the kettle came to the boil, lifted the teapot, slopping its contents over the table and into the saucers. "Sorry," he mumbled, grabbing a cloth.

Nathaniel Baggit sniffed his cup and pushed it away, wrinkling his nose. "I'm not drinking that."

The older Baggit tutted and smiled. "Youngsters! What can you do with them?"

Manx had a few ideas of what he'd like to do with the one pulling faces at the table right now, but remained silent.

"Would you perhaps have some juice for my son?"

Manx grabbed a bottle from the dresser and pushed it across the table.

"What's that?" asked Nathaniel, eyeing the bottle suspiciously.

"Limpet water," said Manx, "there's no juice till the summer."

Nathaniel Baggit pulled out the stopper and passed the bottle under his nose. "Ugh! This place is weird! And there's plenty of juice at the other house."

"Nathaniel!" Baggit looked down the length of his nose at his son. "We cannot expect the same degree of luxurious hospitality everywhere in this delightful town." He turned to Father G. "You must forgive my boy. He so enjoyed the selection of delicious juices served to us this morning."

Manx glared, clenching his fists until he felt his fingernails cutting into his hands. He poured out a cup of the limpet juice for himself and downed it in one. Father G held out a plate of kelp crackers, first to Ninian, then to Nathaniel, who both declined with barely disguised revulsion.

"You're staying with Lugstitch?" asked Father G, attempting to make conversation.

"Mr Lugstitch? Yes," said Baggit. "Such a generous host. How very sensible of this town to have elected him as its Burgmaster."

"He elected himself," said Father G, raising an eyebrow. "There are no public votes in Haarville."

Baggit shrugged and placed his bony hands on the edge of the table. He shook it. "Solid," he said.

"Like most folk in Haarville, we prefer function over finesse," said Father G. "This was constructed by one of Manx's ancestors from driftwood washed ashore after a ship was wrecked on one of the reefs."

Baggit cast his eyes around the room and Manx noticed that despite being so tired-looking and bloodshot, they were green too.

"Running water, I take it?" asked Baggit, raising a hand to point at the sink.

"We are fortunate to have a pump installed, yes." There was a wary edge to Father G's voice.

Baggit nodded slowly, as if absorbing the information word by word.

"And this pump – forgive me, but I am still discovering the, shall we say, *unusual* method this intriguing town uses to power such things – this pump is one of these so-called perpetual machines?"

"Yes," replied Father G. "I take it Lugstitch has shown you some of his many devices?"

"In-deeeeed." Baggit stretched the word far longer than Manx thought possible. "Our host has indulged our curiosity most generously. It will be a wrench to leave such kindness – not to mention luxury – behind."

"You're leaving Haarville already?" asked Manx, realising too late that he sounded a touch too pleased about it.

Baggit glanced at him, his eyes flashing wide for a moment. "Oh, we are most certainly *not* leaving. Not after the trouble we went to reaching this place. You wouldn't believe how hard it is to find a town that nobody's heard of and that doesn't appear on a single map. And as for that causeway! Almost the death of us, wasn't it, son?"

"That's the point," muttered Manx.

"We are, indeed, isolated in Haarville," said Father G, in a grave voice. "Whether you are shipwrecked on a nearby reef, or navigate the causeway on foot, to arrive is to have survived."

Baggit clasped his hands together and lowered his head briefly. "I apologise, my good man. Of course, you must know of the risk to life and limb one takes in getting here. Before us, I understand you were the last to make the journey."

"In one piece and still breathing, yes," said Father G.

"So if you're not staying with the Burgmaster, where will you live?" asked Manx, trying to think of an empty – and habitable – property in Haarville.

Baggit opened his arms wide with a satisfied smirk plastered across his sallow cheeks.

"Why, we shall live here," he said.

"Here?" Father G glanced at Manx, whose stomach was twisting like he'd just swallowed a rancid scallop.

"Correct," smiled Baggit. "Isn't that so, Nathaniel?"

Nathaniel shrugged. "Yeah."

"This is *our* home, Mr Baggit," said Father G, planting his fists firmly on the table. "Mine and Manx's. Our hospitality extends to a cup of tea."

"And a seaweed cracker," added Manx, shoving the plate forward.

Baggit stood, gesturing to his son to do the same. "I apologise," he said. "I seem to have got rather ahead of myself."

"I'd say so!" said Father G.

"You couldn't possibly know why we are in Haarville. Please, allow me to explain. You see, we are come to claim our rightful inheritance."

Neither Manx nor his guardian spoke.

"I'll assume your dumbfounded silence means you need further enlightenment," said Baggit. "To put it plainly, *I* am the lawful owner of Fearty's Perpetuals."

"Impossible!" cried Father G.

"It's mine!" shouted Manx.

Baggit chuckled to himself. "I expected denial," he said. "But it is true. I am the rightful heir to all this." He knocked on the table with his knuckles. "Even the furniture!"

Manx found himself gripping his end of the table. "You can't be."

"I can and I am." Baggit tugged on his coat, snapping the leather collar upright around his neck. "My grandfather was Fabian Fearty."

Father G reached for the back door and flung it open. "Get out!"

Baggit nodded. "We will, but first allow us to show you some proof." He clicked his fingers. "Nathaniel!"

The younger Baggit reached into his coat pocket, then held out his closed fist towards Manx, palm-side down. Slowly, he turned it upwards. Something white glinted from between a small gap in his fingers.

"My great-grandad's," said Nathaniel, unfurling his hand. Sitting in the boy's palm, staring directly at Manx, was an eye. A green eye. Identical to the one Manx had dropped back into the jar only minutes before.

4.

Tittle-tattle

Manx hardly slept more than a few winks that night. Father G had tried to reassure him that the Baggits couldn't lay claim to Fearty's Perpetuals on the strength of a glass eye alone, but a nagging doubt had lodged itself inside Manx's mind. And if the dark circles under Father G's eyes that morning were anything to go by, his guardian wasn't all that confident either.

"I'll go to Burgh House after breakfast," he said, yawning as he placed some kale toast on the table.

"What if that man's there? Do you want to risk seeing him again?" Manx shuddered, picturing Baggit and his claw-like hands thrusting out of that creaking leather coat.

"No, I do not," said Father G, "but a word with Lugstitch will clear this up."

"The Burgmaster!" Manx almost choked on his toast. "What's he ever done to help you? Apart from try to ban you from performing."

"That was years ago, Manx. And besides, he was outvoted by the Elder Council."

"Only just," muttered Manx. It was no secret that Burgmaster Lugstitch didn't care much for Father G.

Father G cleared their plates and cups from the table. "Even Lugstitch couldn't believe such a ridiculous claim as Baggit's." He ruffled Manx's hair. "I'll have all this sorted by the time you're home from school." Out in the shop, the perpetual carriage clock chimed. "Talking of which, you'd better get going – unless you want the professor to hand out another detention!"

Manx laughed. "I've got so many already, even Oilyphant's lost count."

"I hope you never call Professor *Oliphant* that to his face," said Father G, trying to hide a smirk. "I know you don't think much of your professor, but you should show him some respect. They say he crossed the causeway during one of the worst storms Haarville has ever seen. If he hadn't survived, you wouldn't be so lucky as to have someone who once lived in the Out There as a teacher. Anyway, I'm sure he has better things to do than keep you in detention – like teach you and Fantoosh something useful."

Manx smiled to himself as he hurried through the shop to the entrance. Their esteemed professor wasn't known for teaching anything useful, so it was unlikely he'd be doing that today.

Stepping outside onto Kipper Lane, Manx gasped. An eye-freezing chill had crystallised overnight. Winter had clearly decided not to skate away just yet. It was so cold even the haar appeared static, as if frozen mid-air in foggy swirls. The town librarian, Tina, had once told Manx about the deathly cold winters her ancestors suffered in Siberia, where the caviar would freeze in their stomachs. Manx hoped the extra goat-wool jumper he was wearing under his oilskin smock would stop his kale toast from doing the same.

Plunging into the teeth-chattering haar, Manx climbed through town, zig-zagging up the steep wynds and narrow braes lined, like elsewhere in Haarville, with granite cottages. Despite knowing every loose cobble and cracked gutter on his route to the academy, Manx still managed to slip a couple of times on the ice and was grateful to finally emerge on to Nethergate. Here, at the top end of town, the streets were wider, the houses taller and the air just a bit fresher. Manx paused and gazed up at Gushet House, Haarville's grandest building, and home to Ma Campbell. He noticed how the haar appeared to linger just above the building's step-gabled roof, but then his eye was drawn, as always, to the round top-floor window, set into the apex of the wall. It was formed of six segments of different-coloured glass, and more than once, he fancied he'd seen a pair of unblinking eyes gazing through the dandelion-yellow pane.

This morning, the glass was coated frosty white, but Manx still found himself whispering the old rhyme he and Fantoosh had made up when they were younger:

"Black cat, broomstick, barn-a-cle nose,
Bubbling cauldron, fourteen toes.

Don't look up and catch her eye,
She'll bake you in her winkle pie. "

"Idiot," he muttered to himself. As if an old recluse like Ma Campbell was a danger to anyone! Father G said she was at least one hundred and twenty years old, so she probably couldn't even spread jam on her sea barley bread without help.

Manx continued on to the academy, barely pausing to nod in the direction of the memorial to cannibalised sailors. Nobody really knew for certain whether any sailors had actually been forced to eat each other to survive after being shipwrecked, or even where it was supposed to have happened. It could have been Clam Rock, or the lethal Razor Reef that surrounded it, or for that matter, any of the nearby reefs and rocks that caused so many ships to founder. Whether the story was true or not, nodding to the dark granite memorial was a Haarville superstition that everyone observed – unlike whispering the Gushet House rhyme, which was Manx and Fantoosh's secret.

A minute later Manx walked into the classroom. The professor tutted loudly, peering over the top of his half-moon glasses, which were wedged on his bulbous, and slightly purple, nose. He pointed his narwhal-tusk cane at the perpetual clock hanging on the wall.

"Late again, Mr Fearty?"

Manx didn't bother checking the clock. The device – with its one and a half pebble-weight's worth of amberose – had seized up ages ago, and Oilyphant hadn't got round to bringing it in for repair. He'd probably been too busy with his hair. Father G often said that if the man took as much trouble oiling his perpetuals as he did his last remaining strands, he might have more luck with his devices. It was how he'd earned his nickname.

"What's today's excuse?" asked Oilyphant, as Manx slouched into his seat. "Schoolbag lost under one of Father G's wigs again?"

Fantoosh let out a giggle, instantly trying to smother it with her hand.

"Silence!" roared Oilyphant.

Manx and Fantoosh turned towards their teacher. Their desks sat side by side at the front of the classroom. The only other furniture in the room was the professor's own larger desk, a slate board attached to the mildew-spotted wall, and a single perpetual room heater. This was positioned to the side, providing, in Oilyphant's words, enough heat to "prevent hypothermia whilst maintaining a cool enough atmosphere to encourage alertness". Fantoosh always sat nearest the heater so that she could unplait her pigtails and dry out her haar-soaked hair every morning.

The classroom had once been filled with desks. However, for many years the number of older people in Haarville had far outweighed the younger folk, and it was ages since there'd been more than two pupils enrolled at the academy, so the surplus furniture had been used for firewood long ago.

"Now," said Oilyphant, "have you got the homework

I set you on herring smuggling in the early twentieth century?" He looked up. "Miss Smith?"

Fantoosh got up and placed two slates of writing on the professor's desk.

"Where's yours, Mr Fearty?" asked Oilyphant, eyes peering over the top of his spectacles. The left lens had long since cracked and fallen out, but the professor insisted on wearing them, probably for moments like this.

"The thing is... actually..." said Manx, trying desperately to think up an excuse.

Oilyphant rapped his cane on the floor. "This had better be good, Mr Fearty," he warned.

"It's been hard to concentrate with everything that's going on," said Manx, which was possibly the most truthful excuse he'd ever come up with.

Oilyphant stared back at him, unblinking.

"You know... the outsiders?"

Oilyphant then made a noise which sounded a bit like a seal sneezing underwater. "I do *not* go in for that type of gossip."

"You're not even a little bit curious?" asked Fantoosh. "Everyone else is."

"Until you have actually met Haarville's new visitors, anything you say is pure speculation and therefore a waste of time."

"But I have met them, sir," said Manx. "Yesterday."

"Nonsense," snapped Oilyphant. "I heard even the Elders haven't had the pleasure yet, so why they would bother with you first, I can't imagine. Yours might be the oldest family in Haarville, Mr Fearty, but it ceased to be the most important many moons ago."

The professor took a small hammer and hacked a piece of chalk off the larger lump that sat on his desk, then began to write furiously on the board. Whilst his back was turned, Fantoosh leant across her desk to whisper to Manx.

"Have you really met them?"

"Yes," whispered back Manx.

"And?"

Manx shook his head. "Not good."

Oilyphant dragged the chalk across the board in an ear-splitting screech, underlining the topic he'd chosen for their morning lesson.

"Does whatever you two are whispering about have anything to do with this?"

Manx read the words on the board:

MATING RITUALS OF COMMON ROCKPOOL SHRIMP

"No, sir."

"In which case, may I suggest that you save your tittle-tattle gossiping for lunchtime? Unless you'd prefer to spend your break chasing the rat out of the privy. Again!"

Lunchtime lasted forty minutes, which was just enough time to get to the Sinking Teapot, order two Monday specials, fill Fantoosh in on the Baggits, and get back in time for afternoon lessons.

Unusually for a Monday, the café was almost full to bursting, its bleached wooden tables crowded and noisy. As they weaved their way to the last free table, the excited chatter reduced to hushed whispers and Manx felt every eye follow his progress.

"What's going on?" asked Fantoosh in a low voice once they'd sat down.

"It looks like everyone's decided the Sinking Teapot's the place to hear some tittle-tattle," replied Manx. "About me."

He fell silent as Hamish arrived to wipe their table. "I saved a couple of portions of the Monday special for you both," he said. Then he leaned in and said in an almost-whisper, "Is it true, what everyone's saying?"

"What's everyone saying?" asked Manx.

"That the outsiders came to your shop yesterday."

Manx nodded. If the news was out already, what was the use in denying it?

Thankfully Hamish was too busy to grill Manx for more information and instead scurried off to collect two bowls of lobster whip for them. Everybody knew Hamish didn't use *actual* lobster – Manx had a suspicion he boiled up starfish meat and dyed it with rosehips – and there was no telling

quite what the concoction was actually whipped up with. But it was delicious, and Manx and Fantoosh had scraped their bowls clean within a couple of minutes.

"Right," said Fantoosh, clattering her spoon in her empty bowl, "talk."

Aware that the seconds were ticking away to another endless lecture from Oilyphant on whale reproduction or clam migration or something else equally mind-numbing, Manx quickly told Fantoosh about the Baggits' visit to Fearty's Perpetuals.

"But your great-granduncle Fabian died in the accident with Celeste Monan. Everyone knows that." Fantoosh leant in over the empty bowls. "You've got his eye to prove it," she said in a hushed voice.

"So does Baggit."

Fantoosh frowned. "So, have I got this right? This Baggit man is saying that Fabian and Celeste survived, then somehow managed to leave Haarville without drowning, lived happily ever after, and that he's their grandson?"

Manx shivered just remembering the mantis-like stranger recounting his so-called family history. "Yes. And it's not just the eye they've got. Baggit showed us Celeste's perpetual handwarmer too. It's all rusty and dented, but it's her initials engraved on the lid. It's definitely a Fearty device, Fan." Manx glanced around the café to make sure prying ears weren't picking up their conversation. "He inherited it from his mother, who'd inherited it from Celeste. It hadn't been used for years – until Nathan bit on it as a baby and it sprang apart in his mouth."

Fantoosh gasped. "A baby playing with a perpetual?!"

Manx nodded. He'd been equally shocked to hear it, imagining the calamity that could have occurred if the amberose had 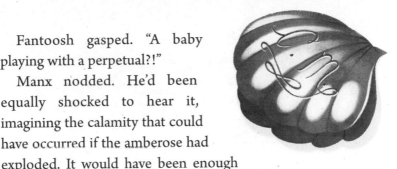 exploded. It would have been enough to wipe the smile off baby Nathaniel Baggit's face. In fact, it would have wiped his face off his face as well.

"Apparently," continued Manx, "there was information about Haarville hidden inside the handwarmer. After Nathaniel's mother died, they set out to find it. Baggit mentioned some rubbish about wanting to track down his long-lost family."

"You don't believe him. Do you?"

Manx shrugged. "If he thinks we're his family, he's hardly jumping for joy to have found us. To be honest, Fan, he gives me the jellyfish wobbles. Meeting them put me completely off my supper, and we were having sea spaghetti as well."

Fantoosh looked horrified. "Manx Fearty misses his favourite seaweed supper! They *must* be awful people!" She punched him playfully on the arm. "And it's taken them all that time to find Haarville?"

"So he said. Ten years to find the causeway and four days to cross it."

"And they're claiming the shop's theirs? No one's going to believe them, are they?"

Manx shrugged. "I hope not."

"But isn't there some sort of document saying you inherited it from your parents?"

"Father G doesn't think so," said Manx. "He said it was never needed because I was the only Fearty left. He went through all of his things last night to try and find something – a note or letter from my parents – but there's nothing."

"So," said Fantoosh, "what do we do in the meantime?"

"We need to find proof that Fabian and Celeste died in Haarville."

"You have proof! You've got his eye!"

"So do they," said Manx. "And Fabian only needed one.

 I know my maths is terrible, but even I know that one false eye plus one false eye equals two false eyes."

"But everyone knows what happened that night of the accident. We've all heard the story enough times."

"Exactly!" said Manx. "We've heard a story. I've never asked what actually happened. I need *real* proof."

"From where?"

"How about we start at the library?" suggested Manx. "After school."

Fantoosh frowned. "I thought we were going to start planning for Death Day."

Manx's shoulders sagged. With the drama of the Baggits' arrival, he'd completely forgotten that Death Day was fast approaching. The whole town would soon be gearing

44

up for the most important day of the year, when they all made their annual pilgrimage over to St Serf's chapel to celebrate their dead ancestors. Manx spent the whole twelve months looking forward to the moment the model of his family's ship, the *Amber Rose*, was carefully lowered from the chapel's vaulted ceiling. Then he'd take out all the heirlooms and trinkets it kept safe, mementos collected over the years by his ancestors, and think of them. And of course, after the memory ship ceremony, there was the massive celebration picnic to enjoy too. He and Fantoosh always took that part of the planning *very* seriously.

But all that was going to have to wait.

"Sorry, Fan," he said, pushing back his seat to stand up. "Right now, finding proof about the accident is more important."

Again, all eyes were on him as they left the café, and Manx had never been so pleased to get out into Haarville's freezing streets. Hamish and his customers were now free to share their tittle-tattle at full volume; Manx and Fantoosh's task was to find some hard facts – and fast.

5.

Up, Periscope!

When Manx and Fan reached the library after school that afternoon, the entrance was closed, but as soon as Manx turned the handle, the familiar warm, amberose-scented air of the reading room wafted out. They hurried inside.

"Hello, my darlings!" Tina waved at them from the far end of the reading room. "Come in! Come in!"

Entering the library always had the same effect on Manx, and despite the urgency of their visit, today was no exception: no matter how cold outside, how heavily the haar pressed down, or how damp and miserable he felt, happiness simply rolled over him here. That, and it was as toasty as five pairs of mittens.

Tina ushered them up onto the raised area of the reading room – once the stage of Haarville's theatre, into which Tina's parents had moved their library years before. The building had become vacant the night the curtain had come down on the theatre's final performance – and on top of the entire cast – crushing most of them to death. Pouncing on the opportunity to protect their books from mouldering away in their damp harbourside house, Tina's parents had managed to convince the Elders to turn the comparatively dry and damp-free theatre over to them.

The librarian drew each of them in turn towards her, wrapping them in her mane of sea-anemone-red hair whilst planting four squelching kisses on their cheeks: left, then right, left, then right. Manx breathed in the soft scent of the dog rose-petal soap Tina always used.

"Come," she said, "warm your young faces."

She led them to the centre of the stage, where two ancient leather travelling trunks were stacked one atop the other. They formed a desk, where, in pride of place, stood the library's source of warmth, comfort and a hundred happy memories: Tina's *babushka*'s Imperial Russian samovar, adapted to run on amberose – a full three pebble-weight's worth – by Fabian Fearty himself. It had been providing heat and hot water ever since.

"We're here to do some research," explained Fantoosh. "In the archives."

"I thought as much," said the  librarian, with the hint of a twinkle in her eye. "But on empty stomachs! *Niet.* No. This I cannot allow."

She sat them down and lifted a copper kettle from the top of the samovar. "First, we drink tea and eat toast."

Manx glanced at Fantoosh and shrugged. Tina never let you choose a book straight away – there was always chat first. And Manx certainly wasn't going to turn down a round of sea barley toast.

"There." Tina poured out two cups of steaming tea – it was dark and strong, the colour of kelp swaying in the surf – then handed Manx a dish of ruby-red jam. "The last of my bramble jelly. Two spoons, I think." She smiled. "To help you grow! Although I think you've both grown taller since last week." She laughed, stirring jam into her own cup. Somehow, Tina's laughs sounded Russian, which Manx always thought impressive considering it had been her grandparents who'd fled their homeland. Tina was born in Haarville, in the library – her crib had been one of the travelling cases they were now drinking tea off.

"And when you have eaten," she said, "you are free to do this vital research. You will discover what you need on the balcony, I think."

Manx stared at the librarian, who was now occupied with wrapping her mass of hair up in a blue tasselled scarf. Tina prided herself on being able to guess exactly the book you were in the mood for, but how could she possibly know what they were searching for right now, when they weren't even sure themselves?

"The archives of the *Haarville Periscope* are on the second and third shelves to the left of the stairs." Tina now looked at Manx with her dark eyes full of seriousness. "Be careful with the older editions, please. The sealskin vellum has become brittle with age."

"*Spasibo*, Tina," said Manx, using the single word of Russian he knew.

"Yes, thank you," said Fantoosh. "And for the tea."

"I've never understood how Tina does that," said Fantoosh, once they'd climbed the rickety spiral stairs to the balcony. "She always gets it right."

"Almost always," laughed Manx. "Last time I was here she chose me a story about a famous Siberian hunter and his lifelong quest to find an albino mountain bear."

"You didn't enjoy it?"

"I couldn't read it," said Manx. "It was in Russian!" He began running a finger along the shelves. "Here they are. Some of these are ancient!" He pulled out one of the old *Haarville Periscopes* at random. It was a single sheet of vellum, and in places you could still see tiny seal hairs embedded within the skin. "This is way too old," he said. "The accident was about a hundred years ago. We need more recent *Periscopes*."

Further along the shelf the copies were made from a different material.

"Seagrass parchment," said Fantoosh, sniffing the stack she'd reached for. They quickly divided them up and began flicking through them. Manx couldn't resist pausing occasionally when a headline caught his eye:

Six More Weeks of Haar Predicted!

Low Tide Reveals New Limpet Bed!

Wreck's Cargo of Tinned Meat Sparks Phlegm Town Riot!

49

"I've never heard of most of these stories," he said.

"Me neither," said Fantoosh. "This one looks interesting."

Manx read the headline Fantoosh had found:

Fearty's Offers Stranger Apprenticeship – Elders to Decide!

Reading on, Manx felt a prickle up his back. This was a report about Father G!

An emergency Burgh-Meet has been called to decide the fate of the outsider currently lodging in Phlegm Town. The young outsider, who goes only by the so-called stage name of Gloria in Excelsis, has so far failed to convince the Elders of his good intentions, but Fairfax Fearty has made a surprise offer to apprentice him. A decision is expected by week's end.

"Of all the tides!" exclaimed Manx. "The Elders really didn't like Father G!"

"Doesn't sound like it," said Fantoosh. "Look, Manx, this is all interesting and everything, but there are a lot of these to get through."

Fantoosh was right. He returned to his stack of *Periscopes*. Halfway through the pile he found what they'd come for.

"Got it!"

Death Day Explosion Rocks Haarville –
Monans & Feartys United in Grief!

ran the headline. They both read the report underneath:

Haarville is slowly coming to terms with last Sunday's tragic accident at Fearty's Perpetuals, in which Fabian Fearty and Celeste Monan lost their lives. Whilst exact circumstances surrounding the explosion are unclear, it is thought that Fabian and Celeste were either killed instantly or perished in the fire which ripped through the backyard workshop, reducing everything to ash. There were no witnesses to the incident, as it occurred during Death Day celebrations, but it is known that neither of the deceased were present at St Serf's for the Lowering of the Ships ceremony.

The reason for Celeste Monan's presence at Fearty's Perpetuals remains unclear – the two clans having been the subject of a recent feud. However, the discovery of a partially melted amberose handwarmer similar to one belonging to Celeste, along with Fabian Fearty's glass eye, is grim evidence that both souls perished. The pungent smell of burnt amberose which still hangs over the site of Fearty's Perpetuals suggests that the substance was once more the cause of an appalling calamity to befall the Fearty family. The *Periscope* understands that the Elders will not be holding an inquest.

Manx banged the edge of the shelf with his fist. "This is it, Fan! Proof that Fabian died in that explosion. Baggit *must* be lying!"

"But then how does he know so much?" Fantoosh started replacing the *Periscopes*. "Who else could have told him about Haarville? And he has the handwarmer and eye. Plus, you said Nathaniel looks just like you."

"I didn't say *just* like me. He's skinnier and his face looks like he's swallowed a barrel of herring pickling juice," said Manx. "Anyway, all that matters is that the Elders back then decided they died, which means Baggit has no claim to my shop. My parents left it to me. And I won't let him steal it."

6.

Marching Orders

Breakfast the next morning was a disaster.

To start with, Father G spilled the last of the gutweed tea on their amberose pot boiler, filling the kitchen with bitter green smoke and the sharp tang of smouldering seaweed. Then, when Olu unexpectedly tapped on the kitchen window, Manx dropped his freshly spread cracker on the floor, where it landed limpet paste-side down. He picked it up, but a woodlouse had got stuck in the paste, legs wriggling and kicking in desperation for release. With no more crackers in the tin, he left his breakfast on the floor, where Olu began pecking at it suspiciously.

Manx had been on edge since returning from the library the evening before. He'd arrived home on a surge of excitement that his discoveries from the archives might help persuade Lugstitch that Baggit was lying, but Father G had soon drained away Manx's hope. The Burgmaster had refused to see him that morning. It was clear, said Father G, that Lugstitch and Baggit were cooking something up.

An uneasy feeling of impending doom had kept Manx

awake all night, and it was still flapping around his thoughts now, like a gull swooping over an abandoned crab sandwich. He sat slumped at the table with his empty plate, whilst Father G scraped and scrubbed the burnt-on leaves off the pot boiler. In the corner, Olu was quietly preening his feathers, but his beak shot up, instantly on the alert, as an insistent banging on the shop door started up.

"That doesn't sound very friendly," Manx said.

"It sounds downright impertinent," said Father G. "Stay here. I'll deal with this."

Manx had no intention of staying there, but he nodded and waited for Father G to vanish through the winkle-shell curtain before following him. He hid in the shadows behind the counter with Olu, who had scuttled through from the kitchen with him. Glancing to the door, Manx saw dark shapes shifting outside in the swirling haar. He steadied himself against the edge of the counter as Father G opened up.

First to stride in was Burgmaster Lugstitch, the clam-shell buttons on his goat-twill jacket straining against his puffed out chest. The Burgmaster was short and stout, and Manx often thought he resembled a barrel – albeit a well-dressed one.

"Finally," he grumbled, wiping haar drops from his long, grey moustache with a yellow pocket kerchief. "Business can't be so good that you can afford to keep people waiting in the gutter."

Manx spotted a mother-of-pearl trident brooch pinned to the lapel of the Burgmaster's jacket – the official Burgh House emblem – which meant he was at the shop on official business.

"It's not yet eight o'clock," replied Father G. "Like most sensible people, we breakfast *before* opening."

"I prefer to rise with the gannets," said Lugstitch, "and dive into the opportunities the day has to offer." He paused and looked around the shop. "It's all about seeing the potential."

"What do you mean?" asked Father G. "What potential?"

"I wasn't talking to you," snapped Lugstitch, his voice tight with disgust. He turned away to the entrance. "Ninian, please join us – there's no need to stand on ceremony." Baggit slinked in, coat-tails glistening with condensed fog droplets. Nathaniel followed, creeping slowly behind, looking up furtively from under his mop of dripping hair. "You'll see possibilities everywhere," said Lugstitch, reaching up to pat the older Baggit on the back. "Sadly, the business has gone downhill since your grandfather's untimely... disappearance."

"Death. Untimely *death* is what you mean to say," said Father G firmly. "And the business is doing perfectly well, thank you. If you've come here to throw insults around like discarded mussel shells, then I must ask you to leave."

Lugstitch, who was peering under one of the dust sheets covering the cabinet of amberose handwarmers and scent diffusers, cleared his throat. "*You've* done rather well for yourself, haven't you?"

Father G was shaking, fists clenched. Manx was convinced he could hear his guardian's heart beating from a few feet away. "Meaning?"

"Meaning," continued Lugstitch, whipping away the sheet, "that you've profited not only from these valuable objects, but also from the demise of several Feartys."

Father G pushed back his shoulders. "I don't need to remind you, *Burgmaster*, that Manx's grandparents sponsored me as their apprentice when none of you would give me the time of day. And his parents named me the boy's guardian in the event of their untimely passing. Everything here belongs to Manx."

"Says who?" asked Lugstitch.

Manx stepped out from behind the counter. "Says me."

A blast of chilled air around his legs reminded Manx that he and his guardian were still dressed in their nightshirts, whilst their unwelcome guests stalked around them in suits and coats and with slicked-down hair. He glanced over to Nathaniel, whose scowl could have scared off a hungry shark.

Every part of Manx's skin was prickling. Father G might be his guardian, he thought, but it was *his* shop and *he* was going to deal with these people. He clamped his teeth together, running his next words through his head. As he did, he felt the tickle of feathers on his ankles. Olu stood, beak raised, between his feet.

"Whatever you're here to say, Mr Lugstitch, just say it,"

he said, hoping his voice didn't sound half as nervous as his stomach felt. "Then leave my shop. Please."

Lugstitch blinked twice before speaking. "Quite the plucky young thing all of a sudden, aren't we?" he said. "But as you wish." He cleared his throat. "The Elders have verified Mr Baggit's claim to be the direct descendant of both Fabian Fearty and Celeste Monan. Furthermore, in accordance with the unwritten, though longstanding, agreement in such matters, it has been decided that his other claim to ownership by nature of patriarchal hereditary lineage and proper rules of inheritance should be honoured."

"What does that mean?" Manx frowned at Lugstitch.

"It means we're being evicted," said Father G.

Manx felt a wave of nausea swill through him. How many hours had he spent labouring over the Burgmaster's vast collection of perpetuals, expertly repairing and servicing the valuable devices, all to be treated like this!

Manx lifted his chin and glared at their unwelcome guests.

"You're stealing our home."

Baggit, who up until now had remained silent, cleared his throat.

"I think 'steal' is too strong a word." He uttered this softly, as if trying to sound kind. The effect was entirely the opposite.

"Is that so?" Father G said bitterly. "And what word would you choose instead? Thieve? Rob? Plunder?"

Baggit ignored him and suddenly lurched towards

Manx, enveloping his hands in a bony grasp. "Thank you," he said, as Olu scurried out of range of Baggit's boot, "for taking care of my family's business for so many, many years in my absence."

"*Your* family!" cried Manx, pulling his hands free. He was starting to feel like a shaken-up bottle of clam seltzer whose stopper had just been popped. "It's *my* family. *My* shop. These devices are *my* responsibility."

Baggit tried to smile. At least, that's what it looked like. But the man's yellow teeth and sunken cheeks made his face look more like a dead dogfish's head on one of Sheila Giddock's fishmonger slabs.

"My dear boy," (words which made Manx's blood run from hot to icy cold in seconds), "the sooner you accept the facts the better."

"Facts!" The word exploded from Manx's mouth. "I'll give you a fact! Fabian died out there, in the courtyard. His sister – my great-grandmother – inherited Fearty's Perpetuals. It's mine!"

Baggit thrust a hand into his coat pocket, and with a flourish whipped out the eyeball and handwarmer. "These, dear boy, are *actual* facts." He waved them in front of Manx's face, then threw him a pitying look. "You seem… shocked."

"We cannot allow this boy's pathetic emotions to hinder this process," said Lugstitch, stepping forward. He turned abruptly to Manx, running his fingers the length of his walrus whiskers. "You are no longer owner of Fearty's Perpetuals. The shop, all items therein, and adjoining accommodation are hereby transferred to Ninian Brontus Baggit, grandson of Fabian Fearty, and therefore the true direct inheritor and heir." He removed a sheaf of parchment from his jacket, flicked through to the end and held it up for all to see. "Signed by the Elders at last night's emergency Burgh-Meet."

"How much did you bribe them, I wonder," muttered Father G, earning himself a sharp stare from Lugstitch.

"But… this is the only home I've ever had," said Manx.

Lugstitch grunted. "I will not allow the whinings of a child and," he curled his lip at Father G, "those of a second-rate entertainer of dubious repute to delay proceedings. You have until lunchtime to vacate."

"Lunchtime!" Father G almost exploded at this announcement.

Baggit smiled, pulling Nathaniel forward and clasping his son by both shoulders.

"We have waited many years and risked our very lives to claim what is ours," he said. "I think a few hours to clear out of *our* home is more than generous."

7.

Room to Let

"'Dubious repute!' That's what he said. 'A second-rate entertainer of dubious repute!'"

Father G kicked the wooden chest he'd been dragging along the street. If their situation hadn't been so disastrous, Manx would be in fits of laughter seeing his guardian decked out in his entire collection of flamboyant scarves and boas, all coiled around his neck. The look was topped off by his most outlandish starfish-pink wig, which he'd refused to squash into the chest. Unfortunately, in the rush to pack as much as they could before the eviction deadline of midday, there'd been no time to dress the wig properly. Manx wasn't even sure Father G had put it on the right way. Strands of fog-limp hair were pasted across his cheeks. Gloria in Excelsis had never appeared so bedraggled. It was just as well the streets were quiet.

"And I am certainly *not* second-rate!" Father G pulled some wig out of his eyes. "*Don't* say anything."

"I wasn't going to," said Manx. "Come on, it's freezing." He pulled his own wig down over his ears. Father G had insisted Manx wear another of Gloria's wigs – the russet red bouffant – rather than have it crushed along with the gowns. These had been stuffed, along with most of Manx's clothes, into the giant sail-canvas pack slung over his back. As long as the pack was balanced evenly, and the wig stayed in place, he'd found he could just about walk in a straight line – though the cobbles on Hithergate were particularly treacherous with a slick of moisture from the fast-dropping haar.

Wearing multiples of everything else made progress even more difficult, but since they weren't allowed back to the shop, it was either take everything now or never see it again. This explained the wig-wearing, and why Manx was layered up in sweaters, cardigans, oilskin coats and three pairs of breeches – and why his best boots were hanging round his neck by their laces.

"Ouch!" Manx yelped as his right foot slid out from underneath him and he careened into the gutter. Thankfully, the mound of gowns in the pack cushioned his fall.

To avoid any more slips, they held onto each other as they picked their way across Parten Brae. Ditchwater Burn had burst its banks again and the street was running with muddied marsh water. Crossing the bridge over the burn itself was equally fraught, and it wasn't until they were in Phlegm Town that they let go. Manx couldn't resist a quick look behind him. Despite the murky air, he could still make out the eerie pulsating beam from the harbour's perpetual light tower, doing its job of marking the harbour entrance for Sheila Giddock when she returned from her daily fishing trip. Then Manx noticed that the fog draped over Haarville seemed to throb with an orange glow, as if a giant heart was beating slowly somewhere inside.

"Is it always like that?" he asked.

"Yes," replied Father G. "It's the amberose afterglow – the haar reflects it back. When you're in it, you don't notice it's there."

"But there's never a glow like that over Phlegm Town."

"It takes a lot of perpetuals to create the afterglow, Manx. When was the last time you repaired a device from this side of the burn? Folk across here will have sold most of their perpetuals years ago, to pay for food or to put coats on their backs in the winter – either that or they don't have the means to repair them."

"I didn't realise," said Manx quietly, as they turned into Ratfish Wynd.

Ice-cold water dripped from the low, overhanging gables either side of the wynd. Trying to avoid them, whilst also side-stepping broken cobbles and decomposing rat corpses, wasn't easy, especially with eyes smarting from the rancid reek of decay and rotting seaweed.

Manx deliberately avoided looking at the dark windows  and doorways, from every one of which he sensed eyes following him. He didn't blame people for staring – he'd no doubt be doing the same in their place. From one doorway he even heard his name being whispered. "It's the Fearty lad," the voice said, "so it must be true."

Gusts of frigid wind whipped around them as they stumbled on, but about halfway down the wynd, they stopped. A paint-peeled sign screeched as it swayed on rusty fixings and a thin curtain of droplets fell from it onto Manx's face as looked up to read it:

Manx shuddered. Everyone in Haarville knew you had to be either desperate or already drunk to want to step a toe inside Phlegm Town's most notorious inn.

"Are you sure I can't ask Fantoosh? Her parents would definitely take us in."

"And sleep in their parlour? Or their privy?" Father G adjusted his wig where it had slipped over one eye. "No. We are quite able to look after ourselves. Although," he added, sighing deeply, "I never imagined I'd end up back at this place."

"What do you mean?" asked Manx.

Father G sniffed. "Remember I told you the Elders sent me here to Phlegm Town when I first arrived?"

"Yes."

"Well, this was all I could afford back then." Father G

shook his head and shrugged. "And thanks to Lugstitch and Baggit, it's all we can afford now."

Grasping the grubby squid-shaped handle with the end of a pink feather boa, he pushed open the creaking door. Before stepping inside, they exchanged the briefest of weak smiles. There was no need for words – Manx knew exactly what his guardian was thinking, because he was thinking it himself: how had it come to this?

"Well, here's a turn-up," croaked a thick, rasping voice from inside. "How the fortunate 'ave fallen."

A sallow, wrinkled face appeared out of the gloom. A halo of dim light surrounded the head, but that was the only angelic thing about the man's appearance: a raggedy cardigan hung limply off knobbly shoulders, whilst a tiny, dusty moth flapped around one of its gaping pockets. Smoke swirled up from a blackened clay pipe hanging from his thin-lipped mouth.

This was Silas Skulpin, the Lange Fluke's landlord. He seemed to match his grim surroundings perfectly.

"If it's a room yer wanting, better bring that in," he croaked, pointing a gnarled finger to their luggage. "I won't be doing no carrying nor lifting for no one."

"When did you ever?" muttered Father G, bending to lift his trunk.

Having heaved their belongings over the threshold, Manx closed the door on the nose-wrinkling stench of Ratfish Wynd. But if the stink of the air outside the Lange Fluke's entrance was memorable, the first intake of the air inside would stay with Manx for ever. He had to fight to keep down even the few drops of limpet water he'd hurriedly swallowed before the Elders had arrived to escort them out of the shop.

There were so many foul smells, it was hard to single them out. But strongest of the lot was the pong of the gull oil which lit the dim, flickering wall lights and lanterns placed on grime-rich tables.

As they followed Skulpin through the bar, the air and its odours thickened, and hissed whispers filtered out from shadowy, smoke-filled corners.

When he reached the bottom of a staircase, the landlord turned to them with a leering smile. "I'll go and select one of our finest rooms for you. Ha!"

He slowly heaved himself up the stairs, muttering under his breath to the percussion of knee clicks, wheezes and coughs. At the top, he turned his head and glowered down at them.

"You just going to stand there like a pair of startled sandpipers all day? I got work to do, you know."

As the landlord shuffled along the landing, Manx grabbed one end of the trunk. Somehow, he and Father G managed to hoist it up the steep flight of stairs, but it was impossible to avoid scraping against the soot-smudged walls.

"You'll be sharing the bed," wheezed Skulpin, kicking open one of the doors on the landing. "And pillows is extra." A fusty waft of stale air and grey dust billowed out.

Skulpin stepped into the room. In the meagre light cast by the small, crud-caked window, Manx saw that the landlord's wrinkles stretched all the way to his long ears, where flakes of skin and wax clung to the bristly hairs sprouting from deep within. There were probably as many life forms in one of his lugs as there were in the lumpen mattress Father G was now poking with a finger. As Skulpin scratched a dry patch on his bald head, a shower of dead skin rained down.

"I want payment up front," he snapped, fixing them in turn with his red-rimmed, watery eyes. "Or perhaps you'd prefer to negotiate an exchange of labour as part-payment for board and lodging. Like the last time?"

Father G raised his eyebrows. "You mean when you made me pay with my few valuable items of jewellery and then forced me to scrub your foul kitchen twice a day when I had nothing left to give you?"

Skulpin merely shrugged, picking at a crusty scab on his whiskery chin. "We'll make our deal over lunch. One o'clock sharp." He stepped out and slammed the door. A wardrobe leaning against the wall wobbled precariously before settling back in place.

Manx threw off his boot necklace and went to the window. Carcasses of dead flies littered the dust-layered sill, and yet more were ensnared in the cobwebs hanging in thick, lace-like curtains across the pane. He grasped the window latch, but after several fruitless attempts gave up trying to shift it.

Unpacking the little that was left of their lives didn't take long, although Father G spent a while carefully smoothing out the creases in his gowns.

"I'm sure you'll fit right in here, wearing those!" said Manx.

Father G looked over and smiled. "After you, these are the most important things I have," he said quietly. "When I came to Haarville I had no choice but to give up everything about my life, but I could never give up Gloria. Without her, I'm half a person."

Manx rummaged in the chest for the two wooden tea caddies they'd found space for. He placed them on the windowsill, having first swept it clear of flies.

"I suppose we'll get hot water somewhere," he said.

Father G grabbed a knotted old wig from the crate, extracting an amberose pot heater from inside it. "Couldn't leave without this." He winked.

Manx laughed, as he thrust a hand into the pile of sweaters and socks he'd emptied out onto the bed. "Tah-dah!"

"Your carousel!" exclaimed Father G.

Manx carefully laid the amberose-powered toy down on the bed's threadbare blanket. "When they searched my sack I was sure they were going to find it."

He set his treasured device spinning for a few seconds to make sure it hadn't been damaged during the move. The ten miniature wooden ships that hung from the domed, sailcloth canopy spun perfectly, just as they always had. The carousel was ancient – quite possibly one of the oldest perpetuals in existence – and had been made by Sarah and Finnick Fearty themselves for their children to play with. The tiny ships were supposed to represent the real *Amber Rose*, and Manx couldn't imagine trying to get to sleep without his precious carousel spinning slowly, wafting its sweet aroma around his room.

Father G put his arm around Manx. "They had no right going through your things like that."

"I don't think anything would have stopped Baggit," said Manx. "You saw his face when he looked at the cabinets. He couldn't wait to get his hands on every last one of our perpetuals. But he wasn't getting my carousel."

Father G sighed and set the pot boiler down on a worm-riddled chest of drawers. "Let's have some tea to settle our stomachs before we eat. If Skulpin's food is as bad as I remember, we'll need it."

8.

Black Cats and Broomsticks

What passed for lunch at the Lange Fluke was every bit as grim as Manx could have imagined. He stared down into the bowl Skulpin had just filled from a bucket smeared with globs of congealed fat. Assorted unidentifiable morsels bobbed around in a thin, brown slick of oil.

"We're paying for this foul soup," whispered Father G, "so we're going to eat it. OK?"

Manx nodded, sifting out a fish fin and something that resembled the sucker end of a leech, then he tentatively filled his spoon with the oily broth. Both he and Father G swallowed at the same time, then simultaneously reached for the salt.

The bar's tables had filled up whilst they'd been unpacking upstairs and Manx risked a quick glance around. The Lange Fluke's customers seemed a motley crowd, hunched over their bowls, slurping and guzzling up the slippery fish intestines and whatever other unsavoury morsels Skulpin had added.

"Everyone here seems to be *enjoying* this," whispered

Manx, removing a thin bone from between his front teeth.

Father G spooned up a fish eye from his bowl. "Phlegm Town's inhabitants can't afford to be picky when it comes to food," he said. "They've always put up with the cheaper parts of fish and the less-than-fresh strips of seaweed. Nothing goes to waste round here, Manx. If it's edible, someone will scoff it."

"Veritable *gourmands,* we are!" Skulpin had crept up on them and now eased himself down onto the opposite bench, sighing heavily as his joints creaked and cracked. "Feasting as we do off the slops and scraps." He placed his gnarled hands on the table and leant in, lowering his voice to a hoarse whisper. "Is it true what they say?" Skulpin looked at them. As watery and baggy as his eyes were, Manx could sense a nervousness in the way his gaze flitted left and right, waiting for them to answer. "This stranger – is he who he says he is?"

"No!" Manx blurted out.

A hush descended over the Lange Fluke's bar. Skulpin turned to his customers.

"Back to your bowls, you gossip-greedy old stickybeaks!"

"Sorry," whispered Manx, "but he can't be. Fabian was killed in the fire. Everyone knows that. And Celeste. They both died."

"Sure of that, are you?"

"It doesn't matter if I'm sure of it," said Manx. "The Elders said they did."

Skulpin made a noise like a fulmar fighting off an egg thief, which Manx guessed was supposed to be a laugh.

"Well, if our esteemed Elders said so, it must be true," said Skulpin, curling his lip.

"Don't you believe them?" asked Manx. "It was printed in the *Periscope*."

Skulpin banged a fist on the table. "Doesn't mean it's the truth, boy." He spat the words, sending spittle across the table. "This town conceals more secrets than there's stones to hide them under. Lies lay dormant for so long, they become truths." He paused to catch his breath, then tapped out his pipe and refilled it with some leaves from his cardigan pocket. "Secrets and lies," he said, "are like spawning salmon. They always return home in the end."

"Exactly!" cried Manx. "Baggit's lying."

"Unless he isn't." Skulpin's eyes glazed over, flicking around in their sockets as if chasing a thought. "And it pains me more than you can know to admit it."

"I don't understand."

Skulpin leaned in, so close that Manx could smell the whelk schnapps on his breath.

"That makes two of us then." He pushed himself up from the table. "Clear your bowls when you're done, and you're both on supper duty tonight." The landlord shuffled away into the kitchen, leaving Manx's head swirling with confusion.

"I don't see why he's so upset by all this."

 Father G stacked their bowls and wiped the discarded fish bits onto the floor.

"Silas Skulpin has more reason than anyone to be concerned by Baggit's claims," he said in a gentle voice. "Perhaps more even than you, Manx."

"Why?"

"Because Silas is Celeste's brother. He was the youngest of the three Monan siblings, and not much older than you at the time of the fire."

Father G's words echoed around Manx's head for a few seconds.

"That means Skulpin would be even more related to Baggit than I would be!" He tried to work out exactly how everyone might be connected if Baggit was telling the truth, but the task required a quill and some squid ink. "Hold on – did you say there were three of them?"

"Yes. Celeste had a twin sister."

"Shame she's not alive," said Manx. "We could have asked her if she knew anything about this."

"She *is* still alive."

"What!" Manx stared at Father G. "But Skulpin's so ancient. Who in Haarville could be old enough?" He thought about everyone he knew, but couldn't picture anyone who looked even a day older than Skulpin... Unless... "Not Ma Campbell?"

Father G nodded gravely. "Yes. Margaret Campbell is Celeste's sister. But I doubt she'll know any more than we do already."

"Why didn't you tell me this before? We could have gone to Gushet House straight away to ask!"

Father G glanced around the bar, then spoke in a low whisper. "The story goes that after the fire, Silas and Margaret cut themselves off from their family, and from each other. Silas didn't even keep the Monan name, and Margaret married and never spoke to her parents again."

Manx flicked a wriggling earwig out of his hair, sensing a rising swell of hope. If anyone knew what really happened that night, surely it would be Celeste's twin sister.

Manx wasted no time in escaping the dank confines of Phlegm Town, promising Father G that he'd be back to help prepare supper. If he hurried, he could intercept Fantoosh on her way home from the academy.

Pausing for a second on the bridge, Manx breathed in a lungful of cold haar to clean out the foul air from the Lange Fluke. Above Haarville's rooftops, the amberose afterglow cast its warm orange halo. It was like a beacon, calling him back, and within just a few steps Manx sensed a familiar sweetness in the air. Smelling the amberose again was like putting on a favourite old jumper.

"Enjoy it whilst you can," he muttered to himself, heading up Parten Brae.

Manx lurked near the memorial to cannibalised sailors for a few minutes, staring at the carved stonework depicting the sorry-looking bunch of starved shipwreck survivors taking bites out of each other's limbs. Maybe a dish of the Lange Fluke's soup wasn't so bad after all, he thought, as Fantoosh came skipping down the academy's steps.

"Hey!"

Fantoosh screamed as Manx leapt out from his hiding place. "That really scared me!" she said. "What are you doing lurking there?"

"Waiting for you, of course. How was Oilyphant today?"

"Don't ask," moaned Fantoosh. "It's awful being in class on my own. I had to answer everything myself. And he made *me* chase the rat out of the privy. That's your job. You'd better be back tomorrow." She grabbed his hand. "You will be back tomorrow, won't you?"

"I hope so," replied Manx, which were not words he thought he'd ever say about going to classes. But if he wanted to avoid another lunch at the Lange Fluke, the academy suddenly seemed like a necessary option.

"I can't believe they kicked you out of your shop like that," said Fantoosh. "And so quickly." She looked at him. "Mum said you're at Skulpin's place. Is it really stinky?"

Manx shrugged. "The food's pretty gross."

"Thought it might be." Fantoosh loosened her patchwork cape and plunged a hand into her dungaree's large front pocket. "I saved these from lunch. Hamish's Tuesday special."

"Crab claws!" Manx practically snatched one from Fantoosh. He sucked the end of the pink claw, allowing the sweet juice to run over his tongue. It was almost good enough to banish all memory of the unidentified floating objects in his lunchtime soup. "Thanks, Fan."

"Take them all."

Manx placed the claws carefully in
his pocket. "I'll save them for later."

"So," said Fantoosh, "where are we
going? Madame Bonbeurre's for a
limpet bun?"

Despite that idea being tempting,
Manx was on a mission. "I'm not giving up that easily," he
said. "Baggit's managed to get Lugstitch under his bony
thumb. It's like he's bribed him, or offered him something.
If there's one thing we know about our Burgmaster, it's
that he never does anything for anyone unless there's
something in it for him too."

"So we need to find out what it is," said Fantoosh.

"Exactly. But first I want to know one way or the other
if Baggit really is a Fearty, and I think I know where to find
the answer."

"Really? Where?"

"Gushet House," said Manx, striding away. "Come on!"

As they headed along Nethergate, Manx told Fantoosh
what he'd found out about Ma Campbell being Celeste
and Skulpin's sister.

"Incredible," said Fantoosh, eyes wide in disbelief. "I
knew Ma Campbell had to be old, but this makes her *really*
ancient. Do you think she'll talk to us?"

"That's what I'm hoping," said Manx as Gushet House
loomed overhead, its dark slate roof slicing through the
haar. His stomach twisted. He'd never been inside the

imposing building before. Without thinking, he started mouthing the words of their witch's song.

> *"Black cat, broomstick, barn-a-cle nose,*
> *Bubbling cauldron, fourteen toes…"*

"What are you doing?" asked Fantoosh.

"Nothing."

"You were singing the rhyme, weren't you?"

"It's just habit," said Manx, spotting movement behind the circular window. They were being watched. "And I don't care. This place still turns my insides to quicksand."

"Go on then." Fantoosh nudged him towards the door. "Knock."

Swallowing so hard it actually hurt, Manx reached for the clam-shaped knocker. He knocked with it twice, then took a cautious step back.

9.

Gushet House

Nothing happened for a moment. Manx and Fantoosh stood and stared at the red door, then they both jumped as the heavy, clunking sound of a bolt being heaved across reverberated from inside. The door swung open with a dramatically long *creeeeak* and a heady rush of sweet amberose-infused air clouded around them.

A stout woman with rosy cheeks on a face almost as white as freshly steamed haddock stepped into the doorway. She wore a grey apron and matching scarf wrapped around her head, from which a few strands of vivid ginger hair had escaped. A collection of keys, cloths and feather dusters swung from a rope belt tied around her waist.

"Maizy!" blurted Manx, who, for some reason, had forgotten that the door would likely be opened by Ma Campbell's housekeeper. Maizy Halfin had worked at Gushet House for decades. It was said that she could spot a fleck of dust at fifty paces.

"Master Fearty, Miss Smith," said Maizy, nodding at each of them in turn. "Come in. We've been expecting you."

Exchanging quizzical looks, Manx and Fantoosh stepped inside, the door's hinges grating again as it closed behind them.

"You need a drop of oil on that." Manx laughed nervously.

Maizy unhooked a small bottle from her rope belt and dripped a thick brown liquid onto the door's hinges. "Any other housekeeping advice for me?" A smile twitched at the corners of her mouth.

Maizy didn't wait for an answer. Instead, she tucked her loose strands of hair back under her scarf and led them across a grand entrance hall. Around the walls, eight identical perpetual lanterns flickered, each containing a half pebble-weight of amberose. Manx might not have been inside Gushet House before, but he was well acquainted with Ma Campbell's perpetual devices, which she regularly sent to the shop for servicing and repair. The lanterns' bright light was reflected back by the elaborate mosaic under their feet, made up of thousands of highly polished mother-of-pearl pieces placed in a circular wave pattern.

"It's beautiful," whispered Fantoosh, spinning around to take the mosaic in.

"It is," whispered back Manx. He'd never seen anything like it – not even in the meeting chamber at Burgh House.

"Your mother, Matilda, loved that mosaic too," said a

deep, gravelly voice from somewhere above. "My ancestors had it laid to remind them of the ocean that surrounded the Mediterranean island they once called home."

Peering up the grand spiral staircase, Manx couldn't see who the voice belonged to through the gorse-golden glow of an intricately latticed lantern which hung by a heavy chain from the ceiling. Then, a figure began to descend slowly, finally joining them on the mosaic floor.

For a woman of her great age, Ma Campbell stood remarkably tall, and was made taller still by a mound of sliver-grey hair pinned up into a snail-like coil. As she smoothed down the front of her long, purple woollen dress, Manx marvelled at how her warm, olive-toned face wasn't nearly as wrinkled as Skulpin's, when it should have been as withered as a piece of sun-dried seaweed.

"You knew my mother?"

Ma Campbell smiled, her hazel eyes twinkling. "Matilda would stop by regularly to deliver or collect one of my perpetuals. She always came in to look at the mosaic."

Manx looked at the iridescent floor again. His mother had stood right where he was now, marvelling at the same tiny, shiny fragments of shell. He savoured the thought.

"Maizy said you'd been expecting us. Why?"

"I may not venture forth from my house these days," said Ma Campbell, "but I am still a keen *observer* of developments." She glanced away, up the staircase.

"So you do spy on everyone from up there!" Fantoosh instantly slapped her hand across her mouth.

Ma Campbell merely shrugged. "They say curiosity

killed the catfish, but it didn't. Curiosity left it better informed. It is, after all, what takes you to the library so often."

Manx stared at Ma Campbell. The question he should be asking her was what *didn't* she see from her spy-hole window!

"The desire for knowledge is a wonderful thing," she continued. "It brings you here, in search of answers before embarking on your quest."

"Quest?" asked Manx.

"Why else risk knocking at my door and being baked into a winkle pie?" said Ma Campbell, laughing.

Manx felt a sudden blush flood his cheeks. His and Fantoosh's silly rhyme wasn't quite as secret as they'd thought.

"Now, we shall talk some more in a moment," continued Ma Campbell, leading them into the large kitchen, where a table had been laid for three, "but first, I believe Maizy has prepared some refreshments."

"Our best hawthorn tea," said Maizy, placing a giant teapot on the kitchen table.

"Very good," said Ma Campbell, indicating for Manx and Fantoosh to sit down. "And I see you have baked a sea-carrot cake, Maizy. Please join us then, dear. If there are to be grand revelations, far easier to avoid having to repeat them."

The housekeeper cut the cake and served Manx and Fantoosh gigantic slices.

"As you have cleverly discovered," began Ma Campbell, "I am indeed Celeste and Silas's sister." She paused a moment to sip her tea. "I assume the one thing you are burning to know is whether Ninian Baggit can possibly be telling the truth?"

Manx nodded, his mouth crammed with the moistest, tastiest cake he'd had in ages. It was almost as delicious as one of Madame Bonbeurre's jam puffs.

"I have to tell you," said Ma Campbell seriously, "that my sister and Fabian didn't survive the fire that night... The truth is, they were never in it."

Manx dropped his slice of cake. "I was hoping you weren't going to say that." He pushed his plate away – he needed to hear whatever was coming next without the distraction of chewing on bits of sea carrot. Glancing over to Fantoosh, he saw that she'd also abandoned her cake and was sitting wide-eyed, waiting to hear more.

Ma Campbell sipped more of her tea, then continued.

Celeste and Fabian, she explained, were childhood sweethearts. However, due to a long-standing feud between the Monan and Fearty families – something to do with a malfunctioning set of perpetual hair curlers and a burning head of freshly curled hair – they were forbidden to marry.

"But they continued to meet secretly," said Ma Campbell, "with me acting as lookout – although it pained me greatly to do so."

"Because you didn't like Fabian?" asked Manx.

"No, my dear. Because I, too, was in love with him. Most of the girls were – as, indeed, were some of the boys."

"So why help them?" asked Fantoosh.

"Love plays wicked games with our hearts. You both have this yet to discover. But believe me, it makes fools of us all eventually." Ma Campbell shook her head sadly. "And so they carried on meeting. Of course, I knew they were plotting to escape and I never once tried to stop them. I'd have done anything for my sister or Fabian."

"Including helping them to fake their own deaths," said Manx.

Ma Campbell sighed. "Yes. Including that."

She explained how Celeste and Fabian had chosen Death Day to make their escape because the whole town would be across at St Serf's chapel.

"If anyone asked where Celeste was, I lied and said she was poorly. And nobody was surprised when Fabian failed to join his family at the chapel – everyone assumed he was tinkering with his perpetuals or in Phlegm Town. He had many friends down on Pollock Row, which was another thing my parents disapproved of." A smile formed on her lips. "Fabian loved rooting around the junk stalls on the Row – he was always on the hunt for quirky objects and rusting old perpetuals."

Ma Campbell said the lovers' plan was to set fire to the Fearty workshop, then leave by the causeway.

"My final task, after they'd gone, was to place Fabian's spare glass eye in the ashes of the workshop, along with a chunk of melted pewter, which everyone would assume was Celeste's handwarmer. My dear sister's hands were always cold and she never left home without her precious perpetual."

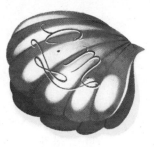

"Why didn't they throw those things in themselves?" asked Fantoosh.

"It was vital these objects were discovered," explained Ma Campbell. "I made sure they were easy for the Elders to find. Which, of course, they did."

"And you're the only one who knew the truth?" Manx wondered how it was possible to keep a secret like that for so long.

Ma Campbell nodded sadly. "I still grieved for them with everyone else," she whispered. "For all I knew, they'd perished on the causeway."

"But they made it," said Fantoosh.

Ma Campbell eased herself from her chair and went to the window.

"It seems," she said, peering out, "that Fabian and Celeste have indeed returned to Haarville in the form of Ninian Baggit."

"And now I understand how both me and Nathaniel have a glass eye – he has Fabian's real one and I have his spare," said Manx.

"I made those eyes myself, you know." Ma Campbell turned from the window. "I blew the glass using sand from Limpet Bay."

"You can make glass?" Fantoosh looked at Ma Campbell in wonder.

"Generations of Monan children were taught to blow glass, including me. It's how my family made their fortune. Alas, I was the last to learn the trade, and I stopped after Celeste and Fabian left."

"Well, they're beautiful eyes," said Manx.

 "Thank you, dear. I was rather proud of them. They certainly made a change from making windows! I was only going to blow one eye, but decided that a spare would come in useful if Fabian ever lost the other."

"Or decided to fake his own death," said Fantoosh, under her breath.

Manx pushed a crumb around his plate for a moment, thinking. "It all seems so risky – faking their deaths and crossing the causeway. Would they really do all that for *love*?"

"Like I said, love can play wicked games." Ma Campbell's eyes seemed to glaze over.

"Well, one thing I'm sure of," Manx said, "is that Ninian Baggit *didn't* risk the causeway for love. If he loved his family, he wouldn't have had us kicked out, or risked himself or Nathaniel drowning. And I bet he hasn't even been to visit you, has he? You're his family too."

Ma Campbell nodded. "I am."

Fantoosh frowned. "So you would be… Baggit's great-aunt?"

"Which makes the boy Ma Campbell's great-grandnephew," announced Maizy.

"Indeed," said Ma Campbell. "And I cannot deny it would bring me some joy to meet the young man. One's family can be troublesome, or distant, or," she turned to Manx, "prone to early deaths. But if you're lucky, they can also bring happiness."

Manx found himself feeling sorry for Ma Campbell. If Nathaniel ever bothered to search her out, he'd probably make a rubbish great-grandnephew.

"If it wasn't for love or family," he said, "then I want to know why Baggit risked the journey here. That's what this quest is about."

"If you want my opinion," said Maizy, "there's only one emotion that blinds people to danger as much as love."

"And what would that be, dear?" asked Ma Campbell.

"Greed," said Maizy. "Some folk would do anything if they're greedy enough." She pushed the cake stand towards Manx with a smirk. "More cake?"

Manx hesitated.

"Ignore Maizy's little joke," said Ma Campbell, "and don't confuse greed with need. If you are hungry, you must eat. Besides, I doubt the meals are up to much at my brother's establishment."

"When was the last time you saw him?" asked Manx.

"Many years ago." Ma Campbell shook her head. "Silas moved out after the explosion. He blamed our parents for forcing our sister and Fabian to meet in secret, and he hated me for helping them to do so. My dear brother even changed his name from Monan to Skulpin. Eventually, I married and left this house too, only moving back after my parents were gone. Over the years, I have tried to persuade Silas to return, but he refuses to even talk to me."

Manx looked around the kitchen and out into the vast hallway with its mosaic tiles and sweeping staircase. It was almost impossible to imagine Skulpin living amongst such grandeur. And such cleanliness.

Maizy cleared the table, while Ma Campbell rose and led Manx and Fantoosh back into the hall.

"What, then, is your next move, Master Fearty?"

"Not sure. Baggit's already got Lugstitch, and probably most of the Elders, on his side."

"You'll certainly need to keep your eyes open and your wits about you as far as the Burgmaster is concerned," said Ma Campbell. "He's another greedy man – in his case, for power." She tapped her lips and narrowed her eyes. "If you want my opinion, you would do better to conduct your investigations from the safety of Phlegm Town."

"What!"

"Friends and allies are what you need right now," said Ma Campbell.

Manx couldn't help laughing. "Friends? At the Lange Fluke!"

"Yesterday," said Ma Campbell, eyes glistening in the light of the amberose lanterns, "you did not expect to find help at Gushet House, and yet here you are." She opened the door for them. "Who is to say that tomorrow you shan't find answers in Phlegm Town?"

10.
Three's a Crowd

"Late again," snapped Oilyphant, as Manx hurried into the classroom the next morning, clutching at a stich in his side, having raced all the way from Phlegm Town. Despite the army of fleas that had been on a night-time offensive across the Lange Fluke's lumpy mattress, he'd managed to oversleep. This wasn't so surprising considering the previous day's exhausting events, and the fact that Skulpin had had Manx scrubbing crud off tables in the bar all evening.

Instinctively glancing at the wall to point out that the clock wasn't working, and that it was impossible to tell if he was late or not, Manx was surprised to find only a round, dust-free circle where the clock used to hang.

"As you have observed," said Oilyphant, "the clock has gone for repair. We shall finally be able to count just how many minutes you arrive late for class each day."

"Gone for repair where?" asked Manx.

"To our shop," came a voice from the doorway. Manx spun around to be met with the unwelcome sight of

Nathaniel Baggit leaning against the doorframe, arms crossed and eyes glinting.

"Indeed," said Oilyphant. "Mr Baggit kindly offered to take the clock yesterday afternoon when he came to register young Nathaniel for classes."

"He can't repair a perpetual," said Manx. "He doesn't know how to."

"How hard can it be?" asked Nathaniel, walking into the classroom.

Manx slid in behind his desk. "Dangerously hard," he muttered.

"Welcome to the academy, Nathaniel," said Oilyphant. "I'm afraid you'll have to share with these two. We're a bit short on classroom furniture at present."

"Thank you, sir. And it's Nathan, not Nathaniel. Only my dad calls me that." He flashed a smile at Manx and Fantoosh. Unlike his father's yellow-stained teeth, Nathan-not-Nathaniel's shone pearly white. To Manx's horror, Fantoosh actually smiled back.

Wondering whether he wouldn't have been better off back at the Lange Fluke helping Father G serve up the

weevil- and water-lice-flecked porridge for breakfast, Manx shunted to the edge of his seat to allow Nathan to wedge himself in place.

With anger threatening to boil over, Manx tried to concentrate on Oilyphant's lesson about the fifty-seven varieties of gut bacteria found in deep-ocean bottom feeders, but it proved impossible. Especially with Nathan whispering to Fantoosh every few minutes.

"What sort of lesson is this?" Nathan asked her at one point, when Oilyphant had his back turned.

"Maths and biology, I think," answered Fantoosh. "It's not always easy to tell."

Nathan sniggered, and, quick as a flash, the professor spun around and threw a piece of chalk across the classroom. It ricocheted off the wall right behind Manx, sending a shower of white fragments raining down on him.

"If you have something to say, Master Fearty, say it out loud."

"It wasn't me!"

"I apologise, sir," said Nathan. "I'm afraid I'm struggling to understand this lesson."

The professor peered over his spectacles. "Did you not learn science at your last school?"

Nathan lowered his head. "We've never really stopped anywhere long enough for me to go to school."

Fantoosh gasped. "You've never been to school?"

"Once or twice I did. My dad's taught me most of what I know."

Manx couldn't help laughing at this. What would Ninian Baggit be good at teaching? How to steal an inheritance?

"Rather than sniggering at this poor boy's academic ignorance," said Oilyphant, "we should instead marvel at the wonderful opportunities his former life in the Out-There has afforded him. If you ask nicely, I'm sure Nathan will share some of his knowledge."

"Would you?" asked Fantoosh, with, in Manx's opinion, far too much enthusiasm.

"Just as," continued Oilyphant, "there are things about our fine town that you can teach him. Might I suggest you start during your lunch break? I'm certain your new friend would be intrigued to try one of Madame Bonbeurre's creations at her bakery."

"*What* are these?" Nathan stabbed at the soft, doughy ball with his finger, pulling it back as if the limpet bun was about to attack him. "They look horrible."

"Shh!" Manx glared at him. "Madame Bonbeurre's very proud of her baking. And they're not horrible at all. They're our favourites." He stuffed two buns into his mouth and chewed.

"Steady on," laughed Fantoosh. "Didn't Skulpin feed you last night?"

"He was serving pickled puffin feet," said Manx, through a mouthful of limpety dough. "They were too rubbery. All I ate was the crab claws you gave me."

He grabbed a third bun whilst Fantoosh bit into her first. A jet of limpet juice squirted out the other side.

"Ooh! They're really good today." She licked her lips. "Madame Bonbeurre boils the limpets in honey then rolls them in sea plantain flour," she explained to Nathan, who was sitting tight-lipped and with his arms folded.

"*Oui!* That's right!" said Madame Bonbeurre, placing a second plate of buns down on the table. Her brown hands and arms were covered in flour, as was her face and curly black hair. Madame Bonbeurre baked delicious buns and pastries, but her kitchen was notoriously chaotic. "Freshly baked *chaque matin* – every morning!" She turned to Fantoosh. "As long as you keep picking limpets, there'll be limpet buns for lunch!"

"Hold on," said Nathan, lifting a bun with the end of his fork as if he was expecting something unpleasant to crawl out. "You pick those slippery suckers and then she bakes them into a yucky bun like this?"

Madame Bonbeurre served up an especially sour look for Nathan.

"Perhaps you'd care to learn some Haarville manners from your friends," she snapped. "And once you've done that, you can teach some to your father. Pestering me like that for my perpetuals when I was up to my eyeballs in plantain dough. It's not on, I tell you! *Non!*" Tears sprang from Madame Bonbeurre's eyes, trickling through the flour on her face. "How am I supposed to make my afternoon batch of buns without my perpetual bun baker?"

"You let him take your bun baker?" Manx said. He and Father G had only ever serviced Madame Bonbeurre's precious perpetual device when the bakery was closed.

"I didn't *let* him do anything!" she sobbed. "He waved

some pesky parchment in my face saying the Elders gave him permission to borrow it. Borrow! Steal, more like. It's an outrage! My poor papa will be spinning in his burial barrel as we speak."

The rest of their lunch break was decidedly uncomfortable, with Manx exchanging daggered looks with Nathan, who continued prodding his bun until Fantoosh snatched it and stuffed it into her mouth before shunting her chair back to leave.

"Everybody here eats limpets," said Manx. "So you might as well get used to them, Nathan. They're our favourite thing about Haarville, apart from Death Day of course. Isn't that right, Fan?"

Fantoosh giggled. "Absolutely. And on Death Day we get to eat double the amount!"

Nathan pulled another sour-looking face. "I hate it here," he muttered, pushing past them both towards the door. "And whatever Death Day is, it sounds ridiculous."

"There's nothing ridiculous about Death Day," said Manx, glaring at Nathan. "It's the best day of the year."

"Better than Christmas?" asked Nathan.

"I don't know much about Christmas," said Fantoosh. "But Death Day is brilliant! We get to go over to St Serf's chapel to spend time with all our dead friends and family."

"What? When?"

"Next week," said Manx. "Everyone gets dressed up and we all pack massive picnics. Then we wait until the tide's really low."

"It needs to be the lowest equinox tide," said Fantoosh.

"It's the only time of the year we can cross to the sea stack without drowning."

"The chapel used to be connected to Haarville until a major storm smashed through the headland," explained Manx. "So now we can only go over on Death Day. That's why it's such a big celebration."

"Once we're inside the chapel," continued Fantoosh, "all the models of our ancestors' wrecked ships are lowered down from the ceiling and we take out and dust off our family treasures, and sing, and dance, and eat…"

"…limpets, of course," said Manx. "Lots and lots of limpets. Fried, grilled and boiled. Baked, juiced or candied." He stared at Nathan. "Yum!"

"It sounds horrible," said Nathan, whose face had drained of the little colour it usually had.

"Wrong!" sang Fantoosh. "It's brilliant. And we get to stay for almost the entire day until the tide drops again, and then we all troop back here."

"For more limpets," added Manx, with a smile.

Nathan looked about ready to throw up, but instead he glared at them. "This place is weird," he said, pushing through the door and stomping off towards the academy. "And so are you!"

11.
Ice Warning!

The classroom had developed near-arctic conditions whilst they'd been at lunch. The windows were coated with a light frosting of ice, and Oilyphant was bundled up in a double layer of jackets. A nose drip had frozen on the end of a hair in his right nostril, and he was frantically puffing onto his blue-tipped fingers.

"Where's the heater gone?" asked Fantoosh, re-buttoning her cape up to her neck.

The professor jerked a thumb in Nathan's direction. "Ask your new classmate," he said, teeth chattering.

Nathan, who'd already sat back down, looked at the empty space where the heater had been. "Did my father come to collect it?"

"Not exactly," replied Oilyphant. "Da Silva's delivery lad performed that task for him. I wasn't aware my classroom heater was in need of a service."

"It isn't," said Manx. "It's not due until the summer." He tried to blow some warmth into his own hands. Fantoosh, meanwhile, was pulling on the gloves she kept inside her desk for use in the depths of winter.

Everyone, Oilyphant included, stared at Nathan.

"Father said the records at our shop have been kept so badly that there's no knowing when the town's devices need to be serviced."

"That's rubbish!" said Manx. Although, even as he said it, he realised Nathan was right. Fearty's Perpetuals had never kept written records of the town's devices – he and Father G knew everything about every device that passed through the shop, including when they were last serviced, the amount of amberose inside them, and how to remove, clean and replace the substance without blowing yourself up. He had a sudden vision of Ninian Baggit struggling to release the sizable chunk of amberose hidden away inside the room heater. Too much handling and the chances were it would explode without warning. "It takes years to learn how to handle perpetuals safely. Your dad doesn't know what he's dealing with. It's complicated."

Nathan shrugged. "You've *obviously* never seen the inside of a computer. Because *that's* complicated." He shoved his hands under his armpits. "Don't you have central heating in Haarville?"

Oilyphant stood up, calling Nathan forward.

"Since your father has seen fit to relieve us of our comfort, why don't you tell us all about the complex world of technology and advanced heating where you've come from." He held out a piece of chalk for Nathan, who clambered out from behind the desk and ambled to the front of the classroom.

"Like computers and stuff?"

Oilyphant snorted, shooting the nose icicle to the floor. "Ah! Computers. I almost got to see a computer once, back when I was enrolled at the Institute of Aquatic Biliary and Digestive Sciences in the Out-There." He tapped a frame standing on his desk with the tip of his cane. It displayed a certificate from the Institute, which Oilyphant polished with his handkerchief at least twice a day. Fantoosh always said the certificate was probably fake.

"How could you *almost* get to see a computer?" asked Nathan.

Oblivious to, or ignoring, Nathan's disbelieving tone, Oilyphant continued. "The caretaker couldn't find his keys to any of the three rooms in which this vast and wondrous machine was installed." A wistful look fell over the professor's face for a moment. "Have you ever been lucky enough to see a computer at work, Master Baggit? Its cogs whirring? Buttons clicking? Ticker tape flying?"

Nathan's eyebrows couldn't have climbed any higher on his forehead without disappearing under his hair.

"Er… that's not what computers are like," he said. "You can hold one in your hand."

Oilyphant snorted again. "Nonsense!" He turned to Manx and Fantoosh. "Your new friend is quite the joker, isn't he?"

Manx stared at Nathan. If there was one thing their new classmate was not, it was a joker.

Fantoosh pulled her cape tighter around herself. "Sir, I know it might be interesting, but what's the point of us knowing about these computer things and how people heat rooms in the Out-There? Wouldn't it be more useful to learn how we can heat a room here in Haarville? You know, like this room? Right now?"

"Yes." Manx blew a breath ring across the classroom. "How are we supposed to stay warm if you've lost your heater?"

Oilyphant took the chalk back from Nathan. "It has been forcibly removed, not lost, and since you obviously have no interest in the wonders of technology we shall return to our topic from this morning and continue with an examination of the digestive tract of the common sand eel."

The students were relieved when class was finally over, and not just because the professor had made them fill both sides of their slates with facts about eel poo. The temperature outside the academy was significantly higher than inside, which meant they could start warming up a bit.

Fantoosh peeled off her gloves as they walked down the street. "Oilyphant will ask you about your computers another time," she said to Nathan. "You're the first newcomers to Haarville in decades – he'll be desperate to hear how things have changed in the Out-There since he left."

"Don't you want to know what it's like as well?"

"What's the point?" said Manx. "We'll never get to use a computer."

Nathan wrinkled his nose. "Of course you will."

"How?" asked Fantoosh.

"When you leave here." Nathan said this with so much certainty, Manx almost felt sorry for him.

"No one leaves Haarville," he said.

"My great-grandfather did," snapped Nathan.

Manx flinched. As if he needed reminding of that fact.

"There's not a single person who would risk crossing the causeway now," he said.

"We did," said Nathan. "Me and Dad."

"You didn't know how dangerous it is," said Manx. "Everyone here does." He was keen to know what their crossing had been like, and now seemed as good a time as any to ask. "How was the causeway, anyway?"

Nathan kicked a stone into the gutter. "Fine."

"Fine!" Manx laughed. "Go on. Admit it. You nearly drowned, didn't you?"

Nathan sniffed. "Maybe. Most of the stupid causeway disappeared twice a day."

"Yes," said Manx, rolling his eyes. "It's called the tide, Nathan."

"Whatever it is, there was hardly anywhere left to stop and sleep. And most of the sand wasn't properly... you know... solid."

Nathan had turned pale, just like he had when presented with a limpet bun.

"I take it you didn't enjoy the quicksand, then?" asked Manx.

Fantoosh gasped. "Did you actually get sucked down?"

Nathan stared at the ground. "Only up to my chest. Dad pulled me out, eventually. Getting here would have been a lot quicker in a helicopter or something." He looked at them both and snorted. "Don't suppose you even know what a helicopter is."

Manx and Fantoosh shared eye rolls.

"Just because we've never seen a helicopter or an aeroplane," said Fantoosh, "doesn't mean we don't know about them, does it, Manx?"

"Of course not," said Manx. "Oilyphant taught us all about them, and Father G said he even flew in an aeroplane with jet engines once."

"You've never seen one!" Nathan stared at them as if they'd just grown fins and flippers. "Not even flying overhead?"

Manx shook his head and turned to Fantoosh. "When was the last time you saw blue sky, Fan?"

Fantoosh shrugged. "Couldn't tell you."

"This fog never lifts?" asked Nathan, shuddering.

"Not completely," replied Manx.

"Oh. So we couldn't have come here by helicopter."

Manx slapped Nathan on the back. "You're catching on. And there's nowhere flat enough to land one anyway."

"What about boats?" asked Nathan. "Couldn't you sail away?"

This time, Manx and Fantoosh exchanged brief 'he-has-no-idea' looks.

"Haven't you been to the harbour?" asked Fantoosh.

"Of course I have."

"So, you know there's only one boat," said Manx. "The *Unfortunate Flounder*."

"Sheila Giddock's the only person with a boat," explained Fantoosh. "She holds the town licence to fish."

"And she's the only person who knows how to navigate around the reefs," said Manx. "Hundreds of ships have been wrecked out there. Where else do you think the town got all the wood to build houses and furniture? There are hardly any trees."

"Most of our ancestors came from shipwrecks," said Fantoosh. "It's impossible to get to Haarville by sea safely. There are too many hidden rocks."

"How much information did Fabian actually leave behind?" asked Manx. "You know, about Haarville?"

Nathan shrugged. "Not a lot. It's not on any maps. No one we asked had heard of it, and even if they thought they might have, they didn't believe it existed."

"That's the point," said Fantoosh. "Some people come here to disappear – like Oilyphant. At least, they used to, when the causeway was still safe enough to cross."

"You must have had *some* information, Nathan, from Fabian. Did you ever meet him?"

"No," said Nathan. "I think he died before my granny was born. He caught a cold, or something."

"That's terrible!" exclaimed Fantoosh. "What a waste after taking all those risks to leave."

"And such a boring way to die," said Manx. "We Feartys prefer something more dramatic, normally."

"What about Celeste?" asked Fantoosh. "How long did she live?"

"Well," said Nathan, "I don't remember her, but she must have been around long enough to tell my granny about Haarville and the shop, because it was Granny who told my dad. And then there's the gobbledegook written on the manky piece of cloth that was found hidden in the handwarmer when I was a baby."

"What exactly does it say?" asked Manx.

"I don't know." Nathan scuffed his foot around in the gutter. "That man Lugstitch wanted to know too. Something to do with what my dad's searching for." He stopped talking and bit his lip. "I'm going home," he said quickly, and slouched off around the corner.

"I think someone just let the fish out of the net," said Fantoosh. "Sounds like his dad's on the hunt for something."

"It does," said Manx. "And whatever it is, I reckon he's looking for it inside perpetual devices."

"So that's your quest," said Fantoosh. "Just like Ma Campbell said."

"What do you mean?"

"You need to find out what Baggit's searching for."

Manx nodded. Fantoosh was right. And it sounded like

Ma Campbell was right about Lugstitch too – he was in on Baggit's plan, which meant they needed to keep their eyes on stalks like a crab to watch them both.

12.

Pollock Row

If Manx had worried that the days in Phlegm Town would drag on, he needn't have. The chores set by Skulpin made the hours slip by like freshly jellied eels. It seemed no time at all before Saturday arrived, and Manx was on his third chore of the morning, having already survived two busy breakfast sittings and helped Father G rinse out a pile of used chamber pots – a task they'd faced by wrapping some of Gloria's featheriest boas around their mouths and noses to deal with the horrible smell.

Manx had just swept an impressive mound of dust, dirt and manky blankets from the bedrooms, along with several mousetraps – some with their victims still clamped in place – and was now busy tipping it all into the kitchen range's burner. He stood back to enjoy the sound of bedbugs fizzing and popping as they roasted – until Skulpin interrupted the entertainment.

"You're to go down Pollock Row," he growled, handing Manx a wrinkled whale-skin pouch and a list. "There's enough coin for that lot, but watch out for old Mabel –

she'd sooner strip the coat off your back than give you a fair price for her rosehip wine. And don't let Brankie fob you off with any lung meat from his fish slops. He knows I only use the good stuff."

Skulpin checked a tarnished pocket watch hanging by a thin chain from his grubby waistcoat. "Best hurry, boy. You're cooking lunch today."

Manx couldn't wait to escape the Lange Fluke's fuggy atmosphere, so hurried off to grab his oilskin smock and headed away down Ratfish Wynd.

The haar was heavy that morning, and had sunk between the overhanging gables. Within less than a minute, Manx had become totally disoriented. He soon found himself in a dark, tunnel-like alleyway, where eye-watering smoke mixed with the fog and caught in his throat. Stumbling half-blindly on, he was suddenly grabbed and pulled sideways into a murky doorway.

As he blinked away smoke-induced tears, Manx found himself staring into a pair of milky-white eyes framed by lank grey hair. A flickering light shone off two stubby teeth and revealed deep wrinkles in the old woman's pallid face. She relaxed her surprisingly strong grip and reached down, lifting the source of light from the ground. It was an actual gull lamp – a fulmar, by the look of it, minus its head and with a burning wick shoved down its neck into the fat within.

A small, yellow-furred tongue uncurled from within the

woman's mouth and licked dryly at her lips. "Ha! Look who be creeping down Crab Gulley," she said in a gruff, breathless voice.

Recoiling slightly from the gum-rotting stink coming from the woman's mouth, it took Manx a moment to realise she meant him.

The woman pursed her cracked lips. "Is he come for the hoard?" she rasped.

Manx was stumped.

"I'm not here for anything," he said, after a pause. "I'm looking for Pollock Row, if you know how to get there from here?"

"Ha!" cackled the woman. "Imagine, a fancy Fearty asking directions from old Leena Cuddie. This be a turn-over."

Manx's skin prickled. He just wanted to get away. "Can you help me?"

"I'll help you when you answer my question," she snapped, suddenly sounding more lucid. "Is he here for the hoard?"

"Who? What hoard?"

"Him that's stolen your business, that's who. Is he come to Haarville for the hoard?"

"I don't know what you're talking about," said Manx, confused.

The woman thrust the headless, burning fulmar towards his face, close enough for Manx to feel the weak flame warming his cheeks. And certainly close enough to get a noseful of singed gull intestines.

"The tastiest crabs hide under the heaviest rocks," she hissed into his ear.

"W... what?" Manx fought the urge to run, but any closer and she'd be licking his ear with that desiccated tongue.

"The juiciest lugworm lies deepest in the sand."

Manx could taste bile in his mouth. He swallowed it back. "I don't like riddles."

"And I don't care for fools," she snapped. "And if you be the fool in this game, the hoard will be his for the taking." Her voice trailed off and she began to back away, sucking her teeth – both of them – impressively loudly. "Roll the stone and dig deep the sand," she murmured, fading back through the doorway into the darkness within, "lest you wish the losing hand."

The door slammed shut with a waft of foul air and Manx hurried away. What had the old woman been trying to tell him? Were her riddling words simply the result of an age-addled mind? And that word: *hoard*. She'd repeated it several times before spouting all that weird stuff about crabs and worms and rocks.

Manx needed fresh air. He hastened down the twisting vennel, then loitered in the shadows at the end of Crab Gulley for a minute. Ahead, stretching along Pollock Row, was the market. Crowds milled around rickety stalls covered with awnings made from fraying sheets of kelp. Dried fish fins hung from hooks at one stall like macabre Death Day bunting, whilst at another, piles of decomposing seaweed dripped thick brown sludge.

The trick here, Manx decided, was to blend in. He took a deep breath, stepped out towards the throng and set about collecting everything on the list.

Half an hour later, Manx was struggling under the weight of a sack of unappealing-looking lumps of bread, two bottles of gull oil and a bundle of mangy sea radishes. He was also laden with a pail of fish entrails. When Manx had asked for no lung meat, the fishmonger, Brankie, growled and looked about to leap over his stall and boot Manx out of the market, until Manx explained that the fish was for Skulpin, at which point Brankie added two extra scoops of fish bits and a handful of eyes for good measure.

All he was missing now was the rosehip wine, and old Mabel drove as hard a bargain as Skulpin had said she would. However, all Manx had to do was mention Skulpin's name and she not only dropped the price, but threw in a free bottle.

Manx staggered back through the market in the direction of Ratfish Wynd, pausing every few steps to put down the groceries and rub his fingers back to life. In the time he'd been out, the haar had lifted slightly and for a fleeting moment, a rare single ray of sunlight shone down. A twinkling brightness caught his eye near where he was standing and he turned to find its source: a stall full of highly polished bottles that lay horizontally in a stepped display. As Manx peered closer, he saw they contained not liquid, but ships. He put the shopping down and marvelled at them for a moment.

"Magical, aren't they?"

Manx almost kicked the wine over as he jumped back from examining an especially elaborate three-masted ship. He'd been so taken by the display, he'd failed to notice the woman sitting behind the stall bench.

"Did you make them?" asked Manx.

The woman laughed, her piercing blue eyes sparkling in her smiling brown face. "Goodness no." She pointed to a sign hanging behind her:

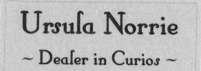

Ursula Norrie
~ Dealer in Curios ~

"They're beautiful," said Manx.

"Indeed they are," said Ursula. "And I've waited a long time for you to come for yours, Master Fearty."

"Mine?"

Ursula nodded.

Manx ran his eyes over the bottled ships. Most of them were mini replicas of tall ships, with their sails unfurled on three masts. Others were simpler sailing vessels, whilst yet more had funnels. One even looked like a paddle steamer, with a large wheel on either side.

"So who did make them?"

"There was a time," said Ursula, "when folk would craft

these objects to remember the ships that brought their families here, and whose wrecking they survived." She beckoned Manx to step even closer. "Look again," she said in a dreamy voice.

Peering more closely at the bottles, Manx realised he recognised several of the ships – larger models of them hung from the ceiling in St Serf's chapel. Then he gasped. Sitting right in the middle of the display was a ship he knew very well indeed.

"It's the *Amber Rose*," he said in a whisper.

Ursula picked up the bottle and handed it to him. Carefully, Manx turned it to get a better look. The miniature tea clipper's three masts were beautifully whittled from tiny pieces of wood. Small squares of sailcloth hung from them,  marked in places, having been sealed inside a bottle for so many years. Whilst this ship wasn't the largest or most colourful of the lot, it was by far the most elegant, and an exact replica of the larger Fearty memory ship from St Serf's.

Painted in tiny fading letters on the front end, Manx could just make out the words *Amber Rose*, and right on the raised prow, instead of the dragons or serpents or mermaids the other ships sported, was a rose, fashioned from a small yellow gemstone.

"It's carved from real amber," said Ursula, taking the

bottle from him and replacing it on the display. "One of your ancestors took great care to craft this."

Manx was mesmerised.

"How did you come by so many of them?"

"My father began acquiring them years ago, in exchange for other curios," said Ursula. "Alas, nowadays people stop to look, but few have the means to buy."

Manx didn't have the means to buy anything either, so instead he savoured a lingering look at the miniature *Amber Rose*. "I promise to come back and buy this one day," he said. "If it's still for sale."

Ursula smiled at him, her eyes twinkling. "It shall be yours."

13.
A Light Tower Alight

After a sweaty hour toiling in the Lange Fluke's kitchen, Manx served up his 'Fish Surprise' to the lunchtime crowd: the surprise being that no two bowls contained the same fish part. Customers either found a fin, an eye, or a length of entrail amidst the chunks of sea beet and rock radish.

Having scrubbed, rinsed and wiped down, Manx climbed upstairs and collapsed on the bed for a nap. He'd just dropped off when Father G came in.

"Wakey wakey!" he cried. "You're down for helping me this afternoon. If we're done quickly, there'll be time to get ready for tonight."

Manx rubbed his eyes and yawned. "What's tonight?"

"It's Saturday, of course! Gloria's on stage."

"We're still going to Lumpsuckers?"

"Why not? We might be *out* of Fearty's Perpetuals temporarily, but we are most certainly not *down*."

111

"Won't we be busy here shovelling muck or something?" Father G pulled a bright pink feather boa off a hook on the back of the door and wrapped it around his neck. "Skulpin's giving us both the night off." He performed a quick twirl. "So you're coming too. I thought you'd appreciate the break from this place."

"What's the catch?" asked Manx.

"There is no catch," replied Father G. "Although I did say we'd do the laundry before we go."

Five minutes later, after Manx had sorted the laundry into three piles of dirty, filthy and soiled-beyond-hope, he decided there was very much a catch. However, it was done soon enough, and at five o'clock Father G was standing in front of their room's dust-streaked mirror, transformed into Gloria in Excelsis. The mother-of-pearl fragments shimmered on his gown, and Manx had brushed the russet-red wig until it shone like mermaid's hair.

Of course, they had to suffer the torment of numerous whistles and raucous jeers as they pushed their way through the bar's schnapps-sozzled drinkers. Father G appeared unruffled though, unlike his feather boas, and turned briefly at the doorway to blow a big kiss to the Lange Fluke's customers.

"I've had worse hecklers than that in my time," he said, as they hurried over the burn bridge, away from Phlegm Town.

They laughed and sang snippets of the songs Gloria would shortly be performing, and for a few delicious seconds Manx savoured the soft-scented air that filled the streets. It was, he thought, almost worth putting up with the foul stenches of Phlegm Town just to be able to enjoy an amberose-infused breath of Haarville air once in a while.

But just as they were approaching the harbour and its row of white, lime-washed houses, Father G grabbed Manx's wrist.

"Something's not right," he said. "Lumpsuckers looks closed."

It was true. Normally at this time of the evening Lumpsuckers' lights would be flooding Front Street and sparkling on the water in the harbour.

Father G hurried along, heels clattering on the cobbles. A snoozing gull took fright at the sound and flapped its wings indignantly.

"Wait for me!" cried Manx, finally catching up by the fish bar's entrance.

"The door's locked!" Father G tried the handle again, then rapped on the window, peering into the darkness.

"Maybe Sheila's ill," suggested Manx.

"Lumpsuckers never closes," said Father G. "Sheila would sooner lose her other arm to a shark, just like she lost the first, than not open to serve her customers."

Nobody actually knew for sure how Sheila Giddock had lost her lower right arm. Depending on the day of the week you asked her, she'd either say it was bitten off by a hammerhead shark, trapped in a sinking lobster pot so it had to be rapidly sawn off, or catastrophically speared on the end of a rusty anchor. But however it happened, two things were guaranteed: every day Sheila would go out to fish, and then fry up her catch to serve at Lumpsuckers.

Manx and Father G stood outside for a bit longer as a cold breeze whipped across the harbour. Then, from around the back of the building, Sheila appeared, balancing a large platter on her upturned left hand. It was covered with a piece of cloth, but Manx could smell the crab cakes.

The gull padded over with a greedy glint in its eye. Sheila shooed it away then stared up at Father G, cheeks flushed as the wind whipped strands of her wiry blonde hair across her weather-worn face.

"What are you doing here? Didn't you get the note?"

"I did not," said Father G.

"That boy!" cried Sheila. "I knew I shouldn't have trusted him."

Manx didn't need to ask which boy Sheila meant. Apart from him, there was only one other boy in Haarville.

"You asked Nathan Baggit to deliver a message?"

Sheila threw Manx an exasperated look. "I've been up to my neck in crab shells and lobster tails all afternoon! The boy was passing by so I asked him to deliver the note." She turned back to Father G. "I'm sorry," she said. "Lugstitch asked me to provide food for the welcome party being thrown tonight for the Baggits." A frown creased her forehead. "But surely you're invited to Burgh House too? The whole town is."

"No. Didn't receive *that* message either," said Father G dryly.

Sheila sighed. "I couldn't turn down an order like that. And besides, Lugstitch wouldn't take no for an answer." She flicked her foot out as the hungry gull hopped closer. "I have to go," she said. "They'll be waiting for these." Sheila bustled past with her platter, leaving Manx, Father G and the gull to breathe in the sweet, salty tang of a hundred disappearing crab cakes.

"Come on! We're going back to Phlegm Town."

Manx held back. "I think I'll hang around here. Just for a bit. Get some fresh air."

Father G fixed him with a knowing stare, which, in full Gloria make-up was quite unsettling. "You mean you're going to Burgh House. You do realise they didn't invite us deliberately?"

"It can't hurt to try and find out what's being said."

"Fine," said Father G. "But I want you back at the Lange Fluke in an hour, and don't get into trouble."

Manx watched him clip-clop away, then he peered glumly across to the harbour light tower. Normally, its bright orange glow made him feel cosy just by looking at it, but tonight there was a burning fury roaring away in the pit of his stomach, and warm and cosy it was not.

A shadow suddenly passed in front of the tower's bright glow, blocking it for a few seconds.

There was someone inside.

Manx instantly abandoned his plan to gatecrash the Burgh House party. Nobody had access to the light tower apart from the keyholders – who, until recently, were himself and Father G. And only Father G was allowed to handle the sizable chunk – a whole seventeen and two thirds pebble-weight – of potentially lethal amberose inside it. The light tower was possibly the most dangerous place in all of Haarville.

Manx sprinted along the harbour wall, slipping on a piece of slimy seaweed and crashing into a stack of lobster baskets.

"For Neptune's sake!" he gasped under his breath, untangling himself from the netting and rope. Looking up he saw that the light had gone out. As he clambered to his feet, Manx could just make out a dark shape emerging from the doorway at the tower's base. Keys jangled, and the shape moved towards him. There might have been very little light, but Manx instantly recognised the mousey squeak of a leather coat.

"What were you doing in there, Nathan?"

Nathan yelped as Manx stepped out in front of him.

"N-n-nothing!"

"You were in the tower. The light's gone out. What have you done to it?"

"I didn't do anything!" said Nathan. There was an edge of fear to his voice.

"You're lying," said Manx.

"I have to go," said Nathan, pushing past and running towards Front Street. Manx watched him vanish into the darkness, his brain fuzzling with questions, then he moved closer to the light tower.

"That's strange…"

The tower was glowing again. But not the usual steady orange glow. This glow *flickered*.

A flame licked at one of the glass panels.

The amberose was on fire.

"No!" Manx's cry echoed back at him from the haar pressing down overhead as he tried, and failed, to pull the locked door open. He scanned the ground for anything he could force it with. "There has to be something!"

He ran around the tower. Below the harbour wall, waves crashed on its outer edge, sending spray up and over, splashing down on him and the row of rusting anchors lined up against the wall. The largest had rusted more than the others and one of the arrow-shaped ends had eroded away. Manx crouched and felt for it in the dark.

"Got it!"

He dashed back to the door, inserted the anchor point along its edge and pushed. It slipped out a couple of times, but then it held fast and he heard the sound of splintering wood as he levered the door open.

A dense cloud of intoxicating smoke billowed out. Manx steadied himself as a wave of dizziness washed over him, then he reached blindly inside the open doorway for the bucket of water that they always kept in place for emergencies – but it had been knocked over.

He grabbed the empty bucket and dropped it on its rope over the wall into the harbour, then hauled it back up. Thank Neptune for the high tide, he thought.

He raced up the tower steps and threw the water at

the base of the flames. More pungent smoke filled the tower, but the fire simply reignited. He rushed for another bucketful, then another. Every bucket he hurled towards the flames created further clouds of smoke that threatened to overwhelm him.

Finally, after at least five more bucketfuls, the amberose stopped burning. Manx emptied several more on the charred and smouldering wreckage of the light to make sure it was well and truly doused.

What had Nathan done to the amberose to cause it to ignite? If Manx hadn't been there, the fire might have burned down the whole tower. Or flames could even have been caught by the wind and set light to the whole town!

More importantly, why had Nathan been in there at all?

Manx decided that he'd have to report the fire. Never mind that the Elders were hosting their welcome party – they had to be told.

He raced up from the harbour, and within a few minutes was tearing around the stone well in the centre of the town's small main square. He took the granite steps leading up to Burgh House two at a time, and hammered on its heavy wooden doors until finally one opened a crack.

"I have to see the Elders," he panted.

"You can't," snapped a voice. The door slammed in Manx's face. He banged on it again.

When it opened a second time, Manx didn't even have time to utter a word.

"You're barred, Fearty," growled a different voice – this time it sounded like Burgmaster Lugstitch. "Leave now, or face the consequences." The door slammed shut. Manx tried the handle but it was locked. He rattled it and rapped again so hard he scraped the skin off his knuckles. But it was no use.

Manx had no choice but to turn and stomp back to Phlegm Town, hoping for everyone's sake that Nathan wouldn't be meddling with any other perpetuals that night.

14.

The Accused

Waking the next morning, Manx lay in bed staring at a damp patch on the ceiling. It was the shape of a flatfish, and a droplet of moisture had formed where an eye might have been. The longer he looked at it, the more it seemed to be looking straight back at him.

Then, with a start, Manx remembered he was supposed to be on breakfast duty. He threw a jumper over his nightshirt and hurried downstairs.

"Why didn't you wake me up?" he asked Father G, who was furiously stirring porridge with a long wooden spurtle.

"I tried."

Manx took over stirring duties whilst Father G lifted another pan off the range.

"Something really weird happened last night—" began Manx, but Father G shook his head.

"It'll have to wait." He headed out of the kitchen with the pan. "They're getting restless out there."

When the second pan of porridge was just the right consistency – thick enough to glue a gull's beak shut –

Manx hefted it out into the bar. He'd dolloped most of it into customers' bowls when the pub's entrance opened a crack and a parchment envelope skimmed across the floor. Manx placed the pan on an empty table and picked it up. It was addressed to him and Father G, and was sealed with a brown glob of congealed gull fat in which a three-pronged spear was stamped.

"Look!" Manx held it out. "A trident. It's the Burgh House seal."

"We'd better open it in the kitchen," said Father G, eyes darting around the bar. "This lot are showing a mite too much interest."

Whilst Father G scraped some smouldering lumps of porridge off the range, Manx tore the envelope's seal and scanned the parchment inside. It didn't say much, but the few words written in sharp, angular letters set a thousand pinpricks jabbing down his neck like a sea urchin's spines.

For the immediate attention of
the erstwhile tenants of Fearty's
Perpetuals

"We weren't tenants! I own that place!" said Manx, knuckles turning white as he gripped the parchment tightly. "Listen to this:

> *Your presence is commanded at an emergency Burgh-Meet this morning at ten thirty, Burgh House. Attendance mandatory.*

Father G groaned. "What can this be about?"

Manx pulled a face. "I think it might have something to do with what happened to the light tower." He quickly told him about Nathan and the fire.

"That explains why our room reeks like a Crab Gulley smokehouse," said Father G. "Why didn't you tell me about this last night?"

"You were already asleep," said Manx. "Do you think they want us to fix the tower's light?"

Father G read the parchment, his face set in a grim frown. "They wouldn't need a Burgh-Meet to ask us to do that." He wiped his hands on his apron. "I'd better find Skulpin and tell him we won't be preparing the soup today."

The meeting was to take place in the main chamber of Burgh House, on the first floor above the entrance, overlooking Burgh Place. A small crowd had already gathered in the centre of the square.

"Never takes these gossipmongers long to sniff out a scandal," muttered Father G as they elbowed their way through to the door.

Burgh House's chamber was smaller than Manx remembered. He'd been inside it just once before, when Oilyphant had decided to take him and Fantoosh on a field trip to "see how the wheels of justice and leadership turn in Haarville". Then, the room had echoed to their shouts and screams as they ran circles around the professor, who'd been attempting to point out the polished wood panelling, rescued from a shipwrecked schooner, and the shiny trident emblem hung high on the wall. Now, the atmosphere was deadly serious.

Two lone wooden stools had been positioned directly below the raised platform on which loomed a long, heavy table. Here sat the Elders. Lugstitch, grim-faced, was centre-stage, with the grocer Da Silva on his left and Mr Pothery, the parchment seller, on his right. They, and the other Elders, seemed uncomfortable, eyes flitting this way and that, not looking at Manx or Father G.

Lugstitch pointed a small wooden hammer at the stools.

"Sit," he said in a low, serious voice, his walrus moustache bristling.

As they sat down, Manx's stool scraped noisily on the floor. For some reason, he felt like laughing and had to swallow it back.

Lugstitch banged his hammer on the table so heavily a loose pane of glass rattled in the window.

"Silence! This emergency Burgh-Meet is now in session."

He cleared his throat theatrically.

"An act of extreme vandalism and sabotage was

committed in Haarville last night. It is the view of the Elders that either one, or both of you, have knowledge of said act."

You could have heard an oyster breathing in the silence that followed. Manx decided to let Father G do the talking.

"Why is that your view?" asked Father G. "I would have thought—"

He was interrupted by a second whack of the hammer.

"You have not yet been invited to speak," snapped Lugstitch.

Father G stood up. He might have been over six feet tall, but the assembled Elders had the advantage of height up on the platform.

"You can't just accuse us without giving us a chance to defend ourselves."

Lugstitch laughed. "This is no courtroom in the Out-There," he said. "Although I have no doubt you were once highly experienced in *their* proceedings."

"How very dare you!" shouted Father G.

"Sit!" roared Lugstitch, making use of his hammer again.

Manx yanked at Father G's sleeve and pulled him down. "Let him have his say," he whispered.

Father G was shaking with rage, but he bit his lip and nodded.

"The light tower was set alight last night. It is the opinion of this Burgh-Meet that you have some knowledge of the incident." Lugstitch paused, as if for dramatic effect. He needn't have bothered, thought Manx – there was more than enough drama going on already.

"Or, indeed, *involvement* in said incident," added Lugstitch, leaning over the table.

Another silence followed, during which Manx noticed a tip-tapping on the window nearest him. He glanced outside. Through the salt sheen on the glass, he could make out a black-and-white shape wobbling along the window ledge. There wasn't much Olu could do to help, but it was good to know he was there. Manx hadn't seen him since the move to Phlegm Town – the wise old bird had obviously decided it was best to stay clear of the Lange Fluke in case Skulpin tried to add him to the soup.

"What is your response?" demanded Lugstitch.

Father G waited for a moment. "Why us?" he asked.

"Everyone else was at the reception for Mr Baggit last night," said Lugstitch.

"Everyone you invited, you mean," said Manx, the words bursting forth before he could stop them. "I bet nobody from Phlegm Town was there."

Lugstitch glared at them, eyes bulging from under his wiry brows.

"We understand you were both in the vicinity of the harbour yesterday evening."

"That doesn't mean you can accuse us!" shouted Father G. "It would be better to ask us to use our expertise and mend the light."

"There will be no need," said Lugstitch, "because the new owner of Fearty's Perpetuals has kindly offered to assist with its repair."

"What does that man know about perpetuals or amberose?" snapped Father G. "It takes years to learn how to handle these devices."

"Perhaps," said Lugstitch, "but Mr Baggit seems enthusiastic. Of course, it may be too late to save it."

"Not if we can dry the amberose out today," said Manx.

Outside the window, Olu piped a single, wailing whistle. It took a second or two for Manx to realise what he'd said. Next to him, Father G's body tensed.

"I don't believe I mentioned any water damage," said Lugstitch, with a sly smile.

"I… I think you did," said Manx.

"Enough!" boomed Lugstitch, banging the hammer down again.

Manx had to admit, things weren't exactly going his way. At this rate, he'd be heading straight to the cells and he didn't even have any spare long johns with him!

"Nathan Baggit is the one you should be speaking to." Manx looked at each of the Elders in turn. "I saw him do it."

"Nonsense!" cried Lugstitch. "From what I have seen of the boy, he couldn't button a waistcoat, let alone set fire to something. And you have already stated that you had no knowledge of the incident, so forgive us if we hesitate to believe you now."

The Elders murmured agreement – the first time they'd

shown any enthusiasm for the proceedings since they'd started. Things were slipping out of Manx's favour – and fast.

"It *was* Nathan," he said, forcefully. "I saw him leaving the tower. He had the keys with him."

"The door was *forced open* when we examined it this morning," said Da Silva.

"Yes! I did that," said Manx. "I was trying to—"

"There!" Lugstitch slammed the hammer again. "He admits it."

"I broke in to put the fire out, not to start it."

"An unlikely story," said Da Silva, looking directly at Manx. "It pains me to say it, but you bring shame on the Fearty name."

"Why would I do it?" yelled Manx. "I would never damage a perpetual or the amberose. They're too precious."

"Revenge," said Mr Pothery, "for losing your shop."

"Jealousy," said Da Silva, "of the Baggits."

Lugstitch lifted his chin, a look of pure triumph on his face, the hammer held firmly in his hand. "Delinquency!" he boomed. "You, Master Fearty, have every reason under the haar for committing the crime."

The hammer hovered. Manx held his breath.

"So that's it," said Father G. "You have no witnesses but still you've made your decision without even bringing in the Baggit boy for questioning?"

The hammer still hovered. The Elders exchanged glances. Manx didn't dare breathe. He was a heartbeat away from being locked up in the dank gloom of Burgh House's cells.

Lugstitch grunted and placed the hammer on the table reluctantly.

"Very well," he said, running his fingers along his whiskers. "We shall withhold judgement until we have spoken with Master Baggit. Pending this, Manxome will comply with all orders we see fit to issue."

"Such as?" asked Father G.

The Elders once again conferred with each other in low mutterings and important nods of their heads.

"Our first order," said Lugstitch, "is that Manxome Fearty be placed under an immediate night-time curfew. He shall not leave the confines of the Lange Fluke between sunset and -rise. This emergency Burgh-Meet is now closed." He gave the hammer one final short, sharp rap. "Now be upstanding and leave the chamber."

15.

Whoever Heard of the Haarville Hoard?

If Skulpin had planned on forcing Manx and Father G straight back to work on their return to the Lange Fluke, they didn't give the landlord a chance. Instead they stomped through the bar and straight upstairs.

Father G slumped onto the bed as soon as they reached their room.

"A curfew!" He held his head in his hands. "I can't believe it!"

"The Elders really don't like us, do they?" Manx slumped down next to his guardian, flicking a surprised bedbug off the blanket with his finger.

Father G sighed. "They've always been wary of me," he said quietly. "For years now, anyone who wasn't born in Haarville has been treated with suspicion, no matter how long we've been here. Look at your poor professor."

"Oilyphant? What about him?"

"That man's desperate to become an Elder," said Father G. "He certainly qualifies: a loyal citizen who has taught generations of Haarville's children. But they'll never have him. Nor me for that matter. To them, we're outsiders and always will be."

"But you belong here just as much as anyone else!" Manx flicked another bedbug across the room to join its friend. "And even if that is the case, why do they hate me so much?"

Father G took Manx's hand and gave it a squeeze.

"You're a Fearty. They're jealous that it was your family who founded Haarville and discovered amberose."

"Maybe," said Manx. "But that doesn't explain why Lugstitch is treating Baggit like he's some sort of pirate king dripping with stolen gold. *He's* the real outsider!"

Father G smiled – for the first time since leaving Burgh House. "That imagination of yours," he said. "Sounds like I read you too many bedtime stories about pirates and hoards of hidden treasure."

Manx stopped trying to clean the bedbug blood off the blanket. "Have you ever heard of a hoard? Here? In Haarville? Because I think that's what Baggit's searching for inside everyone's perpetuals. And the Elders are helping him – or at least Lugstitch is."

Father G actually laughed. It was good to hear.

"I definitely told you too many stories." He yawned and closed his eyes. "Time for a rest. That charade of a court case has worn me out and I'll need all my energy to scrub Skulpin's pots and pans later."

Manx let him sleep. But the mention of a hoard, for the second time in as many days, had got him thinking of his "quest", as Ma Campbell had put it. What had that creepy old woman from Crab Gulley asked him? *"Is he come for the hoard?"* Manx wondered if he should have taken her seriously. After all, the Elders weren't taking him seriously and *he* was telling the truth.

The curfew didn't start for ages yet, so there was plenty of time to try to find the old woman again, even if just the thought of the stench from her mouth made him shudder. It wasn't much to go on, but it was all Manx had for the moment. He headed down the stairs, crossing his fingers that Skulpin didn't stop him on his way out and force him to do some revolting chore.

"Thrown you to the sea wolves, have they?"

Manx hadn't noticed Skulpin as he crept through the Lang Fluke's dingy bar area. The landlord had an unnerving habit of blending into his dank and grease-ridden surroundings, but there he was, polishing a glass with a filthy rag.

"Who has?" asked Manx, uncrossing his fingers.

"The Burgh-Meet," replied Skulpin. "I heard they put you under curfew. You couldn't be in more hot water if you were a shrimp being boiled up in some broth." He wheezed as he laughed to himself.

"News travels fast here," said Manx.

Skulpin licked his lips with his gutweed-stained tongue. "If you haven't learnt that by now, Manx Fearty, you surely will soon. We might not be rich in Phlegm Town. We don't boast of no finery nor frippery, but what we do have about us is our wits. We know to listen, to watch, and to sniff." He made a show of inhaling the air around him. "What I smell right now is trouble."

"Who for?" asked Manx.

"For us all," said Skulpin. "But mostly for you."

"Thanks." Manx walked over to the bar, careful not to touch its greasy surface. "You know a lot about what goes on in Haarville, don't you?"

Skulpin raised an eyebrow, the merest hint of a smile on his lips as he put down his polishing rag and reached for a bottle, then poured out two glasses. He slid one over. Manx carefully selected the least sticky part of the rim and lifted the smeared glass to his lips. It was clam juice, and a good one at that. Far tastier than the watered-down bottles they usually found in Da Silva's.

"Fresh this morning," said Skulpin, knocking his glass back in one go. "Squeezed the life from them myself."

"You must hear all sorts of rumours and gossip from the customers in this place," said Manx, trying not to think about Skulpin's filthy fingers squeezing out the juice he'd just been gulping.

"Rumours, gossip, secrets, half-truths – aye, my waxy lugholes have heard the lot."

"Have they ever heard about a hidden Haarville hoard?"

Skulpin's eyes suddenly widened. "A hoard?"

"Yes."

A peg-toothed smile crept across the landlord's wrinkled face. "I take it you met Leena on your little excursion to Pollock Row yesterday?"

"Who?"

"Old Leena Cuddie," replied Skulpin. "She's been harking on about a Haarville hoard her whole life to anyone who'll listen. If you want to know more about Haarville's legends," he continued, with something like a glint in his tired eyes, "I suggest you pay old Leena a return visit." He reached behind to the shelf and took down a small keg. "She's partial to a drop of my finest cockle schnapps. It'll loosen her tongue for you."

Manx hesitated before speaking again. "Talking of visiting old ladies," he said, "your sister misses you. Did you know that?"

The glare Skulpin threw him was sharp enough to turn the keg of schnapps sour.

"Been snooping round Gushet House, have you?" he growled. "A word of advice: you've enough on your plate without meddling in matters outwith your concern. I'll deal with my affairs in my own way, and you deal with yours."

Knowing he was chancing his luck with Skulpin's patience, Manx carried on.

"Isn't Baggit *both* our concerns? He's related to both our families, after all."

Skulpin's nostrils flared. "It isn't *my* business that man has pulled from under my feet. And in any case, I'm doing my bit to help by having you to stay under my roof."

Sensing that he was unlikely to survive another of Skulpin's acid glares, Manx chose not to point out that he and Father G weren't exactly guests, but more like live-in, unpaid staff.

"Away with you, lad!" grunted the landlord. "And one more word about my sister and I'll have you swilling out the latrines all week."

16.

The Storyteller
of Crab Gulley

Despite it only being afternoon, lantern flames flickered behind grime-coated windows along Crab Gulley, throwing sinister shadows across the broken cobbles. Thick grey smoke billowed down from Leena Cuddie's chimney, stinging Manx's eyes and catching in his throat. With the keg wedged under his arm – and with his stomach feeling like it was full of sandhoppers – he rapped on the rotting door.

He'd expected to be kept waiting for the old woman to answer, but to his surprise, the door opened seconds later.

"About time, lad," croaked Leena. "I've been stewing the tea since lunchtime."

She shuffled away towards a dimly lit room at the end of a short, dark hallway. Manx, his heart thundering in his chest, followed her in, closing the door behind him.

The source of the chimney smoke was the first thing he spotted in the tiny parlour: a soot-thick fireplace where lumps of black seaweed were slowly burning. Dangling over it was a gannet, feathers singed and smouldering. A ribbon of rancid smoke drifted through the parlour.

"Sit down," said Leena, in a dry, rasping voice. She pointed to a threadbare armchair opposite an even more dilapidated one, into which she eased herself, its shoogly legs creaking almost as much as her bones. A rickety table laid with cups and a teapot sat between the chairs. A crack ran down the side of the teapot, and a small pool of water was gathering underneath it.

Leena reached for a rusty oil lamp on the table. She struggled for a moment with a lighting flint until Manx got up and struck it for her. The flame increased the light in the parlour room, and Manx spotted several tea caddies arranged haphazardly on various shelves. One or two were incredibly ornate, with carved ships on the lids. They reminded him of Ursula's ships-in-bottles.

"Take a look if you like," said Leena.

Manx wandered over and picked up a small wooden caddy. He blew off a layer of dust, revealing a two-masted ship inlaid in the lid. All that was needed was a good polish and the caddy would gleam and shine.

"Dug that one up myself,'" said Leena. "Found it one day buried in the sand when I was out harvesting ragworms."

"It's beautiful."

"That it is," said Leena. She closed her eyes for a moment. "The stories these caddies could tell you of far-flung places and stormy oceans and terrible shipwrecks." She pointed to another. "See that one?"

Manx hardly dared touch it – the carved ship on its lid looked fragile and had actual sails hanging from two of its three masts.

"It's always been missing a sail," said Leena, "ever since Fabian gave it to me shortly before he left Haarville. He said he found it in a junk shop by Pollock Row – claimed your ancestor Finnick had carved it."

"So you did know Fabian?" Manx looked at Leena. Her gnarled and age-twisted fingers fiddled with an empty teacup, and when she smiled, Manx was treated to the sight of her gummy mouth with its two lonely teeth. Her milky eyes became translucent in the lamplight as she spoke.

"Everyone in Phlegm Town knew Fabian," she said. "He came for my mother's stories and, after she passed, for mine. He paid for them too, repairing my perpetuals when they needed fixing." The dreamy smile vanished from Leena's face, replaced with a sorrowful shake of her head. "I missed him dearly when he was gone. And without him, I could barely afford to keep my few perpetuals in working order." She nodded towards a tarnished carriage clock with no hands, balanced precariously on the soot-covered mantlepiece. "Even my poor mother's precious clock no longer ticks." Leena leant across the table and fixed Manx with her watery eyes. "More than anything, Fabian was a dear friend. Had been since childhood."

"You know he didn't die in the fire, don't you?"

Tears began to seep from the corners of Leena's eyes. "I've always felt it to be so," she said in almost a whisper. "And when I heard of the new arrivals in town, I knew it to be so. And that they had come to continue the search Fabian abandoned."

"Fabian was searching for something before he left?"

Leena nodded slowly. "Aye, but he never told me what. The hours he spent scouring through curios and junk down on the Row!"

"Do you think it was the hoard?"

Leena shrugged, shoulder bones clicking.

"What is it anyway – this hoard?" asked Manx.

Leena held up a hand.

"I shall come to that," she said. "First, would you do this weak old lady the honour of pouring her tea?"

Manx poured her a cup of yellow-looking tea, then one for himself. It was dandelion, or Poor Man's Camomile, as Haarville folk called it.

"And if you're hungry, the bird will be smoked in no time," said Leena, lifting the cup to her mouth with a shaking hand.

"The tea will be enough, thank you." Manx sipped from his cup. It was surprisingly tasty. Then he remembered the keg and placed it on the table.

Leena's eyes twinkled. "I see Silas hasn't forgotten that the storyteller always takes payment first."

"And is it *just* a story you're going to tell me?"

Leena sipped from her cup again. "The best stories have truths at their heart," she said. "And I only tell the best stories. But I shall finish my tea first. This old throat needs softening."

Manx drained his cup and waited for Leena to do the same. Finally, she clattered her cup onto the saucer and dabbed at her mouth with her threadbare sleeve.

"In this lifetime," she said, suddenly speaking in a clear voice, "I've never travelled further than Limpet Bay. Indeed, these last years, my legs couldn't carry me further than Pollock Row. But it is in the storyteller's soul to listen and I've always been alert to whispered tales of ages past, even if I have to strain to catch the words these days." She tapped the side of her head with a calloused finger. "The stories are all safely locked away in here. Some are yarns to be spun with one beginning and one ending, but more interesting are those with two beginnings: one we think we know to be true, and another, more mysterious beginning. In these tales lies the real intrigue."

"I've never heard a story with two beginnings," said Manx.

"Who needs to, when their very family *is* the tale?"

This was no time for more riddles, but Manx sensed there was no point in rushing the ancient storyteller.

"Your family's story is known to all," began Leena. "At least, the version we *think* we know to be true." She picked at a thread on her cardigan. "That of your brave ancestors' shipwreck en route to a new life. How they managed to survive, and then thrive, harvesting the sea for whatever it offered, to eat, wear or build with. It is a Haarville tradition which continues to this day. Even the counter in your shop

was originally part of the *Amber Rose* – the story says that the couple clung to it until they washed up on the beach." Manx smiled. Father G had always said the counter was probably a piece of the *Amber Rose's* wreck. No wonder it had been installed in pride of place – it had saved his ancestors' lives.

"And of course," continued Leena, "they discovered the very thing that made life here possible."

"Amberose," whispered Manx.

"Aye," said Leena. "Amberose." She pulled a crusty handkerchief from her cardigan sleeve and wiped at the white spittle forming in the corner of her mouth. "Over the years," she continued, "the population bloomed. Most folk were wrecked on one of the reefs. Others came in search of a mythical place they'd heard tell of – somewhere to live their lives far from prying eyes or, in some cases, out of the reach of the law. And so Haarville grew, with different families taking responsibility for something vital to the town's survival, like the Bonbeurres with their baking and the Lugstitches providing clothing."

"And the Monans," said Manx. "They made the glass, didn't they?"

Leena chuckled to herself. "The way I recall it, Celeste never showed much interest in blowing glass. It was Margaret who took on that task."

"And my family made perpetuals," said Manx.

"Indeed," said Leena. "And from what my ancient ears have heard, you are as skilled as any Fearty with them."

"I was," muttered Manx, glumly, "until Baggit stole my shop."

Leena yawned, rubbing her watery eyes with her grubby fingers.

Not wanting her to fall asleep before she'd finished, Manx decided to hurry Leena on. "So, that's the first beginning that everyone knows about," he said. "But you know another, don't you?"

"The other beginning," said Leena, bending over the table and talking in a much lower voice, as if the smouldering gannet in the fireplace might be listening, "may be the stuff of pure fantasy. On the other hand, it might not."

Manx had to steady his knee from jigging up and down. Leena certainly liked to string out her yarns.

"The alternative beginning to this story says Finnick and Sarah did not wash up in Limpet Bay after their shipwreck, but instead landed on a windswept rock."

"What?"

Leena shrugged. "I am simply recounting a tale I once caught on the breeze. It is up to the listener to see the truth or lies hidden in the telling. Now, where was I?"

"Finnick and Sarah on a windswept rock," Manx supplied impatiently.

Leena nodded and licked her cracked lips with the tip of her tongue. "No doubt you are familiar with one of Haarville's more colourful tales – that of how a shipwrecked crew and their passengers survived on a reef out there beyond the haar, declining in numbers, one by one, as they devoured each other, limb by limb, until not one remained alive."

"Everyone knows that story," said Manx. "They built a monument to it. But I didn't think it was true."

Leena chuckled to herself. "And maybe it's not true that Finnick and Sarah were also wrecked on a desolate reef, maybe even the same one, fending for themselves, braving the wild elements. And yet that is the tale I am sharing with you now."

Once more she fell silent. Manx didn't like to rush her, but at this rate the curfew would fall and he'd be spending the night.

"Well," he said, "at least we know *they* didn't eat each other, because they ended up here."

"Indeed," said Leena. "The story ends by saying that Finnick and Sarah made a daring escape, and when they did so, they carried with them not only a piece of what came to be called amberose – after the ship that almost killed them – but also knowledge of something else. A thing they swore never to speak of."

"The hoard," whispered Manx. "But they did speak of it, didn't they? Otherwise there would be no story for you to tell. Is that what Fabian was searching for before he ran away? The hoard? He found something, didn't he? A clue?"

Leena smiled. "Fabian promised that he'd have a story

to tell *me* one day, just as soon as he found the rest of the clues to it." She closed her eyes and sighed deeply. "But it was an empty promise. His desire for Celeste was stronger than his need to find a story to tell his friend Leena." Her head lolled again, then she jerked back up. "I sense his story may finally be told, but by whom I cannot tell." A dreamy look passed over her face. "As a river from a raindrop flows," she whispered, "so a story from but one word grows."

Leena's eyes closed, and she began to snore gently. Manx stoked the fire's embers, then made his way to the door. He was leaving with more questions than answers, but three of those questions rang louder in his ears than any others: Was there really some sort of secret hidden hoard? If there was, what was it? And had Ninian Baggit somehow caught the thread of this fantastical story too?

17.
Repelled and Expelled

A ferocious storm blew hard and heavy that night, rattling rotten windows and snatching slates from roofs to smash on the ground. Manx and Father G, wrapped in blankets, coats and boas against the ice-sharp blasts of wind that stabbed through cracks in the walls, spent the early hours scampering around the Lange Fluke catching leaks in pots and pans. Skulpin then ordered them out into the yard to help him shore up a wall which threatened to come tumbling down.

None of this excused Manx from his Monday morning breakfast chores. Even the back end of the storm howling down Ratfish Wynd couldn't deter the morning customers who appeared at their tables, bedraggled and buffeted by the weather, but still impatient to scoff some gloopy porridge.

So it was with bleary eyes that Manx stumbled into the classroom when he finally made it to the academy.

"Yes, I know," he said, not bothering to look in the

professor's direction. "I'm sorry I'm late."

"It's not me you need to apologise to," said Oilyphant. "It's Master Baggit you've kept waiting this morning."

Nathan was standing at the front of the classroom, chalk in hand. On the board, he'd scrawled:

POWER AND ENERGY
IN THE REAL WORLD

Manx turned to Fantoosh as he sat down, and she immediately answered his unasked question.

"Nathan's taking this morning's class, on energy sources in the Out-There."

"Or the *real* world," added Nathan, underling the 'real' with two thick lines of chalk.

"Thank you, Master Baggit," said Oilyphant. "I believe you were going to begin by telling us about power stations."

Two hours later, Manx had to begrudgingly admit that Nathan's lesson had been quite interesting. First, he'd told them about coal and gas and oil. Then he talked about what he called "forever energy", or energy that you could harness from the sun and wind. It was, he said, becoming more important in the Out-There.

Nathan then spent ages talking about how cars ran on petrol, and how there were even ones now that were fuelled by electricity.

"I can't believe you guys don't have electricity here," he

said. "Not even for lights. I mean, what you use is basically medieval."

"There's nothing wrong with fish or gull oil," said Manx. "And I bet they don't have anything like amberose in your 'real' world."

Nathan was adamant that solar power was infinitely superior to amberose.

"Not in a place like Haarville," said Fantoosh. "Have you actually seen the sun since you've been here?"

"And amberose works perfectly well as long as nobody tampers with it," added Manx, staring daggers at Nathan.

"I suppose," said Nathan, "amberose *might* be popular where I come from." His eyes slowly widened. "Especially if there was lots and lots of it. It would save people a fortune on their bills."

"But there isn't lots and lots of it," explained Manx grumpily. "That's why it has to be looked after. Carefully. By people who know what they're doing."

"Wait, people in the Out-There have to pay for the electricity they use?" asked Fan. "Even if it comes from the wind or sun?"

"Yes," said Nathan. "I'm not sure it's that easy to turn the wind and sun into electricity. It's not like amberose, which just works automatically."

Manx could have argued more about how hard amberose was to handle, but his mind ran elsewhere. He'd always known how attached people were to their perpetual devices, but since meeting Leena, and seeing how much she missed hers, he felt he understood just how important they were to everyone in Haarville. And now here was Nathan saying how valuable amberose could be to people in the Out-There.

The thought settled in his stomach, and was still there when Oilyphant told them to go for lunch. Manx had planned to spend their break telling Fantoosh about his expedition to Crab Gulley, but Nathan insisted on joining them, which sunk Manx's mood even deeper. Worse still, Nathan insisted on talking.

"How does the amberose stuff work?" asked Nathan as they headed though the haar to the Sinking Teapot.

Manx ignored him. He couldn't stop him tagging along, but that didn't mean he had to answer.

"Did you hear me? I asked how amberose works."

Despite clenching his teeth together until it felt like they were sinking into his gums, Manx couldn't help himself.

"You should know! You had a good enough look at the light tower!"

"Was it really you, Nathan?" asked Fantoosh. "Because Manx is in so much trouble for it."

Nathan stopped walking.

"I... I didn't mean to," he said quietly. "I was just supposed to have a look inside the tower, but I tripped on a stupid bucket and crashed into all the workings. It wasn't on fire when I left. I swear it."

"Amberose doesn't always react instantly to being disturbed like that," said Manx. "And what were you *supposed* to be looking for exactly?"

"Not sure," said Nathan. "Whatever my father's been

looking for in all the other stupid machines I suppose."

So he was searching in devices! "How many has he looked at?" asked Manx.

Nathan rolled his eyes. "Loads. It's so boring. Yesterday we went to at least ten different houses to look at pot boilers and hair curlers and water pumps. And now that he's offering free services to anyone with a perpetual machine, he'll be spending weeks looking at them."

"You'll be spending weeks putting out fires then," muttered Manx. "You do know that nearly my whole family have died in amberose accidents, don't you?"

They'd reached the café, but Nathan paused before going in.

"Is that what happened to your parents?"

Manx looked at him. "My dad, yes."

"What about your mum?"

"She caught fish fever just after I was born," said Manx.

"My mum died when I was really young too," said Nathan solemnly, before opening the door.

Their usual table was free today, but before they'd got to it, Hamish hurried over.

"Sorry. It's reserved."

"Reserved?" exclaimed Fantoosh and Manx simultaneously.

"That's right." Hamish was barely looking at them as he said it. In fact, he seemed to be especially interested in some dried-on food stuck to his apron, which he kept picking at.

"Nobody ever reserves!" cried Manx.

"Well, that table is taken," said Hamish in a voice so quiet it was obvious he didn't want any of the other customers to hear.

"Who by?" asked Fantoosh.

Hamish didn't answer – he just shook his head sadly.

"We'll just leave," said Manx. "It's fine."

Once outside, Fantoosh held Manx back for a second. "What was all that about?" she asked quietly.

"It's me," said Manx. "Hamish has been told not to serve *me*."

"Rubbish!"

But five minutes later, after Madame Bonbeurre had rushed to close her bakery's door as they approached, spinning the sign hanging in the window to *Fermé*, Fantoosh had to agree.

They stood outside, staring in at the piles of limpet buns steaming on the counter.

"This is all your fault, Nathan," said
Manx. "No one trusts me any more."

With hunger gnawing at his stomach and anger boiling in his veins, Manx stomped back to the academy, where Oilyphant was waiting for them with a grave face.

"Fantoosh and Nathan, take your seats. Manxome, you are to go home."

"What? Why?"

"Because I said so," snapped Oilyphant. "And I told you two to sit."

Fantoosh and Nathan slid reluctantly into their seats.

"I'm not leaving until you tell me why." Manx remained rooted to the spot, glaring at the professor.

Oilyphant shifted on his feet, deliberately not looking at Manx.

"Please do not make this any more uncomfortable than it needs to be," said Oilyphant. "You are to go home, like I said."

"Why?" cried Fantoosh. "What's he done?"

"This has nothing to do with you, Miss Smith," said Oilyphant.

"Yes it does! Manx is my friend."

Manx threw Fantoosh a weak smile.

"Don't worry, Fan," he said. "We'll catch up later."

Manx turned and left the academy. A few weeks ago, the thought of being chucked out of classes would have been unimaginable. Yes, he was nearly always late, and yes, he was always bottom of the class – with Fantoosh as his only competition, he'd never stood a chance! But he turned up and did his lessons, even if he didn't always do his homework.

Until he knew what was going on, there was nothing Manx could do but add being thrown out of the academy to his rapidly growing list of catastrophes. He slumped at the foot of the memorial to cannibalised sailors. Things could always be worse, he thought. He could be stranded on a rock surviving off someone else's leg.

Then a passing gull swooped low and spattered an especially large dollop of drippy poo on his head. As it slid down his forehead and onto his nose, Manx realised there was only one place he wanted to be.

"Sent home!" Tina's voice hit a high enough decibel to shatter a crab claw. "Oh my poor *malchik*! My poor boy! Come! Sit! Drink tea!" She brushed some torn pieces of parchment off her travelling-case desk and ushered Manx into a seat next to the samovar, then opened its lower hatch to let out some heat and began spooning tea into the pot.

Tea and heat were exactly what Manx needed, which was why he'd gone directly to the library after being dive-bombed by the gull. In any case, Father G would almost certainly have made a huge fuss and marched straight to the academy for a showdown with Oilyphant.

"Here." Tina handed Manx a handkerchief. "Wipe that off your face. You know this is good luck, of course – to be selected by a gull for its deposit."

"Doesn't feel like it," said Manx, glumly.

"I'm so sorry, Manx." Tina shook her head. "All this on top of losing everything else." She poured the tea and pushed a dish of glistening jam towards him. "Tell me," she continued, "is Silas treating you well? The grime is thick at the Lange Fluke and his smiles are thin, but he has a good heart."

"You know Skulpin?"

Tina smiled. Her teeth gleamed in the golden glow cast by the copper samovar. "Admittedly, he does not visit the library now, but there was a time even Silas Skulpin would sit with me, sipping from that very cup." She winked at him. "He preferred five spoons of jam in his tea."

Manx pictured Skulpin's miserable mouthful of teeth. "I can imagine."

"Never mind," said Tina. "You and Father G will be back where you belong in no time, of this I am certain. But for now, I think we require some of my freshly made pancakes – they will take but a few moments to prepare. Pour yourself some more tea, warm your hands and choose a book." She disappeared into the small kitchen off the back of the library, leaving Manx to breathe in the sweet-scented air flowing around him from the samovar.

But the amberose-infused air didn't seem to be working its usual magic, and after a minute or so he still felt as wound up as a tightly rolled ball of flax twine. Even the prospect of Tina's always delicious pancakes slathered in oozing jam didn't excite him. Manx suddenly realised that sitting there sipping tea wasn't going to get him anywhere, so he stomped up the staircase and began looking along one of the shelves.

Manx had always been grateful that Tina's ancestors had managed to save not only themselves, but also the samovar and their massive collection of books from their sinking ship, the *Testy Tsarina*. He always loved searching the library for something interesting to read, but right now he was on the hunt for a book about hoards and, more importantly, how and where people went about hiding them.

He was halfway along a shelf of heavy-looking volumes when he had to stop and shrink into the dark recess of the balcony as the library entrance was thrown open, and the unmistakable, sneering voice of Ninian Baggit carried up the stairs.

18.

The Edge of the Ledge

"I can't say I had much time for libraries before arriving in Haarville, and seeing this sorry collection of boring old books isn't going to change that."

Manx clenched his teeth and fists as he listened to Ninian Baggit. He'd crawled to the balcony's edge and was crouched low, hidden by its wooden panelling.

Next to speak was Lugstitch, whose pointed and precise tone jarred with the soft, comforting, amberose-tinged atmosphere of the library.

"Unlike my wife, I've never seen the point of reading," he said. "Time spent not making a profit is time ill spent. Oh, and you'll need to watch Tina. She'll snare you with her tea and bore you with her interminable book blethering." He laughed in a sharp, tittering kind of way which made Manx's blood pump so loudly in his temples he was worried they might hear it too. But it was vital he remain hidden to discover what these two conniving creeps were up to.

"There's no one here," said Baggit. "The librarian has

perhaps left on an errand."

"She'll no doubt be aware we are here," said Lugstitch. "She'll have seen us coming in her tea leaves."

"Is the librarian an expert in fortune telling?"

"These types of women always are," said Lugstitch. "I should know – I'm married to one!"

Manx had to brace himself against a bookcase before the blood actually boiled out of him.

"Ah, is that the famous samovar I see up there?"

"It is indeed, Ninian. If the information you have is correct, and there are clues to be found inside the town's perpetuals, then I would imagine the samovar is an obvious place to look. You are sure your information is correct?"

"My grandmother Celeste whispered the words to my mother on her deathbed, and she in turn to me in her final hours," said Baggit. "That my grandfather Fabian found a clue to a hidden fortune, and that more clues would be found inside amberose devices. And indeed, we found the first inside Celeste's amberose handwarmer."

Manx froze at these words. Baggit was searching for clues. Clues to a hidden fortune. Or, as Leena Cuddie called it, a hoard.

"Goodness, this samovar certainly looks to be a marvel of design," said Baggit.

Manx could just picture Baggit's spidery fingers quivering as they reached out towards

155

Tina's precious perpetual device. With any luck, he'd burn them on the hotplate.

"Gentlemen!" Tina's surprised voice rang out across the old theatre. "Might I ask you to step away from my samovar?"

"Miss Pomorova, may I introduce Ninian Baggit? Or perhaps you had a chance to meet properly at the reception on Saturday?"

"*Da*. Yes," said Tina. "Unfortunately."

"I told Mr Baggit that you would be expecting us, did I not, Ninian?"

"Indeed," said Baggit.

"I was not expecting you at all," said Tina.

"But those delicious pancakes in your hand," said Lugstitch, "surely are not all for you?"

Manx peered over the balcony as far as he dared and winced as he saw Lugstitch examining his abandoned half-full teacup. Tina placed the pancakes down then reached for some clean cups.

"Silly me," she said, sliding Manx's cup away from the men. "I must have left this one out. Please help yourself to a pancake. I… er… always make some in the afternoon for visitors to the library." She glanced over their heads up to the balcony, searching for Manx. Her frightened eyes met his for a split second, then she turned back to Baggit. "I take it you wish to choose a book?"

"Book?" Baggit pronounced the word as if it were some sort of deadly virus. "No, I am here to view the famous samovar," he said.

156

"Famous?"

"Is it not one of Haarville's more elaborate perpetual devices? I have been led to believe its mechanism is a sight to behold."

"Mr Baggit, my library may be housed in an old theatre, but I am not staging a show of perpetual devices. I can offer you either a book or the door. Take your pick."

"I think I *would* like tea," said Baggit, stretching his words menacingly. "And then you will permit me to examine the samovar."

"No, I shall not," snapped Tina.

Lugstitch cleared his throat. "I really think you might."

"And I really think I might not," said Tina. "You have no business messing with my samovar. My ancestors took a huge risk in rescuing it from their wrecked ship and I will not permit your meddling hands to touch it now."

"Dear lady," began Lugstitch, "you can't have been listening on Saturday night when we said that Mr Baggit is now in possession of the sole licence to handle amberose devices. It is the wish of the Elders that he be permitted access to all the town's perpetuals in order to gain a more intimate knowledge of their function."

Liar! Manx nearly blurted the word out, but stopped himself. Baggit wasn't interested in how the samovar worked – he wanted to ransack it for some clue.

"And as I said, it is my wish that no hands shall touch my samovar. Certainly not yours."

There was a moment of silence. Lugstitch stepped back from the travelling-trunk desk and suddenly looked up to the balcony. Manx ducked.

"How many years is it since the Elders gave your family permission to move their library here?" He turned back to Tina. "Thirty? Maybe forty?"

"Perhaps," she replied.

"These permissions are, as I'm sure you are aware, for the Elders to award as they see fit, which means they are also for us to retract. Should we see fit."

Up on the balcony, Manx's blood had all but boiled dry.

"I am as much the sort of woman to give in to threats," said Tina, "as I am the sort to anticipate visitors to my library by sifting through the dregs of a teacup."

Manx didn't dare look over again, but he imagined Tina and Lugstitch facing up to each other like two angry sea lions fighting over the best spot in the sun.

"I shall leave you both to come to an arrangement regarding access to this most precious samovar," said Lugstitch. "Meanwhile, perhaps you will permit me to peruse your books, Miss Pomorova. One can't help but wonder what *surprises* may lurk amongst the shelves." Footsteps approached the bottom of the stairs. "I always find balconies so very intriguing. I think I'll start up here."

Manx didn't hesitate.

If he'd been a bit smaller he might have been able to squeeze in behind one of the bookcases. Instead, he scurried along the balcony, keeping as low as possible, ducking into the narrow aisle between the fifth and sixth row of books. High up on the balcony's back wall was a small, round window. Tina had asked him to open it for her on the very few occasions the weather was mild enough. "My books like to breathe fresh air as much as we do," she would say.

With blood pounding a beat in his temple, Manx clambered up using the shelves either side of the aisle as a sort of ladder, carefully avoiding the large, dusty volumes. It wasn't easy with his legs stretched between the bookcases, but he could just about reach out for the window latch. The glass itself was salt-encrusted – he had to hope the hinge wasn't as well.

It was.

Manx heaved against the window.

It didn't shift.

Meanwhile, behind him, Lugstitch was making his way along the balcony.

Manx leant as much weight into the window as he dared to without losing his balance. He could almost hear the salt crystals on the outside cracking under the strain. With a final effort, it opened.

As a ribbon of haar coiled in, Manx quickly lifted himself up and stuck his head out. There was a ledge directly underneath, about the width of a couple of street cobbles laid end to end. He pulled himself through, legs wriggling like a hermit crab trying to fit into a too-small shell. Somehow, he managed to crawl out onto the ledge, keeping as close to the outside wall as possible. Then he inched backwards and

pushed the window shut. He rubbed a tiny peephole in the salt and looked inside, dipping his head as he saw Lugstitch looming into view at the far end of the aisle.

There was hardly a breeze, and as Manx squatted on the ledge, the thick haar closed in, pressing him against the stone wall. High above, the sound dulled by the fog, gulls called to each other as they soared.

Hearing the window creaking open, Manx scurried further along the ledge into the haar. Even if Lugstitch managed to stick his head out, he wouldn't be able to see a thing.

"Well, this is interesting." Lugstitch's sharp voice sliced through the haar. "The window appears to be open. How careless! I'd better shut it. We wouldn't like anything to crawl in, would we?"

There was a grating sound as the window was pulled closed. Manx waited for at least five minutes before shunting back, but he knew before trying that the window would be locked.

Hunkering in against the frigid stone wall, he began to wonder how long he could last in the biting cold. Would he be found in a few days, rigid and frozen? If so, would anyone try to retrieve his body? Or maybe the Elders would order it to be left there to be slowly pecked at by hungry gulls – a grim warning to all Haarville not to fall foul of them.

A familiar high-pitched whistling call broke through Manx's nightmare vision, and from out of the haar, just along the ledge, poked Olu's vivid orange beak. The bird waddled closer and gave Manx a quick nudge on his hand.

"Olu! Have you come to keep me company?"

Olu nudged him twice more, then settled down on the ledge.

"Don't suppose you know about these clues, do you? Hidden inside perpetuals?"

Olu didn't move.

"It was worth asking." Manx smoothed some feathers on Olu's head. "Whatever they're for, I reckon the clues have got something to do with the Haarville hoard. If there even *is* a hoard."

Olu remained statue still. Then he bent forward slowly and pecked at the ledge.

Once.

Twice.

"Wait, is that a yes there is a hoard, or a yes the clues are connected, or both?"

But Manx didn't get an answer, as at that moment the window was suddenly flung open, and Olu flapped away into the haar.

"Manx! Are you there?" came Tina's nervous voice.

"Yes! Just a second." He shuffled back to the window. "I hope there's some tea left. I can't feel my fingers."

"Thank goodness you didn't tumble off." Tina helped Manx crawl back inside. "And what a silly question – there is always tea with Svetlatina Pomorova!"

"Did he make you open the samovar?" asked Manx, once they were back downstairs and the amberose warmth had begun to seep into his bones.

"*Niet*. Not this time," said Tina. "Although he will try again. Of this I am sure." She stirred four heaped teaspoons of jam into Manx's cup, giving him a theatrical wink at the same time. "How can I trust a man like that to look after my precious samovar? I suppose he means to learn by exposing her internal workings, but without your or Father G's intimate understanding of her eccentricities, imagine the damage he would cause."

On cue, the samovar hummed and vibrated slightly, and steaming tears began to drip from a small overflow valve on its side. Tina stroked the samovar, making a soothing sound as if the machine were a baby, whilst her own tears dribbled down her cheeks.

She and the samovar were still sobbing when Manx closed the library door behind him. As he forged a path through the haar, he made a decision. It was too late to persuade the Elders that Baggit was up to no good – if Manx was going to stop him, he was going to have to find these clues first.

Wherever they were hidden.

19.

Smash and Grab

Father G had insisted that Manx was not to get up early the next morning, saying he'd gone through enough trauma in being expelled from the academy without also having to dollop out the Lange Fluke's critter-crawling porridge.

Unfortunately for Manx, a luxurious lie-in wasn't on the cards, seeing as the fleas were still waging their war and attempting to gain new territory on his side of the mattress.

"You're supposed to be catching up on your sleep," said Father G, as he attacked the caked-on porridge at the bottom of the breakfast pan with a hammer and chisel.

"It's safer down here." Manx pulled up his sleeve to show his collection of fresh flea bites. From a certain angle, they almost looked like the outline of a humpback whale.

"Snap!" Father G laughed. "Only my bites are in a place that's making it uncomfortable to sit down."

On the kitchen's dusty dresser,

shoved under a teetering tower of dirty bowls, Manx spotted the familiar trident-sealed envelope used by Burgh House.

"What's that?"

"Oh, yes." Father G wiped his hands on his apron. "There are two of them. Delivered this morning."

Manx eased them out and opened the top one.

"That one confirms your expulsion from the academy," said Father G. "It says you broke the terms of your curfew."

Scanning it, Manx gasped. "I was seen in Crab Gulley after sunset? They're spying on me!"

The order was signed with a quite unnecessary flourish by Lugstitch. Manx could just imagine him wielding a long feather quill as he scratched his name onto the parchment. He'd probably plucked it from an albatross's tail especially for the occasion.

The second order was written in the same angular hand, with an equally elaborate signature underneath.

"I'm banned from Haarville completely?" Manx re-read it just to be sure he hadn't misunderstood.

"You're to stay this side of Ditchwater Burn," said Father G.

"I can't even go to the library?"

"Sorry, Manx. It's too risky, and not just for you. Tina could get into trouble as well."

Manx slumped against the dresser, forcing Father G to steady the tower of dirty bowls. How was he supposed to search for the clues and keep an eye on Baggit and Lugstitch if he was stuck in Phlegm Town?

"I suppose this explains why Hamish kicked me out of the café yesterday," he said. "And why Madame Bonbeurre locked the door in my face. They'd already been told not to serve me."

Father G sighed. "I'm afraid so."

"Tina let me in though." But even as he said it, Manx remembered the pieces of parchment he'd seen her sweep off her desk when he'd arrived. She'd obviously decided to ignore the order to keep him out.

"Tina would sooner go swimming with a frenzy of starving sharks than banish you from her library," said Father G. "And if Lugstitch's spies were doing their job, she'll no doubt suffer the consequences."

"They're scared I'll find out what's really going on," said Manx.

"Who?"

"Lugstitch and Baggit of course."

Father G rested a hand on Manx's shoulder. "I think you should hold off on the snooping for a while. It's too dangerous."

Before he knew what was happening, Manx was shouting.

"Don't you want to be back at the shop? Don't you want things to be how they were before?"

"Yes, of course I do," said Father G. "But I can't allow you to put yourself in danger."

"I don't know enough yet," snapped Manx.

"Knowing too much can be dangerous." Father G sighed again. "I miss our old life too, Manx."

"Then let me do this," pleaded Manx. "I have to stop Baggit!"

Skulpin grunted from the doorway. Manx jumped and almost knocked the pile of bowls off the dresser again.

"Do you even know what you're stopping him from, lad?"

Manx glared at the old man. "Not yet."

"Then your guardian is right," said Skulpin. "We must allow time to reveal more of his game."

"Time!" The word spouted from Manx like spray from a whale's blowhole. "What if there is no time? You've seen how fast the Elders are issuing all these orders. How am I supposed to stop them when I'm stuck here counting flea bites?"

"Putting yourself in harm's way is one thing," said Skulpin, "but others will suffer. They already are."

"Who do you mean?" asked Manx, although, with his stomach sinking, he realised he already knew.

"They've been to the library, Lugstitch and Baggit," said Skulpin. "Paid Tina a return visit."

"What about her samovar?" asked Manx, dreading the answer.

Skulpin lowered his head. "They spilled out its insides like they was gutting a seal."

Manx should have known this would happen. Baggit was never going to let anything stop him seeing inside Tina's precious perpetual.

Feeling that he might retch, Manx knew he had to get out of the grease-thick air of the Lange Fluke.

"I'm not banned from Phlegm Town yet, am I?"

"Not during daylight," said Father G.

"I'm going out then," said Manx.

"Watch yourself, lad," growled Skulpin, as Manx squeezed past him. "Cos *they'll* be watching *you*."

The air might have been fresher outside, but Manx sensed a jittery atmosphere. People flitted from door to door along Ratfish Wynd, whilst wide eyes peered through windows and loud whispers leapt overhead between the overhanging houses. But whatever was causing the stir, Pollock Row was the best place to glean information, so Manx picked up the pace. He ran the length of Crab Gulley, dodging out of the way of a stream of people dashing in the other direction.

As soon as he reached the market, he understood why.

Pollock Row was in uproar.

Screams filled the air as stallholders hastily pulled their kelp awnings down over their wares. Market-goers scattered this way and that. Bottles rolled into the gutters and parcels of food were crushed under foot. Two or three stalls nearby collapsed in the mayhem, prompting a sudden stampede towards Manx. He wasn't quite fast enough to dodge out of the way and someone barged into him, slopping their dish of gloopy fish entrails down his front.

And then he saw them.

The Elders.

They were marching through the market in a 'V' formation like migrating geese, with Lugstitch out in front clad in a long, dark green, billowing cape. A few steps behind, and dragging a wooden cart, were two younger men with sullen faces. They were Da Silva's sons, and they didn't look too pleased to be there.

Meanwhile, confusion raged all around. A short woman wearing a grubby brown headscarf suddenly grabbed hold of Manx to steady herself and catch her breath. It was Mabel, the wine-seller.

"What's happening?" asked Manx.

Mabel panted and looked nervously over her shoulder.

"It's a raid, is what it is," she said, gasping. "Them Elders is raiding our perpetuals!"

"What?"

But Mabel shook her head. "No time to chat!" She hobbled away towards the Gulley. "Got to go and hide me stocking-dryer. They isn't getting their greedy fingers on the only perpetual I've got left."

Had he heard right? Did Mabel say *a raid on perpetuals*? Manx had to be certain, so he forced a path through the wave of people rushing away from the Row.

He crouched by a dried-seaweed stall as the Elders loomed closer. Peering out through the gap, he spotted Brankie, the fish vendor, on the other side of the market – he'd crawled under his own stall and was hurriedly trying to cover something with a sheet of kelp. At that moment, the Elders drew level with them. Da Silva had obviously been elected to make their announcement, which he did in loud, severe bursts.

"People of Pollock Row! This is not a raid. I repeat, this is not a raid. We are effecting an audit of non-registered perpetuals. Bring out your devices for documentation."

One of the Elders bent down and peered under Brankie's stall, dragging out both him and a large perpetual fish boiler.

Manx could hear Brankie pleading his case, offering desperate apologies and promising to appear at Burgh House to fill in the necessary parchments. Lugstitch simply shook his head and clicked his fingers. One of Da Silva's sons stepped forward and lifted the boiler onto the cart. Momentarily transfixed by what he was witnessing, Manx realised someone was missing from the scene: Ninian Baggit. But then his eye caught the familiar flash of shiny leather a few stalls further up the Row.

Manx ducked into the crowd in pursuit of his prey, but Baggit proved as tricky to trail as a darting sand eel. He caught one or two glimpses of Baggit's coat-tails, but eventually lost sight of him completely.

Meanwhile, all around him, market traders continued to close up. Others, like Mabel, were simply abandoning their stalls.

Manx stopped next to a stall he hadn't noticed on his last visit to the market. It was laden with piles of rusting perpetual devices, old cogs and bits of wire. This must be where Phlegm Town's devices ended up when its residents had to sell them, Manx thought – left to moulder and fall to pieces in a sort of perpetual graveyard.

A thickset man sporting a bushy grey beard rushed up behind Manx and began sweeping some of the junk into a large reed basket.

"He'll not be laying his thieving hands on my stock," he said. "How dare that smarmy creep threaten to have me arrested!"

"Tall man, leather coat, face stuck in a sneer?" asked Manx.

"That's the devil." The man hefted the basket to his shoulder and hurried away.

It appeared that Baggit had no intention of patiently waiting to examine Haarville's perpetuals for clues. Instead, he'd somehow convinced the Elders to either force townsfolk to show them, or confiscate them. It was no wonder people were panicking – most folk in Phlegm Town had precious little as it was without their few perpetuals being seized. With a gut-churning thought, Manx wondered if they'd already raided the Lange Fluke and found his carousel.

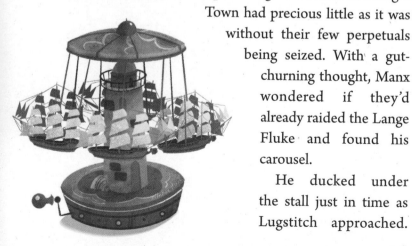

He ducked under the stall just in time as Lugstitch approached.

From his hiding place, Manx heard the Burgmaster pick up several devices and drop them back with a clatter.

"Dirty, useless junk," muttered Lugstitch.

Then Manx spotted Baggit's boots joining Lugstitch's right in front of him. If Fantoosh were there, she'd be egging him on to reach out and tie their laces together.

"You may cease your activities," said Baggit. "Our mission is complete."

"How so?" asked Lugstitch.

Before answering, a large cog dropped off the stall and rolled underneath. Manx held his breath. If either of them stooped to pick it up, he'd be discovered.

"Suffice to say that I am now considerably closer to achieving my goal and, therefore, yours. I'm leaving this revolting place immediately before it makes me ill."

"Yes, yes," said Lugstitch, "you must be getting back to the shop."

"Surely you've understood by now that I didn't come all this way to run a junk shop?" snapped Baggit.

"Should I call off the raid?" asked Lugstitch.

Baggit grunted. "Do as you wish. I suppose watching these wretches panic is moderately entertaining."

Manx waited until he was sure Lugstitch and the other Elders had abandoned Pollock Row completely. Then he set about discovering what had prompted Baggit to stop his search.

It didn't take long.

He heard Ursula crying before he saw her. Great bellows of grief punched through the damp air, drowning out the chaos of the market. The sight that met him when he finally managed to weave his way through the panicking crowd made him want to cry too.

Ursula was standing amidst the ruins of her stall. Scattered at her feet were a thousand shards of glass, whilst lying capsized upon this sea of destruction were the beautiful, lovingly constructed miniature ships, masts snapped and funnels smashed.

And in her trembling hands, she held the remains of the *Amber Rose*, its sails flapping woefully in the breeze.

20.

Sail Away

"Who did this, Ursula?" asked Manx, although he was certain he knew the answer already.

"A man," said Ursula, between sobs. "Scary... slimy... stranger."

"And he just came up and destroyed everything?"

Ursula's eyes welled up. "Not quite. He noticed the *Amber Rose* and grabbed it. He refused to put it back so I managed to get one end of the bottle. We both had hold of it, but then..." She paused, tears flowing down her cheeks. "It fell and the bottle smashed. He picked the ship up before I could and had a good look at it. It was strange because he only seemed interested in the sails. Somehow I pulled the ship back off him before he could steal or completely destroy it." She let out a huge heaving sob. "I'm so sorry, I knew you had your heart set on it."

Manx shook his head. "Doesn't matter. At least you stopped him taking the ship. Did he hurt you?"

Ursula shook her head, still sobbing.

"What about all these other bottles? Did he just smash

them too?"

"No!" wailed Ursula. "That's the worst part! He accidentally crashed into my display when he ran off after I called for help."

Manx could feel the vein in the side of his neck pumping wildly, but there was nothing to be done. It sounded like Baggit had found what he was looking for. And then added a little extra chaos for good measure.

"Can I see it? The ship?" asked Manx, gently.

"Take it," replied Ursula, welling up into a fresh release of tears. "It's no good to me like that. None of them are."

Manx found a brush and helped Ursula sweep up the broken glass. Then, having fetched her a cup of wild thyme tea from one of the few market stalls still open, he headed round the corner to Bladder Wrack Quay, cradling the delicate ship in his hands.

Apart from a few bedraggled gulls, the quayside was deserted. It was stinking, of course, due to the mass of decaying seaweed piled up in what had once been Phlegm Town's working harbour, so Manx took the precaution of breathing through his mouth to avoid the pungent whiffs wafting up from below. He raised the *Amber Rose* towards the light. Up close like this, he could see the intricate and delicate work that must have gone into creating the mini replica. It was perfect in every detail, just like its larger sister

ship hanging in the chapel of St Serf's – it even had a tiny foremast from which an even smaller piece of sailcloth was suspended. Miraculously, the model had survived Baggit's attack almost intact.

With a gasp of delight, Manx realised why Baggit had been so interested in the sails. There were some words scribed onto one of the squares of fabric. The ink was faded, but still just about clear enough to read. Whoever had written them had used a fine-pointed quill and a very steady hand.

Cruel Neptune – so our story goes
Chose to sink the Amber Rose.
We two survived to tell the tale
That here is writ upon the sail.

"I think I've got it!" said Manx, spooking a nearby gull, who dropped the slimy length of seaweed it was attempting to suck up. The so-called clues Baggit was searching for might not be hidden *inside* amberose devices at all: they could be *on* actual models of *Amber Rose* ships – or rather, written on their sails. As soon as Baggit had smashed the *Amber Rose* ship-in-a-bottle and seen the handwritten clue, he must have realised the same thing.

It was too late to save Tina's samovar, but finally, Manx felt he was making progress. There *were* clues, just as

 Leena said, and here was the first one! If Manx had had a plate of Lumpsuckers' fish balls in front of him right now, he'd have bet half of them that the fragment of cloth from inside Celeste's handwarmer was in fact sailcloth as well. And he'd have bet the rest of them that the gobbledegook Nathan said was written on it was another part of the same poem.

Manx rested the model in his lap and stared into the curtain of haar hanging just beyond the harbour, imagining a fleet of tall ships sailing past. But then he pictured them veering onto the lethal hidden reefs, where they'd be smashed to pieces in minutes, just like the tea clipper his ancestors Finnick and Sarah had journeyed on.

Had the *Amber Rose* ever carried a cargo of tea, he wondered? Or had it foundered on its maiden voyage? Manx would never know, but thinking about tea reminded him of Leena's tea caddies, and in particular, the one with the carved ship on the lid. The ship with a missing sail that, now he considered it, could easily be another miniature *Amber Rose*. She'd said it had been made by Finnick, hadn't she?

So, the fragment of cloth in the handwarmer could be the missing sail from Leena's tea caddy. In other words, it might be the one clue Fabian had found before leaving Haarville with Celeste. Somehow, Manx was going to have to sneak a peek at it. In the meantime, there had to be other pieces of sailcloth with more clues or verses on them, and as sure as cod roe was eggs, Baggit would be searching for them too.

Then, with heart-racing certainty, Manx realised exactly where another section of the poem would be found: the Fearty Death Day memory ship. And with Death Day fast approaching, he had to make sure Baggit didn't get the chance to wrap his spidery fingers around it.

The first thing Manx did when he got back to the Lange Fluke was check Baggit and Lugstitch hadn't raided there too. Satisfied that his carousel was safe, he joined Father G in the kitchen to help prepare lunch. Not an easy task when all they had was a couple of mushy marsh carrots and a bowl of festering fish heads even a half-starved herring gull wouldn't deign to peck at.

As they peeled and chopped, Manx described that morning's events on Pollock Row and what he'd discovered on the model ship.

"And Baggit's not interested in the shop," he said. "I heard him say so to Lugstitch. He's only after clues that lead him to this hoard."

Father G dropped the last of the fish heads into the pot, then wiped his hands on his apron. "Your family's memory ship is safe for the moment.

No matter how desperate Baggit is to get his hands on it, he can't get to St Serf's until Death Day itself. And we'll be there to stop him. Unless he can walk on water!"

The way things were going, Manx wouldn't put it past Baggit to try even that, but surely even he wouldn't risk trying to get across to St Serf's chapel before the equinox tide? There was a reason Death Day had to take place when the tides were at their lowest: it would be far too dangerous to attempt it any other time.

Having fed the impatient customers their soup – and a thinner and more meagre bowl of soup had surely never been served in the Lange Fluke – Manx set about tidying the kitchen.

"Want a hand?"

"Fan!" cried Manx, spinning around and almost slipping in the greasy puddle of washing-up water at his feet. "What are you doing in Phlegm Town?"

"Well, I'm not here for the food!" exclaimed Fantoosh. "What *is* everyone slurping out there?"

"Don't ask!"

Fantoosh picked up a soaked dish towel and held it at arm's length. "I think this might bite." She dropped it to the floor with a shudder. Manx rummaged in the dresser and threw her a dry, if not clean, replacement.

"I'm surprised Lugstitch hasn't blocked the bridge over to Phlegm Town yet," muttered Manx, plunging his hands back into the bowl.

"He has," said Fantoosh. "I had to

cross the burn up by the marshes to avoid the guards." She pointed out her muddy boots. "These are going to stink for weeks."

In the time it took to finish the dishes, Manx updated Fantoosh, and there was a lot to cover: Leena's story, the Haarville hoard, the raid on perpetuals, and Baggit's shocking bottle-smashing spree. Plus of course, Manx's suspicion that another verse might be hidden on his Death Day ship.

"Even if Baggit is there on Death Day," said Manx, "it'll be me lowering the *Amber Rose* in the chapel. No one can stop me doing that."

Fantoosh squeezed his arm. "I can't believe Death Day's nearly here. And you'll be sharing our picnic up at St Serf's – my parents are packing double of everything."

"Including barnacle nuts?"

"Especially barnacle nuts!" laughed Fantoosh.

"Sorry to interrupt your friendly little *tête-à-tête*."

Skulpin was loitering in the doorway. "Don't forget the rest of your chores, Master Fearty. Perhaps Miss Smith would care to stay and assist you cleaning out the privy?"

As Skulpin lurched away, she shook her head. "Miss Smith would not like to go anywhere *near* the privy."

Fantoosh dried the few remaining bowls and helped Manx stack them.

"What next, then?"

"Looks like I'm on cleaning duty," said Manx. "Sure you don't want to help?"

"Quite sure," said Fantoosh. "I meant, what next about Baggit and this hoard?"

"Simple," said Manx. "We just need to wait until we're inside St Serf's. If I'm right, there's another clue on my ship. There must be something written on one of the sails and I've just never noticed. Or maybe the ink's faded or it's hidden under the decking. I just wish I knew why Lugstitch is so involved in all this. I'm missing something. Something big."

Fantoosh began to button her cape. "Whatever Baggit and Lugstitch think this hoard is, whatever they're up to, we're going to stop them. But Manx—"

"I know." Manx interrupted her. "There might not be anything at all. It might be a wild herring chase and a complete waste of time." He sighed. "I don't care if it is. The Baggits are in our home, sleeping in our beds. They haven't got a clue about perpetuals and they've already damaged some of them. Baggit's ruining years of my family's hard work – look at what happened to Tina's samovar and the harbour light tower. If there's something to be found at St Serf's, I'm doing the finding before them."

After Fantoosh had left, Manx braced himself to face the stinking privy. He had the brilliant idea of trying to get Father G to swap one of his chores, but his guardian didn't even look up from the washtub out in the yard, where he was pounding clothes against a washboard. "I'd rather stick to these," he said, lifting a up huge, saggy pair of woollen underpants.

"Whose are those?"

"Skulpin's," replied Father G. "Can't have been washed in months."

Resigned to cleaning out the privy, Manx was in the kitchen trying to find a spare clothes peg for his nose when Skulpin – who Manx could hardly look at without thinking about the giant pair of pants now dripping on the line – handed him yet another envelope.

Manx's heart raced as he slipped a knife under the Burgh House seal and opened up the parchment.

Notification of restriction on movement

It is hereby affirmed that one Manxome Fearty, currently residing at the Lange Fluke, Ratfish Wynd, Phlegm Town, is prohibited from attending the annual Death Day ceremony at St Serf's chapel. The Fearty family will be represented by registered heir, Mister Ninian Baggit, of Kipper Lane, Haarville. Any attempt by Manxome Fearty, or his guardian, to attend will result in immediate sanction, with due punishment to be decided by emergency Burgh-Meet.

Manx felt like an elephant seal had just sat on top of him.

"Lugstitch might as well have used my own blood to write this." He handed the opened parchment to Skulpin, who in turn handed it to Father G, who had come in from the yard.

"It would indeed be a serious thing if you were to break the terms of this order," said Skulpin, with a gleam in his watery eye.

Father G ripped the parchment in two and held each half over the flame of a nearby lamp. As they caught light, he dropped the pieces to the stone floor, where they curled and crackled like crispy dried seaweed on a beach fire.

"I feel I should warn you, Manx," his guardian said in a low, serious voice, "that I will be for ever disappointed if you don't."

21.
When Snoozing Means Losing

Father G's words were still running through Manx's head on Death Day Eve, even as he stood, shivering, on the headland facing St Serf's.

An especially cold and sponge-thick haar had dropped to street level that morning and hung around all day – the sort of fog that only a stiff wind would chase off. According to Skulpin, the heavier-than-usual haar was a good omen and would make Manx's attempt to get across to the stack without being seen that much easier. The dense fog had certainly helped him creep undetected from Phlegm Town, although he'd first had to slosh through the marshes to avoid Lugstitch's sentries who were still guarding the bridge.

Now there remained the small matter of crossing over to St Serf's. The equinox tide wasn't due until the morning, so making the journey now, when the tide wasn't quite low enough to reveal the rocky path – and with waves still sweeping across it – was risky.

Father G hadn't been keen on Manx's danger-filled plan

to start with, until Skulpin reassured him that when he'd been Manx's age he'd often raced across to St Serf's before the equinox tide. Apparently it was a game generations of bored Haarville children had played. As long as Manx timed his dash carefully, Skulpin said, there was no reason he shouldn't make it across without even getting his feet wet. Manx just had to hope he was right. The one thing they all agreed on was that Baggit couldn't be allowed to get his hands on the *Amber Rose* memory ship hanging inside St Serf's, and unless Manx tried to cross to the chapel now that's exactly what would happen.

Once there, Manx would have the entire night to retrieve his ship, find the clue, put the ship back, and return before the Death Day procession began the next morning. And with haar as thick as this, he'd be free to light as many lamps in the chapel as he liked and no one would see them burning.

A sudden burst of laughter carried across the harbour from Lumpsuckers. It sounded as packed as it always was the night before Death Day. Any other year, Manx would be there too, laughing and joking with Fantoosh as they stuffed themselves with squid rings and puffed whelks and fish balls. Not that Fantoosh would be enjoying herself too much right now – her job this evening was to help Sheila keep the drinks flowing and the fish balls frying, and to try and stop anyone leaving. Even with the haar, Manx couldn't risk being seen. This mission had to remain secret.

Fantoosh's task would be aided by Gloria in Excelsis. Father G had decided that since he hadn't been placed under the same strict curfew as Manx, and was still allowed to leave Phlegm Town, Gloria would be making an impromptu appearance at Lumpsuckers – a sure-fire way of guaranteeing that Haarville's streets were as empty as possible. Father G had spent the entire afternoon getting ready and Gloria had never looked more spectacular. As the sound of music floated across the harbour, Manx felt a twang of jealousy – there was nowhere else he'd rather be right now.

He felt for the pocket watch Skulpin had lent him. Timing was everything and the moment to move was now. He carefully climbed down to the water's edge, pausing on the bottom step to peer through the murk. He could just see the sea stack and reckoned he could make it in about fifteen seconds. Waves were still breaking over the rocky path, even as the tide reached its lowest point of the evening – but too bad. He wasn't giving up now. He'd just have to run even faster between one wave and the next.

Manx stepped down and began his sprint, sploshing through shallow water. So much for not even getting his feet wet, thought Manx, as he stubbed his foot on a submerged rock. Plunging forward, he somehow stayed upright and ran on, but he'd lost vital seconds and was only about halfway across when the wave came.

He dropped low, grabbing hold of whatever his fingers could find: a rock in one hand and a cluster of limpets in the other. With his feet braced, Manx

turned his head away from the wave, closed his eyes and took a deep breath.

The water smashed against him, cold and heavy. It rushed over him, under him, into his ears, filling him with ocean noise. Pebbles and shells pelted his body. Seaweed tangled over his face and eyes – yet still he held firm.

Bedraggled, soaked and snorting seawater from his nose, Manx blinked sand from his eyes. He tripped and slipped the rest of the way to the stack, reaching the first step just as another wave crashed over.

Dripping and heavy with water, he began to climb.

It was a long, exhausting effort to reach the chapel. The path was tricky enough to negotiate in fair daylight conditions, carrying only a Death Day picnic. On a fog-filled night, weighed down by ocean-soaked clothes, boots awash with water, and pockets full of sand and pebbles, it seemed to take an eternity. The haar was dense, but Manx was all too aware of the sheer drop he knew lay a mere foot's width to the side of the path. This was no time for an attack of the jellyfish wobbles.

A couple of times he heard a bird calling somewhere within the haar. Was it Olu? The fog quickly swallowed the sound, but sure enough, there the oystercatcher was at the top of the path, perched on an ancient moss-covered headstone.

"Thanks for coming," said Manx, allowing the bird to nip his finger in greeting. Then, as the wind picked up seemingly out of nowhere, they crossed the old cemetery to the chapel entrance, Olu leaping and fluttering over broken bits of headstone. By the time they'd reached St Serf's wind-beaten wooden door, the haar had almost cleared. Across the water, lights from Lumpsuckers gleamed, and the amberose afterglow of Haarville's perpetuals pulsated golden orange in the remaining wisps of mist.

"Typical," whispered Manx. The unexpectedly clear night would mean he couldn't risk lighting even one of the perpetual lamps inside the chapel – it would shine like the North Star through the altar window and his quest would be over. He was going to have to sit out the clear skies and hope for the haar to return.

However, even if the perpetual lamps were off limits, the heater sitting just inside the chapel vestibule wasn't. There was just enough light from the newly exposed moon shining through the tiny window for Manx to open the heater's panel and trigger the amberose inside. Within moments the device hummed and clicked into action, sending waves of sweet warmth into the cold and fusty air.

Realising he was soaked almost to the bone, and that there was every chance he would die from hypothermia unless he took immediate action, Manx decided to strip off and dry out.

Whilst he peeled off his waterlogged clothes, hanging them from door handles and rusty hooks, Olu ruffled his feathers and plonked down in front of the heater for a nap.

It didn't take long for Manx to feel the effects either. As the vestibule filled with steam from his drying clothes, his body began to warm through and relax. The glorious, sweet-scented amberose filled the space and he felt his eyes drooping shut. It wouldn't hurt to join Olu in a quick snooze – just whilst his clothes dried – and so Manx lay down on the vestibule's stone bench…

"Ow!" Manx woke himself up yelling. Something had bitten his ear.

He sat up, rubbing sleep from his eyes and pain from his earlobe. Olu flapped to the other end of the bench, this time nipping Manx's toe. The bird whistled, strutting around in a frenzy. Manx was struggling to work out why he was completely naked when a bead of sweat trickled into his eye. Wow! It was *hot.*

The heater! It was literally glowing, a haze of heat shimmering around it. Manx leapt up, sending Olu flying across the vestibule, grabbed one of his now perfectly dry socks, and used it to open the heater's panel to switch it off. Then he opened the vestibule entrance, letting in a blast of cool air. The haar was back, but Manx could tell dawn was fast approaching.

"Olu! It's morning! It's Death Day already!"

Olu paced round the vestibule as if to say "I know! I know!"

Manx rummaged for Skulpin's pocket watch. It had stopped.

"What's the time?" cried Manx. "The procession!"

He threw on his clothes, but there was no time to savour the warmth from them being heated all night. Olu let out a shrill call and sprang over to the chapel door, beating his wings impatiently whilst Manx fumbled with the latch.

"Come on! Open!"

Finally, the rusty old latch caught and he rushed inside. His first task was to turn on a lantern. He needed at least some light to see by, and with the haar returned, nobody would spot it glowing in the window. Meanwhile, Olu flew up to the chapel ceiling, where he perched precariously on the *Amber Rose's* deck. The model ship swayed as Olu shifted his weight to balance himself, which set the nearby ships swaying too, as if caught in a swell at sea.

The memory ships were raised and lowered on a pulley system – a bit like laundry drying racks – each model being tethered to a rope. These led down the chapel wall, where they were secured on a row of large hooks. The ropes criss-crossed overhead like a complicated game of cat's cradle, which meant Manx would have to be careful not to get the *Amber Rose* snagged on its way down. The tangle of ropes also made it hard to pick out which ship was connected to which.

With daylight beginning to appear at the altar window, Manx unhooked a rope. High above, a red-funnelled cargo vessel, the *Testy Tsarina* – Tina's Death Day ship – slipped its mooring, lurching down, bow first. He pulled it back into place quickly, sweat dripping again into his eyes, made the rope fast, and picked another one.

This time, Fantoosh's family's two-masted dhow

plunged down, its elegantly curved sails almost getting entangled in the rigging of a nearby schooner. His heart pounding as he imagined what Fan would say if he damaged her ship, Manx carefully winched it back into position. He then took a deep breath and tried again.

It was third time lucky. With the correct rope finally in his hands, Manx began to carefully lower the *Amber Rose* closer to the ground. Olu assisted by perching on the deck, nudging other ships out of the way. Hardly daring to breathe for five long minutes, Manx eased the rope through his fingers until, finally, the *Amber Rose* was almost within reach...

"*What* do you think you're doing?!"

Manx spun round to find Lugstitch glaring at him, his boiled lobster-coloured cheeks fit to explode. This lapse in concentration caused the rope to slip, and the *Amber Rose* plummeted, snagging on other ships. Every memory ship in St Serf's quivered on their ropes, as if a great tsunami were about to overcome them. Then, with a whiplashing snap, one of the mooring lines sprang free from its fixing, setting off a chain reaction. Several ships slackened on their ropes, others were pulled taut, and under the strain, a few were left hanging by a single line, swinging like pendulums above the chapel floor.

Rings, letters, locks of hair, plus several tiny cameo portraits of long-lost relatives fell overboard as the ships pitched and swayed violently overhead, spilling their keepsakes and mementos. Manx ducked as one of the memory ships swung especially low, but, miracle of miracles, none crashed down.

Manx held his breath as the sounds of rigging creaking, ropes rubbing and hulls knocking together echoed around the vaulted chapel roof. But he couldn't have been holding his breath hard enough, because out of the turmoil and disaster above, the *Amber Rose* finally broke free.

With lightning-fast speed, he threw both arms out wide and caught his family's ship as it nosedived to the ground.

There was silence, then, "I'll take that from your thieving fingers, thank you."

Manx looked up as Ninian Baggit strode across and grabbed the *Amber Rose* with a triumphant sneer. Behind him, the rest of the Elders assembled, and behind them he saw Fantoosh, her mortified eyes flicking from the ceiling and back to Manx.

And then, with one last deafening smash, a ship crashed to the hard stone floor, splintering in a mess of sail, rope and wood. Manx peered behind. There, in pieces, lay the wreck of the *Sodden Seamstress*, Lugstitch's memory ship.

"You're finished now, Fearty," growled the Burgmaster furiously. "For good."

22.

Jailhouse Rot

For the second night in a row, Manx found himself sleeping on a stone bench. Unfortunately, Burgh House's icy cell was nothing like the toasty vestibule at St Serf's, and the musty, thread-thin blanket he'd been given was no match for the freezing draught. It hadn't taken long for the damp stone to chill his bones, leaving him feeling like a semi-frozen fillet of mullet.

Pulling the blanket up to his chin (which exposed his bare feet), Manx wondered what the time was. It felt like days since he'd been led up to Burgh House, his wrists bound, and even longer since the calamity at St Serf's.

Manx winced, picturing himself the day before, forced by the Elders to sit in the chapel's rear pew like a criminal awaiting trial. From there, he could only watch helplessly as

everyone had rushed to rescue their memory ships and try to get on with their Death Day celebrations. Occasionally, they'd thrown him angry glares, egged on by Baggit, who'd stalked around pretending to commiserate with everyone.

Fantoosh, meanwhile, had tried valiantly to sit with him, but the Elders wouldn't even let her near enough to throw him a couple of barnacle nuts.

A loud gurgle from Manx's stomach confirmed that it was at least a full day since he'd eaten. Lugstitch had shoved a bowl of unidentified mush into his hands before bolting the cell door, but it smelled so rancid Manx had decided that it would probably be safer to eat the blanket.

In the silence that followed his tummy rumblings, Manx began counting the water drips as they *ploshed* from the ceiling. He'd reached thirty-six when he suddenly stopped and held his breath, sure that he'd heard voices from… *inside* the wall? Maybe the vile limpet water he'd been given to drink was doing something to his mind.

But no. There were the voices again.

Manx leant his head against the cold brick, feeling a sudden draft of air from above. He crouched on the bench and felt with his fingers. Right at the top of the wall there was a hole, possibly put in for ventilation. Manx shivered. What was the use of having fresh air to breathe if your lungs had already frozen solid?

It took a few moments, but eventually Manx recognised the voices – Lugstitch and Baggit. The ventilation shaft had to be connected to the meeting chamber upstairs. With all thoughts of hypothermia banished from his mind, Manx concentrated on their conversation.

"*So, may I tell the Elders that we are agreed, Ninian?*"

"*Indeed you may, Sheldon, indeed you may.*"

Manx had never heard anyone call Lugstitch by his first name. He usually insisted on "Burgmaster". Even his wife, Betsy, referred to him as Mr Lugstitch. The two men were now obviously as thick as pirate thieves.

"*Good. We shall release the boy into your custody, on the understanding that he returns to Kipper Lane with you.*"

"*And you're sure he will cooperate? I must learn from him how to manipulate amberose safely. I cannot risk showing the substance to my contacts on the outside if it's simply going to explode in our faces.*"

Lugstitch laughed menacingly, sending a shiver through Manx's already freezing body.

"*He'll have no choice but to cooperate, or there will be consequences for his nearest and dearest. As Burgmaster, I will make sure of that.*"

"*And you are quite sure, Sheldon, that no one will hear about the location of the hoard?*"

"*My dear Ninian, there are but two beings on this earth who know where this bounty is to be found – us. We shall keep it that way until we can guarantee maximum profit falls into our open pockets and nobody else's.*"

Manx couldn't have been more stunned had a stingray lashed him with its tail. Baggit had obviously found the information he'd been looking for on the *Amber Rose* model from St Serf's, and he'd struck a deal with Lugstitch not to share it with anyone – even the other Elders. He carried on listening as the sound of parchments being shuffled and the scratch of sharp quills ripping across them came to his ear down the shaft.

"*There.*" Baggit's voice suddenly sounded businesslike. "*I will have the boy. But I can guarantee, my son will not take kindly to sharing a room with him.*"

Never mind what Nathan felt about it, thought Manx. If having to bunk up with the younger Baggit was the only way out of the Burgh House cell, then he'd rather stay locked up.

Unfortunately, that wasn't an option. Moments later the cell door's bolt was wrenched aside with a grating rustiness.

"Get up! You're leaving."

Blinking at the sudden light, Manx made out Lugstitch's barrel-like silhouette in the open doorway. He climbed down from the bunk, stepping straight into a puddle.

"Where are my boots?" he asked.

Lugstitch threw Manx's boots on the ground. They were still soaked from the day before, when they'd crossed back over from St Serf's. With his teeth gritted and his toes squelching, Manx followed the Burgmaster up the stairs to where Baggit stood waiting.

Lugstitch shoved Manx in the back, sending him tripping across the entrance hall.

"You are to accompany Mr Baggit to your former shop on Kipper Lane, where you will do as you are told, when you are told."

"Says who?"

Baggit brandished a sheaf of parchments under Manx's nose.

"Says I." A sly grin stretched across his sunken cheeks. "It's not just the shop that's mine now – *you* are too."

23.

Baggit & Son's

It was clear within moments of arriving back in Kipper Lane that Baggit was going to make full use of having Manx to order around.

"Sort that pile of junk," he barked, as they entered Manx's old home.

On the shop's counter, in a jumbled heap, lay countless perpetuals – or rather, parts of perpetuals – collected, most likely, on one of Baggit's recent raids. Manx instantly recognised bits of clocks, pot boilers, lanterns and even one or two moustache curlers. The precious and cherished devices had been broken apart, their mechanisms and casings separated, and, he realised with a jolt of horror, their hidden chunks of amberose exposed.

"What have you done to them?"

"Never mind what I've done to them," sneered Baggit. "You're going to fix them. All of them. Today."

Knowing there was little point in trying to explain to Baggit that it was going to take weeks, not hours, to mend the broken perpetuals, Manx hoisted himself onto the stool behind the counter. He had to at least appear to be obeying Baggit's orders. Besides which, Manx realised he was now in the best place to discover whatever it was Baggit had already unearthed about the location of the hoard.

So, gritting his teeth, he set about the delicate task of putting a perpetual egg peeler back together, first identifying its parts from the pile, carefully examining the tiny sliver of amberose that powered it, and finally dusting and replacing the cogs and levers of its mechanism.

He'd almost completed the repair when Baggit interrupted his concentration by poking his long nose over Manx's shoulder.

"What calculation do you use to determine the amount of amberose required to power each device?" he asked. "How much is inside that, er..."

"Egg peeler," muttered Manx.

"Is it? How charming!"

Of course, Manx knew there was precisely one twenty-fourth pebble-weight of amberose in the small peeler, but he had no intention of being *that* helpful.

"There's no calculation," he said, which was completely true. "Once you've worked with amberose for as long as I have, you just know."

Baggit sniffed. "No, no, no," he said. "You'll need to do better than that, Fearty. How about the larger devices, like the water pump in the kitchen here? How much do they take to power?"

"Looking to power something big, are you?"

Baggit slammed his hand down on the counter. "Just answer the question."

"Every device is different," said Manx. "You just need to have a feel for it. I have it. Father G has it." He turned to look Baggit in the eyes. "No one else has it."

A low growling sound reverberated from Baggit's throat and his hairy nostrils flared. Manx held his breath – had he gone too far? If he had, he was saved by the timely appearance of Lugstitch, striding past the shop window and rapping on the glass with the end of his cane.

"A word, Ninian," he shouted from outside, before treating Manx to a triumphant leer.

Baggit pulled his nose away. "Don't even think about trying to escape," he said, making for the door.

"I take it I can go to the privy?" asked Manx. He pointed to Baggit's hat, which was lying on top of a display cabinet. "Or I could use that if you prefer?"

"You've got two minutes," snapped Baggit.

Manx jumped off the stool and dived behind the shell curtain. For a split second he actually did ponder his chances of escape, maybe through an upstairs window or by leaping over the wall in the backyard, but no, this was the perfect chance for a quick snoop.

Dashing into the kitchen, Manx began a rapid rifle through the dresser drawers, but found nothing interesting. He climbed onto a chair and swept his hand along the top shelf, which dislodged a family of spiders from their web but nothing else. He even checked the pantry, poking his fingers into the tin of marsh plantain flour in case Baggit had hidden something there, but all it contained was soft flour and a few indignant weevils.

Manx knew he was unlikely to find the whole of the *Amber Rose* memory ship from St Serf's, but maybe a sail or piece of decking – whatever part of the ship the clue might have been written on. He'd need to find more opportunities for a poke around, but in the meantime he really did have to pee, so he hurried outside to the privy.

It was on his way back to the kitchen that he spotted a wooden crate outside the back door. Manx quickly lifted the lid. Inside was a set of new, neatly folded oilskins and some flax twine sacks – also folded – whilst lying on top was a gleamingly sharp chisel and a small iron hammer.

"Manxome Fearty! Where are you?"

Baggit's bellowing voice shook the thin pane of glass in the kitchen window. Manx dropped the lid and scurried back indoors just as Baggit marched into the kitchen.

"I was in the privy, like I said. What did Lugstitch want?"

"None of your business." Baggit grabbed Manx by the arm and pulled him back through the curtain. "Get back to work."

"What about lunch?" Manx must have easily passed his record for the longest ever stretch without eating.

"You'll take your supper with Nathaniel after you've earned it by working a full day. Talking of my son," continued Baggit, flashing his yellowed teeth, "I've another little job for the two of you when he's back from school. Give you a chance to get to know each other. You are sharing a bed after all. Ha!"

Manx's heart spiralled down to his feet. He'd been wondering how his day could get any worse – and now he knew.

The "little job" Manx and Nathan had been lumped with that afternoon was to repaint the sign hanging above the shop's entrance. In reality, this meant Manx balancing on a rickety ladder whilst Nathan held on to it – a role he wasn't particularly good at.

"You're supposed to be holding it steady!" yelled Manx, bracing himself against the wall as the ladder wobbled precariously, sploshing red paint onto the cobbles below.

"Sorry," said Nathan. "I can't stop shivering."

"Well, every time you shiver, this thing wobbles and I end up making a mistake."

"And we don't want that, do we?" growled Baggit, who'd appeared in the shop doorway. "Any mistakes on that sign and you'll be going without supper." He clamped a hand to Nathan's shoulder. "Doesn't it make you proud, Nathaniel? Our own shop: Baggit & Son's." He smiled, licked his teeth, then glared at Manx. "You've missed the apostrophe. Fix it!"

Fighting the urge to flick paint down over him, Manx instead smiled his very best fake smile.

"I'm going out," said Baggit. "I'll be back shortly and I want to see that sign finished." He slammed the door hard enough to set the ladder swaying and stomped away. Nathan planted a foot on the ladder's bottom step and looked up.

"You okay up there?"

"Well, I haven't tumbled to my doom yet, so yes." Manx dipped the brush in the paint. It was thick and deep red, made from crushed sea locusts. As he stirred it, Manx imagined it was actually made from Ninian Baggit's blood.

"Can I ask you something?"

Manx stopped stirring and peered down at Nathan. "Go on."

"What were you really doing at the chapel?"

"Trying to destroy everyone's ships, of course," said Manx. "Isn't that what everyone thinks?"

"Maybe. I don't." Nathan sniffed and wiped his nose with the back of his hand, which set the ladder wobbling again.

"Careful!"

"Sorry." Nathan steadied it. "Why is that ship so important?"

"You tell me!" Manx replied. "It's your dad who ripped it out of my hands."

Nathan shrugged. "Dad never tells me anything."

"Do you know where it is? My ship?"

"In his room, I guess. Dad locked himself in there with it as soon as we got back and told me not to disturb him."

Manx painted on the missing apostrophe and dotted on a full stop with a hard stab of his brush. "So you wouldn't know if your dad was planning a sea voyage?"

"What? No! Why are you asking me that?"

"There's a set of new oilskins sitting in the backyard," said Manx. "And him and Lugstitch are obviously planning *something*."

"I hadn't noticed."

"I take it you've noticed it's your name I've been painting onto this sign?"

"Great!" mumbled Nathan.

"Great as in fantastic, or great as in you'd rather eat a plate of pickled limpets than work here?"

"Can we just go inside?" said Nathan. "It's freezing."

Manx scoffed. "This? Freezing? Just wait till next winter. You'll know what real cold is when your pee freezes before it hits the pot."

"That's not even possible," said Nathan. "If it was, polar bears would pee popsicles."

"Who says they don't?"

Manx looked down at the sound of Fantoosh's voice. "What are you doing here?" he asked, as she appeared out of the murky fog.

Fantoosh smiled up at him, taking hold of the other side of the ladder. "I've come to make sure you're alright, silly! I managed to creep past the bridge sentries and went to Phlegm Town. Father G sends his love and says as soon as he can escape his curfew, he's coming to rescue you. Although I couldn't actually get into the Lange Fluke because Lugstitch has put more guards on the door to stop Father G leaving – he shouted the message through an upstairs window."

"Skulpin won't be pleased about his inn being under guard."

"He's not," said Fantoosh. "When I left, he was threatening them with an old whaling harpoon. He said they were spoiling the warm and friendly welcome his customers have come to expect." She turned to Nathan. "And Manx is right about the winters here. A few years ago it was so cold Sheila's boat was iced into the harbour and gulls kept falling out of the sky, frozen solid."

"Rubbish!" exclaimed Nathan.

"Not rubbish, actually," said Manx. "A frozen fulmar landed on Lugstitch's head outside Lumpsuckers." He smiled at the memory. Sometimes, fate managed to get things right.

"Don't worry, Nathan," said Fan, taking the paint tin from Manx as he climbed down, "you can borrow some mittens. Just remember not to pee outside!"

Their laughter was silenced by Baggit's sudden return. He was holding a long roll of parchment under his arm.

"No slouching on the job!" he barked. "And clean up those drips on the pavement!" He glared at Fantoosh and Manx. "Colluding with others is forbidden too." Then he turned to Nathan. "Don't get too friendly with these miscreants, son. You might catch something." Baggit went back inside, slamming the door so hard that the glass in the window practically jumped out of the frame.

"The only thing you're likely to catch from us is better

manners," said Fantoosh. "Is he always like this?"

Nathan stared at the ground. "Mostly," he mumbled, scuffing some dirt into the gutter. He blew on his hands. "It really is cold out here. I don't suppose you've fixed any of those handwarmer thingies yet, have you?"

"No, I haven't," said Manx. "Why don't you go indoors and warm up? Fan can help me clear up."

"You don't mind?"

Manx smiled. "To be fair, Nathan. You weren't really much help."

He waited until Nathan had gone back inside.

"Don't suppose you saw what was on that giant parchment, did you?" he asked Fantoosh.

"No, sorry. Do you think it's important?"

"Everything Baggit does is important." Manx added the mystery parchment roll to the list of things he urgently needed answers to. "You know he's been asking me how much amberose is inside the largest perpetuals?"

"Because he wants to know how to mend them?" asked Fantoosh.

"Baggit! Repairing perpetuals?" Manx looked up at the sign. It swayed as a cold gust blasted down the lane. "He's only pretending to be interested in this place."

"Go on."

"I don't think the hoard is treasure or gold, Fan. It's more amberose! That's what Baggit thinks, and he wants to get rich by selling it in the Out-There. And Lugstitch is in on it with him. I heard the two of them talking. They know where the hoard is and once they've found it, they're going to share the profits."

"And Baggit needs you to show him how amberose works so he can leave Haarville with this hoard and make a fortune?"

"Exactly!" cried Manx. "Amberose is worthless to him in the Out-There unless he knows what it can do. That's why I've been forced into a lifetime of drudgery – so he can steal my knowledge and get rich."

Fantoosh put her hands on her hips. "Manx Fearty, do you honestly think you're still going to be stuck here this time tomorrow, let alone for a whole lifetime? Don't forget – you're not alone. Although, actually, I'm leaving now before I ice-bergify."

"Fine. Go! Leave me to my lifetime of toil!"

"I am!" Fantoosh smiled. "Until we have a plan."

"A plan for what?"

"To stop Baggit and Lugstitch, silly! That is what we're going to do, isn't it? No, actually, that's not a question. That is *exactly* what we're going to do."

24.

Rhymes of the Ancient Mariners

Fantoosh vanished into the haar and Manx finally returned to the warmth of the shop, almost colliding with Baggit, who was stalking back out. He still had the parchment roll wedged under his arm, but this time Manx noticed an inky dark red 'X' soaking through the parchment from the other side.

"Watch yourself, boy," snarled Baggit, poking Manx with a red-stained finger. "And get back to work!"

Before fixing any more devices, Manx went in search of Nathan to check if he'd seen what his dad had been up to.

"There you are." He walked into the kitchen, where he found Nathan fiddling with a handwarmer. "Careful!" Manx lunged across the table and grabbed the device. "I know we haven't been the best of friends, Nathan, but that doesn't mean I want to see your brains splattered all over the ceiling." He carefully placed the handwarmer in front of him. Elegantly curving letters were engraved in the tarnished pewter: C M. "Is this Celeste's?"

"Yes. Can you fix it?" asked Nathan. "I can't even get it open."

Finally, Manx had a chance to look at the infamous handwarmer! He ran a finger over the initials, put there by Fabian for his sweetheart. "I need something sharp." Manx went to the dresser and rummaged in the drawer for a quill, inserting the pointed end into a small hole on the handwarmer's side. "It's seized shut," he said, wiggling the quill around.

"Dad's never managed to get it open." Nathan peered over his shoulder. "Only that one time when I was a baby."

Manx gently worked the quill a bit deeper until the lid finally popped up with a satisfying *click*.

"Oh!" He fished out a piece of cloth from inside. "Is this…?"

Nathan smiled. "It must be! The cloth I nearly swallowed! Dad must have put it back for safekeeping."

Casting aside all thoughts of repairing the handwarmer, Manx smoothed out the fabric. The words weren't nearly as faded as those on the sailcloth from the ship-in-a-bottle, but the ink was the same, as was the handwriting itself:

A place not quite as it first seemed,
This trove of power beyond our dreams.
Of the hoard that blinds with lure so strong,
A piece we took, be it right or wrong.

Manx's head spun. Here was another clue!

"See – just a load of gobbledegook," shrugged Nathan. "Like I said."

"Maybe," said Manx, wondering how many more parts there could be to the poem. "Maybe not. Can I keep this?"

"If you promise to fix the handwarmer?"

"Deal." Manx folded the cloth and put it in his pocket, where it joined the other clue he'd already found.

He picked up the handwarmer, then put it straight back down.

"Can you smell smoke?"

"On no!" Nathan dashed to the back door. "Dad told me to keep an eye on it."

"On what?"

"The fire! He's burning some rubbish." Nathan hurried outside, Manx right behind him.

In the middle of the yard, a small pile of woodchips, parchment and leaves was smouldering, a ribbon of smoke coiling this way and that. Olu had made an appearance and was flitting around the yard, performing a sort of mid-air dance. He whistled when he spotted Manx, dropping to the ground and pecking at his feet.

"That's supposed to be a fire?"

Nathan picked up a stick that had slipped from the pile and prodded it. "It's almost gone out."

"You either start fires you don't want," said Manx, "or can't keep the ones you do want going. This

209

needs a drop of gull oil." He nipped back inside, returning with a small dish. As he tipped the oil onto the pile, Olu screeched and flapped into the air, narrowly missing a flame as the blaze took hold.

"Watch out!"" cried Manx, as Olu dive-bombed the fire. "What are you doing?"

Olu repeated his daring manoeuvre, this time soaring back out of the smoke with a small piece of cloth clasped in his beak. He dropped it by Manx's foot, where it lay gently smouldering at the edges.

"It can't be!" Manx stamped on the cloth before it could properly catch light, then picked it up. "It is! Well done, Olu!"

Olu whistled happily, flying up to sit on the wall out of the smoke now filling the yard.

"Let it burn down, then douse the fire with water," Manx told Nathan. "I'm going in to read this."

Back at the kitchen table, he stared in wonder at the small square of age-yellowed sailcloth, a shiver racing up the back of his neck. Ninian was getting careless, thought Manx, because here was yet another verse of the poem:

Our lonely home, five months no less,
The rock that stands beyond the Ness.
Two lives sustained on air alone,
Stranded on that towering stone.

With shaking hands, Manx laid out the other pieces of cloth. First the one from the ship-in-a-bottle. Underneath that, the piece he'd just saved from the fire – which Baggit must have ripped off the *Amber Rose* memory ship. Finally, the verse from Celeste's handwarmer. Then he read all three together.

Cruel Neptune – so our story goes
Chose to sink the Amber Rose.
We two survived to tell the tale
That here is writ upon the sail.

Our lonely home, five months no less,
The rock that stands beyond the Ness.
Two lives sustained on air alone,
Stranded on that towering stone.

A place not quite as it first seemed,
This trove of power beyond our dreams.
Of the hoard that blinds with lure so strong,
A piece we took, be it right or wrong.

Another excited shiver rippled through Manx. Finally, he was piecing the clues together! It was just a shame Baggit kept getting there first.

"What was that? In the fire?"

Nathan was standing in the doorway, dripping.

"You're supposed to throw the water on the *fire*," said Manx.

"I did!" cried Nathan. "Mostly. Anyway, the fire's out. So..." He pointed to the table. "What is it?"

"This, Nathan, is what your dad dragged you all the way to Haarville for."

"A piece of old cloth?!"

Manx smiled. "It's more where the words on the cloth might lead to."

"Where do they lead?"

"Not sure," said Manx. "Yet. But I do know your dad is up to no good."

Just then, Olu padded inside, hopped up onto Nathan's shoulder, and let out a short, sharp whistle.

"Ow! What did he do that for?"

"It's a warning," said Manx. "Your dad's on his way back. Thanks, Olu!" He swept the sailcloth off the table and was about to dash back into the shop when he paused. "Nathan, what are you going to say to him?"

Nathan bit his lip whilst Olu cocked his head to the side, staring at him with one unblinking, scarlet-rimmed eye.

"I'll say I was dealing with the fire while you were fixing perpetuals."

Olu flapped off his shoulder.

Nathan looked at Manx. "I didn't need your feathered friend here to persuade me, you know."

"I'm glad," said Manx, smiling at him. "Thank you."

By the time Manx crawled into his old bed, he'd hardly had a second to even think about the clues. Baggit had made him work on the perpetuals until late, leaving out just a small plate of limp sea lettuce and salted winkles, which Manx scoffed before climbing the stairs to his old attic room.

"It's freezing!" Manx tried to pull some of the blanket out from underneath Nathan. "Are you going to share this?"

The mound next to him grunted and turned over, and instantly began snoring like an elephant seal. However, despite being dogfish-tired, Manx just couldn't drop off. Instead he repeated the lines of the poem over and over in his head.

Every time he got to the bit about 'the rock that stands beyond the Ness' he stopped. The only Ness he knew of was No-Hope Ness, site of countless shipwrecks over the centuries. And as far as Manx could remember, the only place marked on the charts anywhere near it was Clam Rock. But, surely, he thought, the poem couldn't mean there – could it?

Was Clam Rock the same rocky outcrop of Leena's

story, where Sarah and Finnick were supposed to have been shipwrecked? Was is really the same ancient towering stone of the poem?

And then, like the freshly oiled mechanism of a perpetual, something clicked into place: the roll of parchment Baggit had been dashing in and out of the shop with – it had to be a nautical chart. Manx would have bet his last barnacle nut (if he'd had any) that the inky red 'X' Baggit had made on the parchment marked the infamous Clam Rock. That must be where he thought the hoard was.

With a growing sense of dread, Manx realised that Baggit was planning a voyage to one of the most dangerous places in the waters around Haarville. Clam Rock was infamous for one reason only: the reef surrounding it. Razor Reef had claimed more ships and more lives than all the other rocks and reefs put together, and was more than likely where all those cannibalised sailors met their gruesome ends.

"Impossible!"

Manx's voice disturbed Nathan, who stirred, and rolled himself up even more tightly in the blanket. Manx shifted to the edge of the mattress, resigning himself to a long, sleepless night full of clues, conundrums and cold toes.

25.

Round and Round the Merry-go-round!

There must have come a time as dawn broke when Manx finally dropped off, because he woke up feeling a sharp prod in his side.

"You have to get up. Come on!"

Manx peered through sleep-filled eyes, finding Nathan's face leaning in rather too close.

"I'm not getting up," he said. "I've only been asleep for about ten minutes. Goodnight."

"No! Not goodnight. It's morning and you're needed downstairs. Now!" Nathan yanked the blanket off the bed. "Now, Manx!" he pleaded. "It's an emergency."

"Alright, alright. I'll come down."

Nathan thumped his way down the stairs and Manx rolled out of bed, threw on his clothes and followed him, thoroughly expecting an immediate dressing-down from Baggit for being late. Instead, he found a desperate-looking Nathan, alone in the kitchen, rubbing his hands and blowing puffs of cold breath.

"Finally! Can you get this stupid heater working? I've

been trying for ages."

"No, Nathan. I can't," said Manx.

"Why not?"

Trying hard not to laugh, Manx answered, "Because it isn't a heater. It's a fish smoker. Did you want to smoke a fish for breakfast?"

Nathan looked confused. "No. I hate fish."

"You're really going to have to start liking it," said Manx. "If you're staying in Haarville." He went over to the range. "Let's get this going instead, shall we?" He fiddled with the perpetual dial. "That'll heat the place up nicely and we can have some tea."

Watching the water come to a boil in the pan, Manx found himself thinking about the rough ocean around Haarville. Then, with a jolt, he remembered what he'd worked out the night before about Baggit and Clam Rock.

"Where's your dad?" he asked Nathan.

"Out already. The harbour, I think he said."

Manx's heart began to race. Was Baggit actually planning on going to Clam Rock *today*?

Despite the risk of leaving the confines of the shop, Manx knew he had to investigate. Getting up from the table, he couldn't stop from yawing the longest, most stretched-open-mouth yawn he'd ever yawned.

"Did you really not sleep at all?" asked Nathan.

"With you bundled up in the only blanket like a boiled lobster stuffed in a bun? What do you think?" Manx rubbed his eyes. If only he could get his carousel back from the Lange Fluke, he'd be sure to sleep better. Just thinking about the comforting aroma it gave off, and the slowly spinning ships, was almost enough to send him to sleep right now, especially with the kitchen becoming warm and toasty. If he could only sit here a while and close his eyes…

"The carousel!" he cried.

"What? What are you talking about?"

Manx's mind whirred. His carousel had ten tiny replicas of the *Amber Rose* hanging from it. But that wasn't all: the canopy covering the spinning ships was made out of a piece of sailcloth. How had he forgotten?

"There's another part to that poem!" he said. "Another clue. I'm sure of it!"

Manx faced a dilemma. He needed to be in two places at once: the Lange Fluke to retrieve the carousel, and the harbour to spy on what Baggit was up to. He briefly considered asking Nathan to go to Phlegm Town, but seeing as Nathan couldn't tell the difference between a fish smoker and a room heater, Manx wasn't at all confident he'd find his way to Ratfish Wynd without getting lost.

"Don't suppose you've seen Olu around this morning?"

"Nope."

Manx stuck his head out the door into the yard and

whistled between cupped hands. Whilst waiting for Olu to appear, he scribbled a quick note to Fantoosh:

Lange Fluke. Carousel. Harbour. Fast!

As he folded the parchment, Olu hopped in through the open door. "Ready for an emergency mission, Olu? Good. Will you take this to Fan?"

Olu tapped the table leg, clasped the note in his beak, and disappeared out the door and up into the haar.

Manx pulled a sweater on. "I have to go out."

"What if my dad comes back and finds you missing?" asked Nathan.

"Shouldn't be a problem." Manx headed for the shop entrance. "It's him I'm going to spy on." And before Nathan could ask him any more questions, Manx dashed out and hurried down to the harbour.

Dawn was just breaking over Haarville, and its weak light was doing its best to push through the haar. But with the light tower damaged, the harbour was still quite dark. There was barely a breeze either, which meant that the sounds of every fish flipping in the shallows or gull squabbling over a mussel carried over the receding tide.

Manx turned his ear towards the harbour, listening for

something, anything that would tell him where Baggit might be.

Within seconds, his ear caught the swishing squeak of a leather coat.

Wasting no time, Manx scurried across Front Street like a crab running for cover from a dive-bombing gull. Baggit was heading out along the harbour wall, so rather than creep along behind, Manx eased himself down one of the flax rope ladders hanging over the side. He dropped silently onto the soft mud and followed the wall round towards its far end, stopping suddenly when he heard Sheila Giddock's angry voice.

"What is it, man? Can't you see I'm busy!"

As he listened, Manx's feet sank into the mud – he didn't dare try to lift them out for fear the squelching would give him away.

"I do apologise," said Baggit in the sort of sarcastic voice that would have earned him a week of detention from Oilyphant. "It is, however, fascinating to see an artisan at work."

"Want to have a go at baiting lobster pots, do you?" Sheila laughed. "Be my guest, although I doubt you'd want those fine fingers of yours to stink of putrefying pilchards for the rest of the week."

Manx wasn't too keen on the smell of Sheila's lobster bait himself – nobody was, which was why Sheila prepared her pots all the way out here by the harbour entrance.

"I merely wish to pick your expert nautical mind, dear lady," said Baggit.

"Is that so?" Sheila's voice had a wary edge to it. "Thinking of doing a spot of seafaring, are you?"

"Perhaps," replied Baggit. "Since arriving in Haarville I have developed a keen interest in tides and wave patterns and such like."

"Tides and waves is what I live or die by. That's all the nautical knowledge you'll be needing."

There was a sound of slimy fish insides being slapped around, and Manx had to silently dodge out of the way as stray bits of guts cascaded down onto the mud.

"I am particularly interested in how the tides react with the various reefs out there," continued Baggit. Manx had to give the man top marks for persistence.

"Reefs? There are thousands of them, and they'll all try to scupper you. Why do you think they've got names like Wrecker and Razor Reef, eh? The ocean's a dangerous place. I should know – I lost my arm to it years ago, sliced clean off by a swordfish."

Manx had to stifle a giggle. This was a version of Sheila's accident he'd never heard before.

"So," continued Sheila, "if it's dangerous to me, the ocean's lethal to them that don't understand it. Now, leave me in peace, man. If you ask any more questions, I'll be forced to charge you for my time. These baskets don't bait themselves."

"One moment and I shall leave you to your labours," said Baggit. "This Razor Reef, as you call it – has anyone to your knowledge ever survived it?"

Sheila's laugh echoed across the harbour and back again. "Survived it! Not a shred of skin has ever been found of them that's had the misfortune to be wrecked on it."

"How odd," said Baggit, "because I have heard otherwise."

"Rumours and riddles told by bored old men over a flagon of limpet schnapps are never to be trusted," snapped Sheila. It sounded like her patience had not just worn thin – it was worn through.

"Humour me," snapped back Baggit, with not a hint of humour to his voice. "In your professional opinion, could you count out the possibility of someone surviving the reef?"

"In theory, I suppose it would be possible." Sheila's tone was remarkably calm considering how annoying Baggit was. "But in my professional opinion, you'd lose more than just an arm if you tried. Like that sneering head of yours, for example."

There was a clopping sound, which Manx assumed was Baggit clicking his boot heels together in frustration. "I see. I anticipate a change in your willingness to assist me, Miss Giddock, when I return at high tide. I take it you will be going out to farm the seas as usual?"

"Course I will."

"Then do not be surprised to find you have an extra passenger or two."

"The *Unfortunate Flounder* does not carry passengers," said Sheila.

Baggit laughed. "I would imagine an order from the

Elders will soften that stance soon enough. Good day to you."

Manx waited until the sound of Baggit's bootsteps faded. Then he tried to free himself from the mud, but he'd sunk almost up to mid-calf and after several futile attempts, he gave up and called out to Sheila for help.

Sheila's face appeared over the edge of the harbour wall.

"I might be wrong, young Manx, but I'd guess there's several people in this town who wouldn't care to find you eavesdropping down there like some mudlubber." She threw a rope over the edge and Manx grabbed hold of it, his feet belching free from the thick harbour silt as he pulled himself up.

"Baggit means it, you know," he said, stomping some mud off his boots. "He'll be back at high tide."

"Nay, lad. A menace that man surely is, and a wrong he has done you and Father G, but that was mere idle threats. I expect no less of Baggit. However, I'll give him his due – he has more guts about him than I have in this pail of fish innards."

"Even so," said Manx, "don't be too surprised when Baggit actually does turn up later on." He kicked some more mud off his boots. "Sheila, have you ever heard a story about my ancestors surviving on Clam Rock after the *Amber Rose* was wrecked?"

Sheila looked grimly at him. "You heard what I just said to that man about the folly of believing in dusty old tales told by dusty old people!"

"Alright, but say they – or anyone – were wrecked on

Razor Reef: Is there any way they could have made it to the rock?"

"This is dangerous talk, Manx."

"Sheila, please! I need to know. It's important."

Shaking her head, Sheila sighed. "Are the desperate deaths of a thousand sailors on the reef not enough to convince you?"

Manx shrugged. "Maybe," he said. "But Baggit won't stop until you've taken him there – him and Lugstitch."

Sheila snorted. "I'd sooner see my boat sink to the bottom of the harbour than let that man aboard – or Lugstitch, for that matter." She placed her hand on Manx's shoulder. "I pride myself on being able to sniff out a storm before it's even had a chance to brew. But it's no storm I'm sensing right now – just plain old trouble."

Having issued her gloomy prediction, Sheila asked Manx to help her carry the leftover fish intestines back to Lumpsuckers, where Fantoosh was already waiting for him.

"You got my note?"

"I was halfway to the academy when Olu caught up with me," said Fantoosh. She held out a bundle of jumpers. "Father G was confused about why you wanted this. Actually, so am I."

"Not here!" Manx looked over his shoulder.

Sheila laughed. "Since the two of you are clearly in cahoots about something of prime importance, I think you'd both better come inside. Secrets are always best shared over a good meal. I've time to fire up the fryer before the tide turns." She turned to Manx and winked. "Last I heard, you were banned from pretty much everywhere, so you'd best take a table at the back where you won't be seen from the street."

As soon as they'd sat down, Manx unwrapped his carousel from the jumper bundle whilst updating Fantoosh on the clues, and his theory that another was hidden on his device.

"Whereabouts?" Fantoosh leaned in closely to examine the carousel.

"On the canopy," said Manx.

He'd already worked out that there was only one way to remove the canopy quickly without dismantling the entire carousel. He picked up a knife from the table.

Fantoosh gasped. "You can't!"

Manx didn't hesitate. "No choice," he said. "Hold it steady for me, Fan."

He ran the point of the knife around the edge of the canopy until he was left with a perfect circle of sailcloth.

Hardly daring to look, he flipped it over. Despite it being stained orangey-yellow by thousands of hours of exposure to warm amberose, he could just make out another verse of the poem.

"I was right!" he cried, holding the cloth up to the light. He read it out loud to Fantoosh:

Lest the reef our lives would swallow,
To flee the rock this rule we followed:
To bide our time and count the waves.
The ninth did save us from our graves.

"This is it!" said Manx. "This is how to survive Razor Reef. On the ninth wave. That's how Finnick and Sarah managed all those years ago. They must have worked out how to get back across the reef in one piece."

"But why the ninth wave?" asked Fantoosh.

"Some waves are bigger than others," said Manx. "They come in patterns. You know that from picking limpets. So, I reckon that every ninth wave around Razor Reef must be bigger than the rest."

"Big enough to carry you over the reef without drowning you?"

"Exactly," said Manx.

He laid out the other three parts of the poem. Despite their frayed edges, it was easy to see how they'd once been part of a single strip of sailcloth. Fantoosh read, her eyes growing wider with each verse.

"It's almost like they're here now, telling us the story," she said in a hushed voice. "I wonder who tore it up like that and why."

Manx had been wondering the same thing. "Maybe it was Finnick or Sarah themselves," he said, "We'll probably never know. But it's almost as if whoever it was wanted someone to find the pieces and put the poem back together one day."

"Someone like you!"

Folding up the fragments, Manx felt a shiver of excitement tingle down his spine. "One thing we do know for sure now though," he said, "is how Finnick and Sarah survived crossing the reef."

"And why's that important?" asked Fantoosh.

"Because Baggit is going to try and reach Clam Rock today," said Manx. He dropped his voice to a whisper. "And I think he's going to force Sheila to take him. They'll be wrecked on the reef if they attempt to cross it." He went to the window and rubbed a clear patch in the condensation. "The tide's turned. Baggit will be back with Lugstitch soon."

"So you'll tell them about this ninth wave?"

"No. Because then they might actually make it onto Clam Rock. If there's more amberose there, we can't let them find it. Whatever they plan on doing with it is going be bad for all of us, and for Haarville."

"But if you don't tell them," said Fantoosh, "and they go out, they'll drown."

Manx puffed out his cheeks. A Ninian Baggit sliced into pieces and gobbled up by sharks would be a Ninian Baggit he no longer had to worry about – but he wasn't sure Nathan would see it that way.

"We have to stop them leaving the harbour, Fan."

Ideas whizzed around Manx's head, but he kept landing on something Sheila had said: that she'd rather see her boat lying on the bottom of the harbour than have Baggit on board.

"We need to sink the *Unfortunate Flounder*," said Manx. "Right now."

26.
All Aboard!

With the tide already beginning to gush back through the harbour's narrow entrance, Manx knew they couldn't afford any delays, but first there were a few things he needed to fetch for the mission ahead.

There was just time to scoff a couple of Sheila's freshly fried fish balls before Manx crept back to Kipper Lane, whilst Fantoosh remained by the harbour, watching out for Baggit and Lugstitch.

As Manx had hoped, Nathan was home alone. Baggit, no doubt, was at Burgh House, plotting his imminent voyage with the Burgmaster.

Ignoring Nathan's questions, Manx went straight to the toolbox under the shop counter and rifled through its contents.

"Found it!" He lifted out a bundle of oily rags, unwrapping them to reveal a perpetual drill. Normally, it was used to fix lamps and lanterns to walls. Its long, pointed shaft of quartz, about as wide as Olu's beak, could pierce the hardest stone in seconds – but Manx had another use in mind today: to drill holes in the *Unfortunate Flounder*'s hull.

He put the drill in an old sealskin bag he found hanging on the back of the kitchen door, along with a perpetual lantern and some stale, uneaten limpet buns. If there was one thing Manx knew, it was that you never embarked on a mission without proper supplies.

"Tell me what's going on." Nathan grabbed Manx's arm. "You're up to something. Dad's up to something. I want to be up to something too!"

Manx prised Nathan's fingers loose.

"If trying to stop your dad from drowning is being up to something, then yes – guilty as charged."

"What?!"

"No time to explain, but you have to trust me, Nathan."

Nathan looked back at him, confusion and a hint of fear in his eyes.

"Look," said Manx, "I don't like your dad. I hate him. He stole my shop, my home, my life. But that doesn't mean I want to see him sliced to shreds on Razor Reef. So, do you want to help me and Fan save him, or not?"

"Yes."

"Good. There are a few more things we'll need, and then we have to go." Manx reached for an old, black woollen hat of his, which had been hanging on another hook on the kitchen door for years. "Put this on," he said, tossing it to Nathan. "It's freezing out."

By the time Manx arrived back at the harbour with Nathan in tow, the *Unfortunate Flounder* was already beginning to float as the returning tide released it from the silt. They found Fantoosh halfway along the harbour wall, sitting with her legs dangling over the side, whilst Olu paced around nearby.

"I see the gang's all here." Manx bent down to give the bird a quick tickle.

"Is *he* part of the gang now?" Fantoosh nodded in Nathan's direction.

"I'm here to help," said Nathan. Fantoosh's eyebrows practically fell off her face.

"To be honest, my dad's never really been interested in me," said Nathan. "All he's ever done is move us from place to place, searching for this thing that he keeps saying will finally make him rich. Him. It's always *him*. Never me. And I think he's planning on leaving again. But I like it here. I like you two. I… I've never had friends. Never been in one place long enough. So if helping you now means I get to stay in Haarville a bit longer, then that's fine by me. Oh, and, yeah, it's probably better if my dad doesn't drown."

"Good," said Fantoosh. She picked up the bag Manx had brought with him from the shop. "Yuck! Is this sealskin?"

"Yes," replied Manx. "I know it's horrible, but it is also completely waterproof. I think it was Fabian's."

"Really!" Nathan beamed. "My great-grandad's? Wow!"

"The sealskin will keep the perpetuals dry," explained Manx.

"And these." Nathan reached for the bag and pulled out a limpet bun. "There's two each. In case you get hungry." Now he pulled a face too. "Although you'd have to be absolutely starving to want to eat one."

"We'll soon have you slurping down limpets by the dozen," said Fantoosh.

"No chance!" Nathan laughed. "There's a towel in there as well, for drying off."

"Not sure I like the sound of this," said Fantoosh. "Who's getting wet?" She looked at Manx.

"We can't use Sheila's dinghy," said Manx. "The sound of the perpetual motor running or even the oars splashing will echo all the way to Burgh House."

"Especially with your rowing skills," said Fantoosh, then her smile quickly faded. "Oh, I see… We're swimming to the boat, aren't we?" She turned to Nathan. "Can you swim?"

Nathan shrugged. "Haven't swum for years," he said. "Dad would never take me. And I was a bit rubbish at it. But I'm not coming to the boat. I'm staying here to delay them if they turn up."

"And you'll do that how, exactly?" asked Fantoosh.

"I thought I could just… throw myself into the water. I'll pretend I really can't swim so either my dad or Lugstitch will have to jump in to save me." He smiled brightly. "But let me worry about that. Go! Sink the boat!"

Fantoosh puffed out a long breath. "We're really doing this, aren't we?"

"Yep," said Manx. He untied his boot laces and stripped off his breeches, then tugged his jumper over his head. "Don't worry," he added, seeing Fantoosh's growing look of horror, "I'll leave my long johns on."

"Just as well I wore mine as well then," said Fantoosh, as she threw off her cape and began to unbutton her dungarees.

They stuffed their clothes into the bag, which Manx carefully tied with some fishing line.

"Ready?" asked Manx.

Fantoosh wrapped her plaited pigtails around her head, forming a sort of topknot. "Ready to freeze or drown, you mean?"

"I'm hoping we won't be doing either of those things." Manx grabbed hold of the ladder nearby. "Here goes!" For the second time that morning, he climbed down the harbour wall.

"Good luck!" said Nathan, peering over the edge.

Manx let out a yelp as the icy water sloshed over his ankle, then he braced himself and lowered the rest of his body into the murky sea.

The key to surviving, Manx decided as the cold stabbed deep into him, was simply to be in the water for as short a time as possible. But it still seemed to take for ever, especially since he had to swim on his back with the sealskin bag balanced on his chest like an otter holding its pup.

It was alright for Fantoosh, of course – she hadn't been crowned limpet picker of the year without being able to swim at speed. Now, she effortlessly slipped through the water, overtaking Manx with ease, a look of grim determination on her face.

It couldn't have been more than thirty strokes to the boat, but by the time Manx bobbed alongside its blue painted hull, he could hardly feel his arms. And as for his legs, they were so numbed by the frigid water that if a monster sea serpent had come along and bitten them off he probably wouldn't have felt it. Using up every last bit of effort he had left, Manx managed to pull himself up the flax ladder which hung from the deck of the fishing boat. He flopped himself over the railing, landing with an uncomfortable bump at Fantoosh's feet.

"You took your time," she said, staring down at him, dripping.

"I was carrying cargo," panted Manx, taking a quick peek just to make sure his feet were still there.

Fantoosh grabbed the bag and began furiously rubbing herself down with the towel. Once Manx had dried himself off too, he retrieved the handwarmers he'd packed and they each clasped one tightly. The amberose soon did its job, and it wasn't long before a tingling warmth began to creep into Manx's limbs.

"Right," he said. "Let's drill some holes then."

Manx headed along the side of the box-shaped wheelhouse to the foredeck, where there was a hatch, which he knew from having gone out with Sheila on several fishing trips in the past. It opened down into the bilges and net store below.

Some of the anchor chain lay coiled on the deck next to a square-shaped contraption made up of lobster pots, bits of plastic flotsam and old floats, all lashed together with rope.

Fantoosh almost tripped over it as she jumped down onto the foredeck. "What in Neptune is this?!"

"I think it's Sheila's life raft," replied Manx. "It's made up of all the junk that's washed up on the beach."

Fantoosh gave the raft a poke with her foot and one of the lobster pots jiggled loose. "Not sure I'd trust this to save a sardine from drowning, let alone a person!"

They dragged the anchor chain aside, trying to make as little noise as possible – not easy given that it weighed an absolute ton. Olu, who had flitted across to the *Unfortunate Flounder* without having to get soggy, perched on the bow, blinking his red eyes.

"It's alright, Olu," said Manx. "We know what we're doing."

"We do?" Fantoosh asked. "Come on, let's lift this hatch up."

They grabbed the rusty handle and pulled. The hatch didn't budge. They tried again. Still, they couldn't shift it.

"The wood's damp," panted Manx, rubbing his palm where the handle had dug into his flesh. "It's expanded and got stuck. We need another pair of hands."

Fantoosh laughed. "If you mean Nathan, he looks about as strong as a blade of grass in a sand dune."

"Even so," said Manx, aware time was fast running out, "he's all we've got."

Manx turned to Olu. "Fetch Nathan," he told the bird. "Quick as you can."

Olu piped a shrill note and flapped away into the haar which had begun to form around the boat.

"Nathan said it's years since he last swam," said Fantoosh, her teeth chattering as an icy blast of wind rocked the fishing boat. "What if he's forgotten how to?"

"We'll soon find out," said Manx, wriggling his numbed toes.

Manx stood at the stern, listening out for Nathan. Eventually, the sound of bubbling gasps and splashes drifted across the water, shortly followed by the sight of Nathan's flailing arms as he performed a very clumsy front crawl. Olu skimmed the surface around him, tooting and trilling to spur him on.

Fantoosh helped Manx haul a panting Nathan aboard.

"I can still swim!" he cried, beaming.

"Great! But shhh!" Manx threw him the half-wet towel. "Voices carry easily over the water."

"Sorry," whispered Nathan. "I'd forgotten how much fun swimming is! And I only went under three or four times. Once I remembered I had to use my legs as well as my arms, I had no trouble." He spluttered a cough, spitting water over the side. "Could've done without the free drink though." He finished drying off, then looked at Manx. "What's the emergency? Olu practically pecked my eyes out to get me into the harbour."

"The hatch is stuck," explained Fantoosh. "We need your muscles!"

Nathan glanced at his stick-like arms poking out from his sodden vest. "I think you've asked the wrong person."

"We didn't exactly have much choice." Manx crouched over the hatch. "Let's all pull on three. Ready?"

The hatch remained stubbornly wedged in place, but when they all tried a second time, Manx felt it shift a little.

"One more try," he said. "Really pull this time."

With their knuckles white and teeth gritted, everyone pulled, until, with a wood-creaking groan, the hatch finally came free. Manx quickly reached for a short wooden pole lying on deck and wedged it against the hatch to prop it open. He dropped the bag through the hole and jumped down after it.

"Whatever you do, Nathan, don't let it shut," he called back up, as Fantoosh landed beside him.

The two of them crouched in the semi-darkness whilst Manx searched the bag for the amberose lantern he'd packed. Once working, its orangey glow cast long shadows

across the hold and over a mound of old – and extremely pungent – fishing nets in the far corner.

"Let's get this over with." Fantoosh pinched her nose.

Manx flicked the switch on the

drill's base, then pressed a sort of trigger on the side. The quartz instantly began to whir, powered by the whole pebble-weight of amberose inside. He chose a flat spot on the floor of the hold. "I think ten holes should do the trick. Not enough to sink the boat quickly, but too many for Sheila to mend in one go. As soon as she spots the leaks, they'll have to abandon the trip."

"So we're not actually sinking the boat?" asked Fantoosh, holding the lantern over Manx.

"As long as Sheila sees the damage quickly enough, it should stay afloat. We just need to stop Baggit from trying to reach Clam Rock. Right, here goes!"

Manx placed the tip of the quartz bit in the middle of a plank and took a deep breath. How had it come to this? Vandalising Sheila Giddock's boat! Manx just hoped she would forgive them, and that they hadn't eaten their last ever fish balls at Lumpsuckers.

The entire boat vibrated as the drill punctured the hold with all the ease of a narwhal spearing its supper. But it was surprisingly quiet. In no time at all Manx had drilled ten perfect holes, and a sizable puddle was soon sloshing around their feet.

"That should do it," said Manx. "We'll leave the hatch open so that Sheila knows to check it straight away. It'll be obvious someone's been down here."

Fantoosh switched off the lantern and was handing it to Manx when, out of nowhere, the *Unfortunate Flounder* tipped sideways. They were thrown against the side of the boat, whilst above, Nathan screamed as he tumbled down through the open hatch, landing with a splashing thud. A split second later, the hatch crashed shut and the hold was plunged into darkness. As the boat rocked back the other way, there came the unmistakable sound of a heavy metal chain sliding across the wooden deck.

In the dark, Manx felt for the edge of the closed hatch. "Come on! Quick!" he called out.

Together, the three of them pushed up on the hatch, but it was clear that it wasn't going to open. Olu's shrill

whistles reverberated from the deck. It sounded like he was frantically tapping at the wood, but of course there was nothing the bird could do. There was nothing anyone could do.

"It's the anchor chain," said Manx. "It shifted across the hatch when that huge wave rocked the boat."

"So we're trapped." Fantoosh didn't sound surprised.

Nathan made a sort of high whining sound. "Er... didn't you just drill holes in this boat?"

"That's right," said Manx. "Ten of them."

"The good news," said Fantoosh dryly, "is that your holes are working really well. They're letting in tons of water already."

"Thanks," said Manx.

"What's the bad news?" asked Nathan.

"The bad news? Oh, that's easy," replied Fantoosh. "The *Unfortunate Flounder*'s going down. With us in it."

27.

Anchors Away!

No one said anything.

Then Nathan broke the silence.

"On a scale of one to ten," he said quietly, "how bad is this?"

"Well," replied Manx, "I'm not really that experienced in how long it would take a boat this size to fill with water and sink, but I'm going to hazard a guess and say this is really very, *very* bad indeed."

"I agree," said Fantoosh. "And I feel I should point out that the water's up to our ankles already."

"What are our options?" asked Nathan.

It was a good question and Manx gave it proper consideration.

"How about panic?" he suggested.

"Or scream?" said Fantoosh. "Someone might hear us."

"From inside this boat," said Nathan, "no one will hear us scream."

Manx's brain felt as flooded as the boat's hold soon would be.

"How about we just drill a hole in the side," he ventured, "but this time big enough for us to climb through before the boat sinks?"

"Great idea!" shouted Fantoosh.

"Let's do it!" yelled Nathan.

"Er… there's just one small problem," said Manx. "I dropped the drill when that wave hit us." He knelt down and felt for it in the pool of water around his feet. "Have you got the lantern, Fan? I can't see anything."

Fantoosh groaned. "Another problem," she said. "I dropped that too."

All three of them began searching the water sploshing around their ankles.

"Here's the drill!" shouted Nathan, handing it to Manx, who quickly pressed the trigger.

Nothing.

A wave of fear rippled through him as the *Unfortunate Flounder* began pulling on its anchor chain, rocked by a series of stronger waves rolling into the harbour. The water in the hold splashed off the sides, drenching everyone.

"The drill's too wet," Manx said. "The amberose won't work."

They fell silent again as the boat continued rocking.

"Those holes you drilled, Manx," Fantoosh said quietly, "really are very good."

"Thanks."

"Yeah," said Nathan. "They're not so big that we're sinking straight away."

"That was the idea," said Manx.

"We'll be sinking nice and slowly instead," said Fantoosh. "It'll give us plenty of time to think about it."

Under the weak shaft of light seeping through a couple of the foredeck's planks, Manx caught a glimpse of Fantoosh's face – it reminded him just how scared he was.

"Where are they?" he groaned. "I was sure your father and Lugstitch would come, Nathan. And even if they've changed their minds, nothing stops Sheila from going out, apart from a major storm."

"Or a sunk fishing boat," said Fantoosh.

Nathan made a sound like someone had trodden on his foot. "Please don't say that. There has to be something we can do?"

Manx racked his brain, but there was only one thing he could think of. "I know I only just drilled them, but we need to plug these holes with something."

"Like what?" cried Fantoosh. "We don't have anything!"

"Anything thick, soft and a bit sticky will do,' said Manx.

"Don't say it!" shouted Nathan.

"What?"

"Don't say 'Nathan's brain.'"

"I wasn't going to," protested Manx. "But now you mention it…"

"Not funny," said Nathan. "How about those limpet buns, though? They're thick and soft, and limpets like to stick to things!"

"Not sure steamed limpets still have a lot of stick left in them," said Fantoosh.

"Maybe not," said Manx, "but I think it's a genius idea."

He felt around in the bag for the buns. The sealskin had kept them perfectly dry. He handed the others one each. "You each plug three holes, I'll do the other four."

Finding the holes in the dark of the hold wasn't easy, but after a minute or so, Manx felt a thin bubbling stream of cold water on his fingers.

"You can feel the water coming in from under the boat!" he shouted, ripping off a piece of bun and sticking it firmly into the hole. Miraculously, it seemed to work, and it wasn't long before they'd plugged all ten holes.

"Makes you wonder what these things do to your insides," said Fantoosh.

"Don't care," said Manx. "I love them."

Suddenly, something thudded on the side of the boat. This was followed by another thud. Then a third. A hoarse voice shouted: "Hold her steady, man!"

"Sheila!" whispered Manx.

Then another voice could be heard, along with the sound of scrambling feet on the deck. It was Lugstitch.

"If you refuse to follow my orders," he was saying, "I'll make sure you never fry a fish ball again!"

Sheila's reply was silenced by another crashing wave, which rocked the *Unfortunate Flounder* on her anchor. Manx began to feel distinctly queasy.

"Come on," he said to the others, "let's shout for help."

The three of them emptied their lungs with a desperate effort to be heard. The problem was that at the exact same time, the boat's engine shuddered to life with an ear-splitting, teeth-shattering roar. And if that wasn't enough to drown out their pleas for help, the deafening clanging of heavy chain coiling onto the deck as the anchor was mechanically winched up most definitely was.

Manx's ears were still ringing as they were thrown to the back of the hold when the boat powered forward.

Wherever the *Unfortunate Flounder* was headed, they were going too.

28.

Hatched

Communication with each other in the *Unfortunate Flounder*'s hold was virtually impossible. The engine's constant roar, which increased with a nerve-wracking surge every time they crashed into a wave, thundered in Manx's ears, head and chest. He could even feel it in his fingers.

Fantoosh pulled Manx close and yelled in his ear.

"Are you sure we're headed to Clam Rock?"

Manx braced himself against the hull as the boat whacked into yet another wave, and yelled back. "Yes! I felt us turn west after leaving the harbour."

The boat corkscrewed violently again in a vomit-inducing twisting motion.

"Just so you know, I really hate this!" yelled Nathan.

On they ploughed, roiling around on the angry ocean. It felt to Manx like the fishing boat was struggling to maintain its speed, as if it was dragging something along...

Of course, Sheila's dinghy! So Baggit and Lugstitch were going to use *that* to get to Clam Rock – even they weren't stupid or desperate enough to try and reach it in the *Unfortunate Flounder*. Not that they stood a much better chance of surviving in a small wooden boat.

The endless rocking and pitching suddenly ceased, and the engine's roar lowered to a less ear-splitting drone.

"We've slowed down," said Manx. "Must be approaching the reef."

"This reef you keep talking about," shouted Nathan. "Is it the one from that poem?"

Manx nodded.

"Is it really that dangerous?"

"Yes!" cried Manx and Fantoosh together.

"And it's made of actual razors?"

"Razor clam shells. Sharp ones," replied Manx. "They can shred a boat to splinters in seconds."

Nathan began making an odd quivering, shivering sort of noise, and his teeth chattered. "What would the reef do to a person – you know – a person who only just remembered how to swim?" he asked meekly.

"You could swim like a fish and it wouldn't make a difference," said Manx. "Razor Reef will still slice and dice you."

"Stop saying things like that!" wailed Nathan.

"I agree," said Fantoosh. "It's not helping."

"Why would anyone take the risk?" asked Nathan.

"For the same reason greedy people always do stupid things," said Manx. "To get rich. I'm sorry Nathan, but your father didn't come to Haarville to find his long-lost family, or to claim back the shop. He came to hunt for the hoard. The same hoard Fabian had started searching for before he left."

"Hoard as in treasure?" asked Nathan.

"Maybe not actual treasure," said Manx. "I think it might be amberose."

"And you think it's on Clam Rock?"

"If the poem's clues are right."

Nathan gasped. "But they'll die trying to get to it!"

"Exactly!" cried Manx. "Your dad never found the final clue so they don't know how to survive the reef."

At that point, the engine powered down almost completely, reducing to a deep, low rumble. Above them, someone was making their way across the deck to the bow.

"I'm telling you, it's impossible!" The voice was Sheila's and it was coming from right above them. "If you take my dinghy over the reef, you'll be fish food in a flash."

Another voice mumbled something, but the sudden splash of an anchor being lowered drowned out the words.

"Fine!" shouted Sheila. "But you're on your own. I won't be coming to rescue either of you."

"I can't believe they're going to risk it!" Nathan sounded desperate. "I don't want my dad to be sliced and diced. We have to stop him."

Nathan began screaming, thumping the underside of the hatch.

"Help! We're trapped! Let us out!"

Manx and Fantoosh joined in, and within moments a

shaft of light blasted down into the hold, forcing them all to shield their eyes.

Manx blinked. Sheila's ruddy face looked down at them – it was a picture of confusion and disbelief.

"What? I mean, why? And how?!"

"Surprise!" said Manx, attempting a smile.

Sheila was pushed out of the way by Lugstitch, whose walrus moustache practically jumped off his lip as it quivered angrily.

"This habit of appearing exactly where you are neither wanted nor permitted really must cease, Fearty," he said, spit raining down on Manx. "It is *exceptionally* annoying!"

Manx was about to answer back, but Fantoosh shoved him out of the shaft of light.

"You can't do this!" she shouted up.

A fleeting flash of surprise passed over Lugstitch's face.

"Well, well. I might have guessed. Quite the double act, aren't you?"

"And me!" waved Nathan, taking his turn underneath the hatch. "I'm here too!"

"Goodness, Sheila," said Lugstitch, "you didn't warn me you kept an entire crew hidden away on your fishing boat."

Ninian Baggit's sallow face appeared above them, his dark eyes boring down.

"What is my son doing on board this foul-smelling vessel?" he asked.

Sheila pushed Baggit aside and stood, hand on hip, shaking her head.

"Good question. Better get you lot out of there." Sheila

reached her arm down through the hatch and hauled up Nathan, then the others, with a strength that could only come from a lifetime of heaving lobster pots from the depths, quite literally, single-handed.

The three of them stood there, dripping, as Lugstitch and Baggit, both decked out in heavy oilskins, glared at them. Olu flitted  around overhead, peeping his loud call. He seemed as relieved to see everyone freed from the hold as Manx was that they were out.

"I've a mind to throw you overboard this instant," snarled Lugstitch, all stormy eyes and bristling whiskers.

Behind him, Baggit coughed. "Perhaps just the other two," he said. "My son was surely forced aboard against his wishes."

Nathan stamped his foot in the puddle pooling around his feet. "I wasn't forced to do anything!"

"No? So what are you doing with these troublemakers?" asked Baggit.

"We're not troublemakers," said Manx. "We're trying to stop you from drowning!"

"Ha!" Lugstitch clapped his hands together. "How very thoughtful, and very unlikely."

"It's true!" shouted Fantoosh.

"Come, Ninian," said Lugstitch, "we have no time for this. Time is money after all, and we have a lot of that to make."

"What money?" asked Manx. "From where?"

248

Lugstitch raised his eyes to the clouds. "As if you don't know! Did you really think your family could keep the hoard a secret for ever? Such selfishness! However, once the world learns about amberose and my pockets are filled, I might just excuse you."

"What do you mean, 'the world'?" asked Fantoosh. "Are you leaving Haarville?"

Lugstitch smirked.

"As much as I enjoy laying down the law in this little town," he said, "the Out-There can offer me untold riches."

"Us," corrected Baggit, throwing Lugstitch a narrow glance. "It can offer *us* untold riches."

"What about Mrs Lugstitch?" asked Fantoosh.

"I'm certainly not sharing anything with her!" spluttered Lugstitch. "And anyway, I'm not leaving for ever. Just long enough to find some like-minded folk and strike a few highly profitable deals. Ninian has kindly offered to be my guide to the Out-There."

"In return for a share of the vast profits," added Baggit, staring at Lugstitch.

"Yes, yes, of course." The Burgmaster dismissed Baggit with a flick of his hand.

"Whatever it is you're looking for," said Manx, desperate to stall Lugstitch, "there's probably nothing to find."

"Which again leads me to ask why we've just found you trespassing in the underbelly of this stinking ship?"

"To stop my dad from dying on the reef!" shouted Nathan.

Lugstitch leered. "How very touching. I wouldn't have

thought it possible of a child of Ninian Baggit."

"Nathan's a Fearty!" said Manx. "We do what's right."

"Dad doesn't always put me first," said Nathan, "but I don't want him to die on Razor Reef." He looked at his father briefly, but Baggit turned his head towards the rolling sea.

"Pass me my hanky!" Lugstitch sniggered. "I'm overcome with emotion." Then he stared at Nathan, a sly glint in his eye. "Since you're so concerned with your father's welfare, I think you'd better come with us. We could use the extra pair of hands." Then he lunged for Nathan, dragged him to the stern, and dropped him over the railing.

Everyone, including Ninian Baggit, charged to the back of the boat and leaned over the side. Nathan had landed in the dinghy, where he sat, dazed, rubbing his head.

Baggit grabbed Lugstitch by his collar.

"That was my son you just threw overboard!"

"He's fine." Lugstitch pushed Baggit off. "And if you really want a share of the bounty, you'll climb down and join him."

Meanwhile, Manx had scrambled for a rope on the deck and dropped it over the side.

"Grab this!" he screamed.

Nathan very nearly caught the rope, but Lugstitch shunted Manx off balance and he fell to the deck, letting go of his end. By the time he'd clambered to his feet, both Baggit and Lugstitch were in the dinghy. He could only watch helplessly as Lugstitch untied the line and they began to drift away.

Sheila and Fantoosh joined him at the railing as the wind blasted their faces and tugged at their hair. In the dinghy, Nathan's terror-filled eyes peered back at them. But then his expression changed, and even from a distance, Manx could see him grit his teeth.

The next few seconds passed in slow motion – or that's how it seemed. Manx watched as Lugstitch, struggling to get the dinghy's perpetual motor going, yelled something at Nathan, who grabbed an oar, then, with a final glance towards the *Unfortunate Flounder*, stood up in the bobbing boat and leapt over the side. At the same moment, a current caught the dinghy, span it round, and dragged it away into the swirling mist.

Nathan began kicking out, holding onto the oar, and for a few miraculous seconds, he seemed to be making headway back to the fishing boat. Manx, Fantoosh and Sheila yelled encouragement, but it soon became clear he was struggling.

"Can that boy swim?" shouted Sheila.

"Yes!" replied Manx and Fantoosh simultaneously.

"Doesn't look like it," said Sheila, grimly. "Are you sure?"

"Er, sort of," said Fantoosh.

Manx looked forlornly over the waves – Nathan's head was barely visible. Then it vanished altogther.

"The current!" cried Sheila. "It's got him!"

Manx clutched the side of the boat. If the current had got its hold on poor Nathan, there was only one place it was taking him: Razor Reef.

And there was nothing anyone could do to stop it.

29.

Raft Race

An eerie silence fell over the deck of the *Unfortunate Flounder*. Out where Nathan had vanished, the current swirled and sucked at the waves.

Manx remained glued to the spot, eyes fixed on the surface, as if Nathan might rise up triumphantly on the back of a porpoise. He jumped as Olu let out a sharp *peep*, flitting overhead before dropping to soar just above the waves, calling out every few moments. But it was no use. Nathan was nowhere in sight.

"We have to go after him!" Fantoosh pleaded with Sheila. "Please!"

"Not in this boat we can't," said Sheila. "I'd lose control of the rudder on the currents and the *Flounder* would founder. It's too shallow over the reef anyway. There's no way we can go near it." She stuck her tongue out and sniffed the air. "There's a storm approaching. I need to lift the anchor before it hits."

"But what about Nathan?" It was Manx's turn to plead.

"We can only hope that Lugstitch has the decency to try and rescue him," said Sheila. "But even if he does, the reef will still take them all." She lowered her head, sighed, and made her way to the foredeck.

"What about the ninth wave?" Fantoosh grabbed Manx's arm. "They might survive."

"They don't know about it. I never got a chance to tell Nathan."

"At least he has the oar to hold on to," said Fantoosh, with more than a hint of desperation in her voice. "That floats, doesn't it?"

Manx stamped the deck. "Floats? Of course! You're brilliant, Fan!" He raced after Sheila. "This raft is seaworthy, isn't it, Sheila?" He heaved the life raft up off the deck and shook it. Another lobster basket came loose, but otherwise it seemed sturdy enough.

Sheila shook her head. "I cannot allow it."

"But it's a life raft, isn't it?" cried Fantoosh, joining Manx. "For saving lives?"

"That's not the point. It's too risky. And you're too young."

Manx looked at Sheila. "Haven't you ever taken a risk? To do the right thing?"

"Of course," said Sheila. "Every time I put out to fish I take risks."

"And how old were you when you started doing that?"

Sheila sighed. "Fourteen – no, thirteen. I hadn't long lost my arm,

but my father lay dying from whelk poisoning, so I had no choice but to take the boat out alone."

"See! You were only a bit older than me," said Manx. "But you did it anyway."

"I had to. Nobody else knew the reefs, and the people of Haarville needed fish to eat."

"And Nathan needs to survive." Manx stared out to sea, then turned back to her. "I'm a Fearty. If I don't die in the waves today, it's only a matter of time before the amberose gets me. And anyway, Nathan's my friend, and friends look out for each other."

Short of collapsing to his knees and begging, Manx wasn't sure how else to persuade Sheila. So he collapsed to his knees.

"*Please!* You know it's the right thing."

"Oh, alright!" said Sheila. "But I'm attaching the raft to the *Unfortunate Flounder* with a long safety line."

Sheila expertly tied the line to the raft, way faster than Manx could have managed with two hands, and seconds later she was hauling it over the side. Manx and Fantoosh carefully climbed down and positioned themselves on either side so that the raft wouldn't tip over. Manx readied himself to push off when Sheila let out a yell.

"The oars!"

She vanished for a moment, reappearing at the stern with two battered oars, which she threw down. "Find the boy, then paddle straight back. I'll start winching you in as soon as I can see you. And watch out for the current."

Manx pushed them away from the fishing boat's hull

and they began drifting off into a sea mist. Seconds before it swallowed the raft, Manx remembered the holes they'd made.

"Check the hold!" he yelled. "Your boat needs some urgent repairs!"

"What?"

"I'll explain later! Just go and check!"

And with that, the murk swallowed them up.

They drifted for a minute, wavelets breaking over the raft with quiet splashes. Then, somewhere up ahead, a wave crashed.

"The reef!" cried Fantoosh.

"Let's paddle." Manx dipped his oar into the water.

Paddling was much easier with two of them. Every time the raft tipped to the side, they managed to steady it by one of them leaning the other way. Somehow, in this fashion, they remained afloat.

"What's that sound?" yelled Fantoosh. "That rattling. Listen!"

When the next wave crashed, Manx heard what Fantoosh had: first the roar of the wave smashing onto the reef, then a weird, rolling sort of rattle.

"It's the razors!" he shouted back over the din. "The backwash must be really strong. It's dragging the clam shells back with every wave."

"They sound sharp," yelled Fantoosh, as a sudden gust

hit them. Then the raft dipped violently forward, sending Manx face down onto a lobster basket. He pushed himself upright, braced for another gust of wind, but, weirdly, the sea immediately around them had flattened again, whilst in the distance, waves continued to break.

"I wish the weather would make up its mind," moaned Fantoosh, trying to re-wrap her pigtails around her head with one hand. "And the sea doesn't know what it's supposed to be doing either."

"Must be the currents." Manx cast a wary eye over the surface. "I don't trust them." He peered all around the raft, searching for Nathan. The light forcing its way through the rapidly dropping haar played tricks, casting shadows here and there that might or might not have been a boy's bobbing head.

"Nathan!" he yelled. "Where are you?"

Fantoosh joined in, but the haar seemed to suck up their shouts.

"I can't see him," said Fantoosh. "I can't see anything."

"What's that?" Manx pointed to a dark shape about three rafts' lengths away. But as it bobbed closer, they saw it was only a massive, purple-centred jellyfish. "This is hopeless."

"No, it's not." Fantoosh started calling out again. "We know he can swim a bit, so as long as he can stay afloat before the cold or the current gets to him, we stand a good chance of finding him. Keep shouting."

No sooner had the words left Fantoosh's mouth than she had plunged her hand into the sea.

"Nathan's hat!" she cried, snatching it up. "So where's the rest of him?"

"I don't know," replied Manx, "but right now, we've got a bigger problem. Look." He held up the frayed end of the safety line. "It must have broken with that last gust of wind."

Fantoosh stared, open-mouthed. "The current's going to take us now, isn't it?"

Manx gulped, then nodded. "There's nothing we can do about it, though, so we should keep looking for Nathan."

They paddled on for a minute, until a splintered plank bobbed past.

"That's part of the dinghy." Manx dipped his hand into the icy water. "And here's another bit – from the rudder, I think."

Suddenly, they were surrounded by more broken bits of dinghy, some no longer than Olu's beak, others as large as Oilyphant's desk.

A sense of dread filled Manx's chest and he caught Fantoosh's eye.

"We mustn't give up," she said. "Your ancestors got lucky and washed up on Clam Rock, didn't they? Nathan might still be alright."

They fell silent for a second, scanning the choppy water, when, without warning, the raft spun a quarter turn and veered to the left.

"The current!" Manx plunged his oar back into the water and began to paddle furiously. "It's got us! We have to turn around."

But the raft was caught in an undertow. And all the while, the waves began to grow, each rise and fall more pronounced, thrusting the raft higher, dropping it further. Balancing and steadying the craft took all of their efforts.

"Fan."

"Don't say it."

"We're heading for the reef!"

Fantoosh squealed. "I said not to say it!"

They carried on paddling, but the current was simply too strong.

"This is pointless." Manx raised his oar as a larger wave rolled under them, lifting and dropping the raft with it. He looked behind them – a smaller wave was following fast behind. "The waves are coming in sequence. Start counting." A ripple passed by, so small, it barely rocked the raft. "That's one!" With his eyes glued to the water, Manx watched for the next. The raft gently bobbed up, then down. "Two!"

Manx's heart was beating faster and faster – his fingers and the back of his neck tingled.

"Here comes the next one!" shouted Fantoosh. "Three!"

Waves four and five weren't much bigger, but the sixth rose behind them, surging forward like a surfacing whale, forcing them to brace and grab the raft. Manx's stomach roiled and rollicked with the motion of the ocean.

"That was horrible!" exclaimed Fantoosh.

"Worse to come," grunted Manx, feeling decidedly queasy.

Before they knew it, the seventh wave bore down on

them. Manx grasped the raft tighter. They were basically floating on decaying lobster pots and used plastic bottles from the Out-There – if a dinghy couldn't survive the reef, how would they?

He held his breath, and just when it seemed the rolling wave would break on top of them and smash them to smithereens, it picked them up and carried them forward, plunging them back down with a sickening smash. Spray covered the raft, and before they could even catch their breath to scream, up the raft went again as the next wave barrelled them forwards. This time, though, they kept flying ever higher, ever faster.

Just when it seemed the wave would break with them still on it, the raft plunged back down as the wall of water surged on, smashing into the reef with a roar, sending a billowing mass of spray and foam high into the air. Manx's knuckles were white with the force of holding on so tightly.

"I've lost count," panted Fantoosh. "Was that the ninth wave?"

"Eighth," yelled Manx.

"But it was ginormous!"

Manx peered behind the raft and gulped as a cliff-high wave surged towards them.

"No, it wasn't," he shouted, pointing at it. "*That's* ginormous!"

30.

The Ninth Wave

Fantoosh twisted to look at the ninth wave.

"Oh my sticky limpets," she whispered. She turned to Manx, her eyes frozen in a wild stare.

Beneath them, a deep rumbling moan grew louder as the wave thrust itself up. This was it. The poem had been right. The ninth wave was the biggest.

But would it be big enough to clear the reef?

Deciding it might be a fraction less terrifying not to watch the monster wave expanding behind them, Manx faced forward, and was greeted instead by the sight of a towering white rock looming out of the haar some distance ahead.

"Clam Rock!" he shouted, just as the sea began to surge again beneath the raft. A flash of black, white and orange flapped past, and above the roar of crashing waves and the slicing rattle of the razor shells, Olu's shrill whistle pierced the air.

"*Come on!*" he seemed to say. "*You can make it!*"

The wave kept growing and the raft kept rising – faster

and higher, lifted by the force of water beneath them. And below – so very far below – the sea awaited their crashing return.

"What if that poem was wrong?"

Manx looked at Fantoosh. "Huh?"

"The poem. What if it's just a story? You know – made up. Complete nonsense."

"You're asking this now?!" screamed Manx.

At this point, they stopped rising into the air and the wave began to curl beneath them. As it did, the raft tipped back slightly.

"We're going to slip off," said Manx.

"Well, hold on then!" yelled Fantoosh.

"Not off the raft – off the wave!"

They weren't going to make it. The wave was outrunning the raft and would clear the reef without them. As Manx pictured the two of them being shredded to pieces by the razors, Olu soared ahead, swooping and dipping on an updraft of air over the curled lip of the wave, whistling all the while. He was using the wave to carry him forward.

"That's it!" cried Manx. "We have to ride the wave!" He plunged his oar back into the water. "Paddle, Fan! Paddle for your life!"

He had no idea where it came from, but a burst of energy powered through Manx's body as if twenty pebble-weight's worth of amberose was glowing hot inside him. He plunged the oar in and pushed back through the wave, plunging and pushing, plunging and pushing, until his arms and shoulders seared with pain.

"We can do it!" shouted Fantoosh.

And they were doing it – they really were. Their frantic paddling kept them from slipping back until they'd reached the crest of the wave, and then it felt as if it grabbed them from below and held them whilst it surged on. Manx lifted his oar from the water and clung to the raft for his life. To his side, Fantoosh had done the same. They just had to stay on board and keep afloat.

"We're riding it!" cried Fantoosh.

Manx dared a split-second glance over the side, where a silvery-grey blur shimmered beneath the surface.

"It's the reef! We're over the reef!"

The poem had been right: the ninth wave was big enough to clear the reef without breaking.

"Thank Neptune!" Fantoosh cheered. "But what next?"

The brief feeling of elation Manx had felt at surviving Razor Reef drained out of him. Fantoosh was right. There was no "next" in the plan. As Clam Rock loomed ever nearer, Manx wondered if the wave was just going to throw them at the rock – and at the speed they were travelling, their bones would shatter like hammered crab shells on impact.

Just as Manx decided that a body-pulverising death was imminent, the wave slowed, splitting in two as it surged past the rock. The raft slipped down the back of the wave

and suddenly they were no longer riding it, but instead skimming the surface of the sea until it shallowed and they skidded to a welcome stop on a gently inclining shelf.

Above them towered Clam Rock, white and massive, its peak shrouded in swirling haar.

Manx and Fantoosh looked at each other.

"That was … interesting." Manx tried to catch his breath.

Fantoosh raised a dripping eyebrow. "Not how I'd describe it."

Clambering up from the raft, almost slipping on some rubbery bladder wrack, Manx instantly clamped his hand over his nose. A sharp tang caught at the back of his throat and made his eyes water. "Ew! It stinks here!"

"It's bird poo!" shouted a familiar voice.

"Nathan!" cried Manx, looking up to find him standing near the rock.

"This place is covered in the stuff," said Nathan, soaked hair flattened to his head and bits of seaweed dangling from his ears.

"You're not sliced up!" said Fantoosh.

"Or diced up!" added Manx.

"I know!" Nathan beamed at them. "Not even a scrape!" He'd no sooner said this than he promptly stepped into a pile of seaweed, tripped and fell into it face first. He picked himself up, flicking bits of desiccated bird droppings off his cheeks. "Yuck!"

"But how did you survive?" asked Manx, making his way up the beach, sinking almost knee-deep into the muck-encrusted seaweed with every stumbling step.

"Yeah!" Fantoosh threw Nathan his woolly hat. "We found this. Thought you were, you know…"

"I thought I was too," said Nathan. "But my dad saved me."

"Your dad?!" cried Manx and Fantoosh in unison.

"I know!" Nathan laughed. "I couldn't believe it when he jumped in after me. And wearing all that clobber too."

"Can he even swim?" asked Fantoosh.

"No! But he'd pulled up one of the plank seats in the dinghy and it kept him afloat. Just as well really, because I lost hold of the oar and was almost going under when he reached me." Nathan puffed out a massive breath. "We kicked out for a bit, but then the current caught hold and started dragging us closer to the reef, and the sea was really rough and I could hear the waves crashing and you both calling me, but the haar was too thick and—"

"How did you both survive the reef?" Fantoosh interrupted.

"Give him a chance to tell the story," said Manx, thinking about how Leena liked to string out a tale for maximum effect. This was Nathan's big moment, and he was clearly enjoying it.

"Well," continued Nathan, "we had just said our goodbyes and I was deciding if it was better to drown first or be cut to shreds, when a big piece of wood floated past."

"We saw some too!" cried Fantoosh. "It was the dinghy."

"It was what saved us," said Nathan. "Dad grabbed it and helped me crawl on, and then a massive wave came along and we sort of surfed all the way here."

"You surfed? On a plank?" Manx could hardly believe it.

"Says the boy who just arrived on a pile of old lobster pots!"

"But surfing! You only started swimming again today."

"I know! I'm learning tons of new skills in Haarville."

"How did you know it was a big enough wave to clear the reef?" asked Manx.

Nathan shrugged.

Manx whistled. "You really did survive by luck – just like Finnick and Sarah when they were shipwrecked."

"And my superior surfing skills," said Nathan. "Don't forget those."

Manx had a feeling Nathan was *never* going to let them forget.

"Any sign of Lugstitch?" Fantoosh peered along the beach.

"No," said Nathan. "There are bits of dinghy washing up in the surf, so maybe there are bits of him too."

Manx shuddered at the thought and turned away from the lapping waves, his eye finally drawn by the imposing mass of rock looming over them.

"Maybe he's hiding behind that?" he suggested, and began stumbling through the seaweed to take a look.

"He's not," said Nathan. "We already looked. But my dad's there."

"Doing what?" asked Fantoosh.

"Digging," said Nathan. "For the hoard."

Manx couldn't believe it. "But you almost drowned!"

"I know." Nathan shrugged. "He did at least make sure I wasn't hurt before he started."

Baggit was certainly determined to find the hoard, thought Manx. But not as determined as he was, and there was no way he was going to let Nathan's dad get there first.

He headed for the rock, which was much bigger at the base than it appeared from a distance, and up close it became clear why the towering monolith looked so white.

"It's covered in poo as well," he said, peering up. The thickening haar almost silenced them, but Manx could still hear the insistent calls of hundreds of gulls way above. On cue, a dollop of droppings splatted his shoulder. "Don't look up," he warned the others. "Unless you want an eyeful."

They rounded the rock and there was Baggit, on his knees, frantically shovelling seaweed with his hands like a turtle digging a nest. He must have sensed them all watching him because he turned his head.

"Might have guessed you'd turn up," he spat. "Don't just stand gawping – help me dig!"

"What for?" asked Manx.

Baggit growled, "You know what for."

Manx just shook his head and walked back around the rock. Fantoosh and Nathan followed.

Fantoosh scuffed up a heap of the poo-covered kelp. "You're not going to let him find it first, are you Manx?"

"Of course not," replied Manx. "But we're not searching where Baggit can see us." He stamped his foot on the spongy seaweed. "Might as well start here."

"Anyone got a spade?" Nathan lifted a piece of stinky seaweed between his thumb and finger. "This is revolting."

Manx patted down his long johns. "Let me see…There must be one here somewhere…"

"Alright, alright! I was joking," laughed Nathan. "But we'll never dig through all this with our hands."

Kicking over a matted lump of the kelp, Manx had to agree. It was hundreds of years since Finnick and Sarah were supposed to have been shipwrecked here. The hoard they'd written about in the poem would be buried under metres of this muck by now. They could be shovelling for ever until they uncovered it.

Just then, Olu whistled past in his usual flapping blur. He landed on the rock, perching on a thin ledge, from where he started pecking away with his long beak.

"I know that bird doesn't act like a normal oystercatcher," said Fantoosh, "but that's even more not normal than usual."

They watched as bits of dried-on bird mess pinged off the rock.

"Hey! Look out!" yelled Nathan, ducking out of range.

After a minute of this decidedly odd behaviour, a larger piece of the poo fell away. Olu remained rooted to the ledge, flapping his wings and ruffling his black-and-white feathers. Only, his white feathers no longer appeared white – instead they were now bathed in a golden-hued glow, as if the sun had burst through the thickening haar. But the glow wasn't coming from the sky. It was coming from the rock.

Manx gasped. "I think we just found the hoard... It's the rock. Clam Rock *is* the hoard!"

Fantoosh leaned back, almost falling over. "What, all of it?"

"Yes," said Manx. "It's not a rock at all. It's amberose. A ginormous, poo-covered tower of amberose!"

31.

Clam Rock

Manx, Fantoosh and Nathan stood in stunned silence, staring up at the enormous rock. The notion that it was made of pure amberose was so mesmerising that even the continual bombardment of gull poo from above didn't bother them. Within seconds, the three of them were spattered from head to toe. It was no wonder, thought Manx, that the amberose was hidden so well.

Olu jumped off the ledge and contentedly waddled around Manx's feet, dodging the poo bombs with nifty hops.

"Clever bird," said Manx, eyes still fixed on the pecked-off area of amberose. "You showed us the hoard." He couldn't resist the temptation any longer – he just had to touch it, to be absolutely sure. Stepping forward, he reached up and put his hand through the hole Olu had made in the caked-on poo.

Instantly, his palm tingled. A warm glow crept slowly up his arm towards his elbow.

"Wow!" He pulled his hand away and rubbed his

tingling fingers, releasing the amberose's sweet aroma into the air. "Have a go, Fan."

As soon as Fantoosh placed her hand onto the amberose, she smiled. 'It feels alive," she whispered.

Nathan giggled when it was his turn. "It tickles!" He turned to Manx. "So this is what that poem goes on about?"

Manx nodded. "I think so. It's the 'trove of power beyond our dreams.'"

"They must have seen it before the birds started using it for target practice," said Nathan, his head taking a direct hit on cue.

"I can't believe Finnick and Sarah never told anyone about this," said Fantoosh, eyes wide open with excitement. "Do you think they discovered what it could do straight away, or after they got to Haarville? I mean, they must have worked out it was, you know, unusual. Rock's not supposed to feel alive like that." She shuddered. "It's a bit creepy."

"Who knows?" said Manx. "But I'm glad they worked out how they could use it. There wouldn't be any perpetual devices otherwise."

"I think this place must have scared them," said Fantoosh. "It scares me a little. Actually, it scares me a lot."

"Me too," said Nathan. "It feels like it's breathing."

"Whether they were scared or not, it can't have been much fun being shipwrecked here," said Manx. "There's no fresh water, no shelter, nothing growing."

"How did they survive?" Nathan reached down for a

handful of crinkly bladder wrack. "On this stuff?" Another bird poo slapped him on the cheek. He wiped it off with the seaweed, grimacing towards the sky. "Or maybe they trapped one of these birds for their dinner. That's what I'd have done."

Olu made an indignant screeching noise and pecked Nathan's ankle.

"I didn't mean you, Olu, obviously," he said quickly.

"It's odd Finnick and Sarah never attempted to come back though," said Fantoosh. "They knew about the ninth wave, so could have made it."

Manx laughed. "*You've* just crossed it! Would you do it again, out of choice?"

"Fair point," agreed Fantoosh.

"I quite enjoyed it," said Nathan, "once I'd got over the fear of being ripped to tiny pieces."

"They were probably too busy building Haarville to even think about coming back," said Manx. "Plus, they didn't have a boat. The *Amber Rose* was destroyed on the reef. All that was left was the piece of wood they used to escape from here."

"And now *we're* stranded here," said Fantoosh. "You Fearty folk really are dangerous to be around. If you're not blowing yourselves up, you're eating poisoned food, or risking life and limb on killer reefs."

Manx slumped down in a heap of bladder wrack, crackling the dried-out fronds and popping several of its airbags. "I'm sorry I put you both in so much danger."

Nathan crouched down next to him. "It's not your

fault," he said. "Lugstitch and my dad are to blame."

Hearing Nathan mention his dad made Manx's stomach lurch. He hoicked himself up and stepped around the rock, heaving a sigh of relief when he saw that Baggit was still occupied with his one-man treasure hunt.

"We can't let your dad know about the hoard, Nathan," he whispered when he got back to the others. "You won't tell him, will you?"

Nathan looked up at the rock. "There's so much of it." He still sounded awestruck. "Imagine what it could power!"

"What *could* it power?" asked Manx, curiously. "In the Out-There?"

Nathan whistled. "A city? Or even a hundred? Maybe all the cars in the whole world?"

"When you did your talk for Oilyphant, you said the world was running out of energy."

"It's running out of some sorts of energy, yes. But there are the sun and wind and waves. They don't run out."

"Neither does amberose," said Manx.

Nathan reached up and held his hand over the hole Olu had made. "If anyone in the Out-There knew about this," he said quietly, "they'd come in their thousands to get their hands on it. And they'd look for more – digging, drilling, blowing things up."

"They'd destroy Haarville," said Manx.

Olu, who'd been hopping around their feet, cheerfully pecking at the seaweed, let out a whistle, flapped past Nathan and poked his long beak into the hole. Pincered in the tip was a tiny speck of yellow, hardly bigger than a grain of sand. He flicked it into the air, opened his beak wider, caught it, and swallowed.

"Did you see that?" cried Fantoosh. "Is Olu actually *eating* amberose?"

Manx tickled Olu's head. "I think," he said, slowly, "this might explain quite a lot about our oystercatcher friend – like how he's been around for so long, and where he keeps disappearing to."

"How long *has* he been around?" asked Nathan.

Olu jumped over a seaweed mound and nuzzled Nathan's foot.

"I reckon he's at least as old as Ma Campbell," replied Manx.

"And probably older than that," laughed Fantoosh. "Eating the amberose must make him live longer."

"And I thought eating limpet buns was weird," said Nathan. "Does Ma Campbell eat amberose? Is that why she's so ancient?"

"Of course not," said Manx. "But I think, maybe, just being near amberose might be enough."

He thought about how touching the massive block of amberose in front of them had given him a warm, tingling sensation. He pictured the golden glow that hung permanently over Haarville, and he closed his eyes remembering the sweet-smelling, calming atmosphere in the shop when multiple devices were humming

away at the same time. Then he thought about how most people in Haarville lived until they were very old. Unless your name was Fearty, of course.

"How old do people live to in the Out-There, Nathan?"

"Some people get to a hundred," said Nathan, "but it's not normal. The King even sends a special card to say well done for living so long."

"Loads of people in Haarville would receive one of those cards," said Fantoosh.

Nathan's eyes were wide with wonder. "Have we just discovered the secret to eternal life?"

"Not eternal," said Manx. "But yes – I think just breathing amberose air might be enough. Ma Campbell has more perpetuals than anyone else and she's older than nearly anyone else."

They were silent for a moment. Gulls bickered overhead. Surf splashed at the water's edge. Olu stopped rifling through the seaweed and stared at Manx as if to say, *"What are you going to do?"*

"No one can ever find out about this," Manx said in a low voice. "Haarville as we know it would be finished. I don't want that."

"Nor me," said Fantoosh.

They both looked at Nathan. He was biting his bottom lip.

"I like Haarville," said Nathan. "It's the best place I've ever lived. I don't want it to change."

Manx smiled. "Good. So, we're agreed?"

Fantoosh and Nathan nodded.

"Agreed on what?"

Baggit must have crept around the rock without anyone hearing – now he loomed, eyes boring into them.

"Er, that we should get off this rock right away," said Manx, the back of his neck prickling.

"Before the storm gets here," added Fantoosh. "Sheila said there was one coming."

Baggit looked up, scanning the haar-filled sky. Manx nervously glanced at the rock – if Baggit spotted the glowing hole, the secret would be out. As if realising the same thing, Olu flittered up and positioned himself in front of the bit he'd pecked, shutting his eyes as if he was fast asleep.

"I see no storm," barked Baggit. "And we've the whole place to dig yet."

"When you've been in Haarville as long as we have," said Fantoosh, "you'll learn to smell a storm before it hits."

"We should go, Dad." Nathan stumbled over the seaweed and put his hand on his father's arm. "There's no treasure here. No hoard. There's nothing." A massive bird poo splashed off the end of Baggit's nose. "Except…" Nathan tried to cover up a laugh with a cough. "There is lots of that."

Baggit growled under his breath.

"If the storm hits," said Manx, "we'll be washed away onto the reef. We have to leave now. There's room on the raft for all of us. You too, Mr Baggit. It's the only safe way off Clam Rock."

Baggit muttered something under his breath and stomped away.

"Stubborn, isn't he?" said Fantoosh.

Nathan shook his head, watching his dad shovelling more seaweed. "I don't think he's ever admitted he's been wrong about anything."

"And now," said Manx, "you're asking him to admit he's wrong about something that he's actually right about!"

"I know." Nathan shrugged, smiling at Manx, then pointed out to sea. "How safe is getting away from here going to be? You said me and Dad only survived crossing the reef by luck. What if we're not lucky twice?"

"Because," said Manx, in a voice low enough that Baggit couldn't hear, "we'll be surfing the biggest wave again. It's how our ancestors got away from here in one piece." He pointed to where the waves barrelled towards them. "See? The waves split and go either side of the rock." Then he spun around and pointed to the other side, to where the cleaved waves merged back into one, regaining power and height and surging on towards the reef again. "All we have to do is paddle back out and catch the right wave as it passes by, then ride it to the open ocean." Manx shouted over to Baggit. "Your only chance to leave this place in one piece is with us!"

"And we're leaving now," added Fantoosh, heading back down the narrow beach to where the raft was ploshing around.

"No one is leaving until every square inch of this blasted place has been searched!" shouted Baggit, wincing as a flash of lightning briefly lit the haar-filled sky.

"We'll die here before finding anything other than

276

seaweed and bird muck," said Manx. "The bits of poem you've been hunting for were just a story. Haarville's bursting with them. Hang around long enough and you'll hear a few."

A sharp clap of thunder sent the circling gulls spiralling away.

"Dad," said Nathan, in a low, confident tone Manx hadn't heard before, "I've always done what you've told me to, and gone where you asked me to go. Now it's your turn to trust and follow me."

Baggit stared at his son in surprise. "I've only ever wanted to be rich to give you a better life."

"To give *yourself* a better life, you mean," Nathan snapped back. "I never asked for anything. All I ever wanted was to stay somewhere long enough to make friends and to spend some proper time with you. But this stupid treasure you've been hunting for has always been more important than me. Well, there is no treasure, Dad. But I'm still here." Nathan lifted his chin. "And I'm leaving."

He turned away from Baggit, and he and Manx made their way to the raft, where Fantoosh was busy securing the floats and re-tying knots in the fishing line that was holding the lobster pots together.

As the boys waded into the water to help, a faint "Wait!" drifted down on the breeze, and they all turned to see Baggit tripping and slipping his way to join them.

An odd mixture of relief and disappointment muddled Manx's head. He'd gladly have left Baggit behind as a punishment for everything he'd done, but a quick glance at Nathan's smile reminded him that the man was his friend's only parent. Maybe, thought Manx, a mostly rubbish father like Ninian Baggit was better than no father at all.

Having directed Baggit to lie in the middle of the raft – his extra weight would hopefully stabilise the raft this time – Manx scanned the shoreline.

"Anyone seen Olu?" He picked his way quickly back to the rock, where he found the bird pecking frantically at the hole he'd made earlier. "Easy does it, Olu. You'll break your beak." Just then, a chunk of amberose the size of Manx's fist pinged off. He caught it, his palm instantly tingling with the amberose's warmth. "You can't eat all this!"

Olu hopped down and landed on the chunk, staring intently up at Manx.

"Oh! I see…" said Manx. "Alright, it'll be our secret." He stuffed the chunk down his long johns, hoping the others – Baggit in particular – wouldn't notice.

"Found him!" he called out, hurrying back to the raft. "Let's go!"

Nathan clambered onto the raft next to his dad, then Fantoosh and Manx waded it out until the water deepened, before jumping on either side.

Now it was time to deploy the paddling skills they'd learned that day as they negotiated the currents swirling all around the raft.

But even after some furious dipping and flipping with their oars and an impressive effort from Nathan, whose feet were kicking up piles of foam behind them, they still hadn't escaped the backwash and kept veering back to the rock.

"Kick harder!" shouted Manx. "Both of you."

Nathan doubled his efforts, screaming at his dad to do the same. Baggit groaned, but did as Nathan asked, and eventually the raft cleared the backwards pull and they managed to row closer to where they could pick up a wave.

They bobbed around for a minute as the waves passed. They watched. They waited. They counted. Finally, the eighth wave approached, dividing in two as it passed the rock, joining up again just beyond where they were floating, before rolling on towards the other side of the circular reef.

"Go!" screamed Manx.

With teeth gritted and arm muscles pounding, he paddled like never before. Timing was everything – they had to be in the perfect position to hitch a ride on the ninth wave, which was already powering through the lagoon. They had mere seconds before they missed their chance. It was now or never.

One stroke. Two. Three. With a final huge dip and pull on their paddles, and with Nathan and his dad kicking up a fury, the raft spun and skimmed the wave as it picked them up and thrust them forward. It lifted them higher and higher, easily clearing the reef and its deadly razor shells.

Finally, the wave began a slow decline, gently depositing the raft, and its exhausted crew, to the comparative stillness of the ocean beyond the reef.

"No!" yelled Baggit suddenly. "My boots! I've lost my boots with that blasted kicking."

"Who cares about your boots?" yelled Nathan. "We almost lost each other today. For ever."

Baggit scanned the sea behind them, as if searching for his beloved footwear, then he turned and stared at Nathan for a few seconds, before shunting across the raft and pulling him into a hug.

Manx could see Nathan's eyes peering out over Baggit's shoulder. They looked surprised for a moment, before filling with tears.

"I think," said Manx, smiling, "that crossing Razor Reef twice in one day is enough for one lifetime."

"Agreed," said Fantoosh.

"Definitely," added Nathan, wiping his eyes.

"Good," said Manx, as Olu fluttered down and perched on the front of the raft, like a live figurehead. "Because we're never coming back. Nobody is ever coming back. Clam Rock's all yours, Olu. For ever."

32.

An Eye for an Eye

The shop's counter shone. It gleamed. It practically sparkled. And no wonder – Manx had been polishing it for an hour. Having survived Razor Reef on a raft, he had a newfound respect for his ancestors for having done the same on this very piece of wood. From now on, the last remaining piece of the *Amber Rose* would get a thorough polish every day.

He dipped into his sea-glass jar and took out his great-granduncle's eye.

"Ready for a test spin, Fabian?" Manx flicked the glass sphere gently across the counter. It rolled beautifully, the green iris twinkling and winking with every rotation. "That's enough polishing, then." He dropped the eye back into the jar and turned to the window. Kipper Lane had become dark suddenly. "It had better not rain," he muttered, hurrying to the door. He'd only finished repainting the shop's sign that afternoon and the paint wouldn't be dry yet.

281

He poked his head outside. It was just the haar rolling in, so the sign was safe. He checked his handiwork and smiled. It was good to see the Fearty name back in its rightful place.

Manx closed the door and made himself a pot of hawthorn tea. He'd developed a taste for it since his visit to Gushet House, and Da Silva hadn't even charged him for a tin of his finest blend. In fact, ever since Baggit had apologised and moved out – and Manx and Father G had moved back in – gifts were arriving all the time. Madame Bonbeurre had only that morning dropped by with a plate piled high with freshly baked limpet buns. So far, Manx had resisted the urge, but if Fantoosh didn't hurry up he was going to have to dive in.

Placing his teacup on a driftwood coaster, Manx went over to the table where he and Father G had been busy repairing Tina's samovar. The amberose was back in place and it just needed one last dust down. As soon as Father G was home, they were going to return it to the library. Not that his guardian would be back for a while yet – today the newly elected Elders were holding their first Burgh-Meet, so they were bound to have a lot to discuss.

The recent election – Haarville's first ever – was still hot gossip, which Manx was only too happy about because it diverted attention away from the events at Razor Reef. For a while, all anyone wanted to talk about was that day – there'd even been daily editions of the *Periscope* printed for the first time in years just to satisfy demand for news. The headlines shouted things like:

Baggit Saves Son from Reef!

Treasure Hunt Ends in Tragedy!

Burgmaster Lost Overboard!

The reports managed to get some details right: that Baggit and Lugstitch had commandeered Sheila's boat, that somehow the children had been trapped in the hold and that the *Unfortunate Flounder* almost sank. Otherwise, so-called facts were either sketchy, inaccurate or completely made up.

Manx knew from his investigations in the library archives that the *Periscope* didn't always get the story right, but did people really believe – as the paper reported – that Baggit had come to Haarville to search for a sunken Spanish galleon and its hoard of emeralds? It seemed they did, because that's all anyone talked about for days.

Manx had a sneaking suspicion that Fantoosh had deliberately spread that particular rumour. But it didn't matter where the story had come from. Anything that put people off the truth was a good thing, because the truth had to stay hidden for ever. Only he, Fantoosh and Nathan knew about the amberose, and it seemed that Baggit was too ashamed of risking his and Nathan's lives to admit to having made it to Clam Rock. Or maybe he was just too exhausted after years of endless searching. He hadn't mentioned the rock or the hoard to Nathan since their return. It seemed he really had given up his quest.

Anyway, Haarville seemed willing to forgive Baggit for going after mythical treasure, and instead hailed him a hero for saving his son's life. Baggit certainly seemed to enjoy the attention, especially the harbour-side celebration held in his honour.

Manx, Fantoosh and Nathan enjoyed the party too, even if it was hard work remembering not to let anything slip about Clam Rock and the amberose hoard. And Manx was thrilled to see Ma Campbell and Skulpin sharing a keg of schnapps. There was, he thought, plenty of time for them to make up for all the lost years. After all, Ma Campbell was still only one hundred and twenty!

One thing was for certain: nobody seemed surprised by Lugstitch's display of greed – least of all his wife, Betsy.

"He was never satisfied," she explained to Manx, as she sipped on her limpet juice. "Always parading around as Burgmaster, looking for another deal, and never giving me a hand in the shop. If you'd told him there were steps on a rainbow, he'd have tried to climb them to get his hands on the pot of gold at the other end. No, you won't find me grieving over his gruesome end on the reef. It *was* gruesome, I take it?" Betsy had smiled when she asked this, so Manx said he thought it probably had been, which seemed to cheer her up no end.

The remaining Elders didn't seem that upset to hear

of Lugstitch's demise either. Da Silva insisted that the Burgmaster had forced them to agree to all the emergency orders they had sent to Manx and Father G, but it wasn't enough to save them, and they were forced to resign. It was decided that proper elections should be held to choose the new Elders, and that anyone from Haarville or Phlegm Town could not only vote, but also stand.

Only Father G himself seemed surprised when it was declared that he'd received the most votes. Manx couldn't have been more proud, and he was equally thrilled to hear that Tina and Oilyphant had been elected too. Even more excitingly, Skulpin and Ursula also received enough votes, which meant for the first time in history, Phlegm Town would be represented at Burgh House.

There had been other changes in Haarville too. For example, residents of Phlegm Town were no longer scared to venture across the burn – in fact, they were welcomed with open arms and doors. Madame Bonbeurre was especially happy with all her new customers, saying she'd never known such demand for her rowanberry jam puffs – they were now selling out within half an hour of opening.

Manx and Father G had also begun to welcome new customers into their shop, and there was now a small selection of perpetual devices from Phlegm Town waiting for repair. Some of them hadn't worked for years, and Manx couldn't wait to get them fixed and back to their

owners in pristine condition – and thanks to Olu, he now had enough new amberose to truly bring them back to life.

The shop door swung open. Fantoosh and Nathan tumbled in, pushing and shoving each other, followed swiftly by Olu, who flapped overhead and settled on the counter, apparently admiring his reflection in the newly polished wood.

"Slow down, you two!" Manx jumped in front of Tina's samovar to protect it. After the hours he'd spent restoring it, he wasn't about to let it be damaged again.

"Sorry, Manx." Fantoosh smiled. "We heard you'd had a delivery from the bakery."

"I did." He pointed to the plate of buns. "Help yourself."

Nathan pulled a face. "No jam puffs?"

Manx shrugged. "Not today."

Fantoosh mumbled something through a mouthful of limpet bun, which Manx interpreted correctly as: "What did Father G wear to the Burgh-Meet?"

Manx beamed at her. "Betsy made him a new frock! It's covered in polished scallop shells and fringed with three rows of puffin feathers. Now her husband's gone, she says she's free to make whatever clothes she fancies. She's even offered to make me an equally fabulous outfit!"

"Just imagine if Lugstitch was around to see Gloria in Excelsis perched in his old seat at Burgh House!" exclaimed Fantoosh. "It would almost be worth him coming back just to see the look on his face."

"Almost," said Nathan. "But not quite." He lifted a parcel onto the counter, smiling.

"Is that Leena's clock?" asked Manx.

"Yes. She cried when I told her you wanted to get it going properly again."

Manx unwrapped it. "All it needs is two new hands, a good clean-out of the mechanism and this…" He dipped into his pocket and placed half a pebble-weight's worth of amberose next to it. "It's going to work much better with this inside it."

Fantoosh gasped. "With that much she'll live to a hundred and fifty."

"Hopefully," said Manx. "She deserves to."

"But where did that amberose come from?" asked Fantoosh.

"Some's from my carousel." Manx sighed. "It was in pieces anyway."

"And the rest?" asked Fantoosh, a quizzical look in her eyes. "Or shouldn't I ask?"

Manx shrugged. "Olu might have encouraged me to bring back a tiny souvenir from our visit to Clam Rock."

"I knew it!" cried Fantoosh. "I said he had something stuffed down the back of his long johns, didn't I, Nathan?"

"She did!"

"It's just as well," said Manx. "Or I'd never have been able to repair all these perpetuals from Phlegm Town."

"Don't worry," said Fantoosh. "We won't tell anyone."

"Definitely not," said Nathan. "Oh, and I brought this too." He held out his hand. Fabian's other false eye stared up from it. "Dad says it belongs here, at Fearty's Perpetuals. To be honest, it's always freaked me out a bit."

Manx took the eye and dropped it into the jar, where it nestled alongside Fabian's other one. They peered out, unblinking, unwinking.

"How is it on Crab Gulley?" Manx hadn't had time to visit Nathan yet in his new Phlegm Town cottage. It had lain unoccupied for years, and Nathan and his dad would have to put up with Leena's smoking chimney next door, but there hadn't been many other options. Ma Campbell had generously offered to put them up – they were family after all – and Skulpin had grudgingly suggested they could move into Manx and Father G's old room at the Lange Fluke. Baggit, however, had insisted that he and Nathan fend for themselves.

"I thought Haarville was weird when we arrived," said Nathan, grinning. "Phlegm Town is even weirder. It's dirty, and smelly, and full of the oddest people. Everywhere we ever lived in the Out-There was so boring – Crab Gulley is anything but. I *love* it!"

"Tell Manx about your dad," said Fantoosh.

"Oh, yeah. Now he's finished repairing Sheila's boat, Ursula's asked him to help her set up a new stall on Pollock Row."

This wasn't at all what Manx had expected, but Ursula was a kind person, and if she was prepared to forgive Baggit, then maybe she saw some good in him.

"So you're definitely staying?"

Nathan's eyes gleamed. "Yes! Haarville's the best place I've ever lived. And you're the best friends I've ever had." He laughed. "And before either of you say it, yes, I know, you're the *only* friends I've ever had."

"Tell Manx your other news," said Fantoosh.

Nathan's smile spread wide across his face. "Ma Campbell wants to restart the Monan glass-blowing business, and she's offered to teach me how to do it. Like she says, I'm as much a Monan as I am a Fearty, so I'll be carrying on the family tradition."

"I'm glad you found some family, and that you like it here," said Fantoosh. "I mean, I know you nearly drowned, and your dad and Lugstitch might have ruined Haarville for ever, but we like having you here, don't we, Manx?"

"Absolutely! And I kind of like not being the only Fearty in Haarville." Manx helped himself to a bun and bit into it. Some limpet juice squirted out the other side, only just missing Olu, who let out an indignant whistle before he set about sucking up the juice from the counter.

"Yuck!" Nathan pinched his nose. "That's one Haarville tradition I'm *never* going to like. I am hungry though."

"Let's go for lunch," said Fantoosh. "Where do you fancy?"

"Anywhere," said Nathan. "As long as it doesn't involve limpets!"

"How about a trip to Ratfish Wynd?" Manx smiled. "I hear the Lange Fluke serves an excellent fish fin soup!"

Glossary

aye: yes

bladder wrack: common brown seaweed found on rocky shores, with air-filled pockets or "bladders" to help it float

brae: a steep bank or hill

breeches: trousers

Burgmaster: a mayor or town official

burn: a small stream

causeway: a raised path or track giving access to land cut off by the tide

clam: a type of shellfish that usually lives buried in the sand in shallow waters

clan: a family, or group of related families

dhow: a one- or two-masted ship with slanted triangular sails, traditionally used in the Indian Ocean

fulmar: a grey-and-white seabird

gannet: a large white seabird with black-tipped wings and a long bill

gutweed: a common green seaweed growing in fronds

haar: a chilly, moist sea fog

hawthorn: a hedgerow plant with fragrant white flowers in spring, followed by red fruits, which can be used to make wine or jellies

headland: a narrow piece of land on a coastline that reaches out into the sea

kelp: a large brown seaweed that grows in underwater forests

limpet: species of sea snail with a conical shell, found clinging tightly to rocks

long johns: long underpants

lugs: ears

marsh plantain: a plant growing in coastal areas including rocks, cliffs and saltmarshes

mussel: a bluish-grey shellfish found growing in clumps on rocky shores

oystercatcher: a black-and-white wading bird with a bright orange bill and reddish-pink legs

privy: an outside toilet, often in an outbuilding

reef: a ridge of jagged rock, sand or coral just above or below the sea's surface

samovar: a metal urn used to heat and boil water for tea

samphire: an edible wild plant found on coastlines

scallop: shellfish with a soft body protected by two grooved, hinged shells

tea caddy: a small container in which tea is kept

tea clipper: a nineteenth-century merchant ship used to carry tea and other traded goods

whelk: a sea snail with a cone-shaped shell – they can grow as big as 10 cm (4 in)!

winkle: species of sea snail with a spiral shell

wynd: a narrow street or alley

About the Author

After years spent flying around the world as cabin crew, Justin hung up his wings to focus on writing books children can lose themselves in. His first book, *Help! I Smell a Monster*, won the Fantastic Book Awards in 2021. He is also the author of *Whoa! I Spy a Werewolf*. As well as writing, Justin loves visiting schools to share his stories, which he says is one of the best things about being a children's author.

When not lost in his own imagination (or in someone else's, because he loves to read!), Justin continues his lifelong quest to bake the perfect scone. It's an important endeavour, and one he takes very seriously.

Justin lives with his husband, Andrew, and Sally the rescue greyhound in the shadow of the Forth Bridge in Fife, Scotland.

Find Justin on Twitter @flyingscribbler and Instagram @justindaviesauthor, or check out justindaviesauthor.com.

Acknowledgements

Time to celebrate these fabulous people with some tasty treats:

A bowl of Hamish's luxurious lobster whip for my amazing agent, Thérèse Coen. Thank you for keeping me on an even keel and steering me clear of any razor-sharp reefs!

There's a giant plate of just-steamed limpet buns for the entire team at Floris, whose energy has helped this book come to life. Extra special shout-outs to my excellent editors, Jennie Skinner and Sally Polson; design gurus Richard Wainman and Jenny Skivington; and marketing maestros Suzanne Kennedy and Kirsten Graham.

I've uncorked a bottle of Mabel's rosehip wine to share with illustrator Francesca Ficorilli, whose breath-taking cover artwork captures Haarville's atmosphere so brilliantly. *Adoro le illustrazioni! Grazie mille.*

Maizy Halfin has baked one of her scrumptious sea-carrot cakes, a large slice of which goes to Peta (P.M. Freestone) for all the dog walks, book-world talks and insanely good cold brew coffee; also for the lockdown Zoom writing sessions during which *Haarville* became fully formed.

An equally large slice of cake goes to my other lockdown Zoom writing pal, occasional Edinburgh Botanics buddy and Cheerleader-in-Chief to so many authors, Sarah Broadley.

Madame Bonbeurre has delivered a tray of her famous rowanberry jam puffs for my SCBWI critique group, whose encouragement and enthusiasm were invaluable in this book's early stages. There's an extra jammy puff specially for Geoff Barker, for joining me on pre-pandemic research missions.

I have a bottle of freshly squeezed clam juice for Jayson Byles from East Neuk Seaweed to say thank you for some expert seaweed-foraging advice, a delicious sea spaghetti lunch and the live limpet-picking and -eating demonstration!

There's a bucketful of tasty barnacle nuts for the staff and pupils at North Queensferry Primary School for sustaining (and entertaining) Mr Davies, pupil support assistant, and for giving Justin Davies, children's author, so many brilliant ideas!

Talking of schools... Although time has blurred my childhood like a slow-sinking haar, I clearly remember my English classes with Miss Hardy and Mr Kestrel. None of us might have predicted back then that I'd end up writing for children, but your lessons helped forge my love of words and reading, so I raise a glass of finest whelk schnapps to you both.

I'm raising another glass to celebrate the thrill of random conversations with strangers. It was just such a conversation whilst I was out having dinner that triggered the idea for this book. So thank you to the Courthouse in Kinross for a) your excellent pizzas, and b) for employing people who like to share intriguing factoids about mythical towns that may, or may not, exist.

And finally, I've reserved a table for two at Lumpsuckers and ordered a platter of Sheila Giddock's fried fish balls to share with my wonderful husband, Andrew. Thank you for introducing me to Scotland and the fishing villages of Fife, whose harbours, wynds and haar-heavy skies inspired so much in these pages.